THE WEEPING WOMAN
A Sheriff Lansing Mystery

Micah S. Hackler

Books by Micah S. Hackler

Sheriff Lansing Mysteries
Legend of the Dead
Coyote Returns
The Shadow Catcher
The Dark Canyon
The Mutes
The Weeping Woman

Coming Soon!
A Sheriff Lansing Mystery
Moon of the Blue Mustang

THE WEEPING WOMAN
A Sheriff Lansing Mystery

Micah S. Hackler

SPEAKING VOLUMES, LLC
NAPLES, FLORIDA
2019

THE WEEPING WOMAN

ISBN 978-1-64540-099-8

For Bill Rambin
and to the memory of his beloved wife
Linda

Acknowledgments

If you find something you love doing, you'll never have to work a day in your life.

I have had the joy of writing almost every day for the past year. Not one of those days did I have to "work."

Thank you, Olivia, for helping me make that happen.

For Bobbie and Bill Riggle, Robin and Don Perrero, Jim and Robin Krestalude, thank you for the years of friendship and encouragement. I truly appreciate your comments and critiques.

George Sewell, Dan Baldwin – I'm able to write this because the three of us spent so many nights watching campfires dwindle, while we discussed the craft of writing and downed the occasional shot of brown. *The Factory* lives on.

Continued thanks to the folks at my publisher, Speaking Volumes. I am only able to write because of the platform you provide. Thank you, Kurt Mueller, for taking me on and for the peppy correspondence; Erica Mueller, for the book layouts; and Rick Turylo, for the most spectacular book covers any author could hope for.

Prologue

It was after the Great Pueblo Revolt.

After a dozen years, the Spanish returned with a vengeance.

Povi's husband died defending the *Ohkay Owingeh.*

Povi fled to the river with her two small children. Neither she nor they would be captured to become slaves. She hid them in the bushes and that night sneaked into the Pueblo for provisions. It was winter, the time of the White Corn Maiden, and a great chill swept down from the north.

It was nearly dawn before Povi returned . . . only to find her children frozen to death.

The Spaniards heard a beautiful song coming from the riverbank. That's where they discovered Povi, singing a lullaby . . . sad and sweet.

When Povi saw the soldiers, she grabbed the two small, lifeless bodies and dove into the icy water that she might drown and join her children in death.

To this day, Povi still wanders the river, still crying, still singing to her children . . . inviting all who hear her to join her beneath the waters.

She is called *La Llorona,* The Weeping Woman.

Chapter One

The body was found face down, washed up on the bank of the Rio Grande.

Joseph Aquino, San Juan Pueblo Tribal Police Chief, had been summoned immediately. He wasn't sure why Raymond Mesa was there. He hoped Mesa's presence was as a concerned citizen along with the other three men from the pueblo. Not as the new Pueblo Sheriff.

Mesa's appointment had been made only three days earlier, New Year's Day, when the Winter Chief selected him for the position. He wouldn't officially be sworn in until January 6th, Three King's Day. The Catholic mass certifying his appointment would be conducted after the Winter and Summer Buffalo Dances were completed.

Another fine point Aquino would gladly make was the Pueblo Sheriff had no real authority. These days, at best, it was a ceremonial position. He would hold the slot for twelve months, then it would be the Summer Chief's turn to make an appointment for the next year.

Aquino himself had only been Police Chief for a year, though he had been on the force for over twelve.

"It's Diego Salazar," Aquino said when they turned over the body.

Pauline Dominguez nodded. "The last time I saw him was at Christmas Mass . . . He works for the Northern Pueblo Indian Council, doesn't he?"

"Something like that," the new sheriff agreed.

Pauline, the nurse at San Juan Elementary School, had reported the body. She said she had seen it from the Highway 74 bridge on her way to work. She and four men from the Pueblo had joined the new sheriff on the snow-covered riverbank.

"He might have gotten drunk on New Year's Eve and fell in," the nurse guessed.

Aquino looked up and down the river. Highway 74 was a hundred yards upstream, to the north. The Yunge Owingeh Bridge was a hundred yards to the south. San Juan Pueblo was directly across the Rio Grande. It was possible Salazar had gotten drunk and fallen off the highway bridge. This time of year, the river wasn't deep, but the waters were icy cold. It wouldn't take much to incapacitate someone, especially if they had too much to drink.

"Maybe . . . but why didn't someone see him sooner?" It was Monday, January 4th. New Year's Eve had been four nights earlier.

"It's been snowing," Pauline remarked. "People kept their eyes on the road."

It was Aquino's turn to nod. It had already been a raw winter. In the 10 days since Christmas, they had already had more snow than all of '97-'98. January of 1999 looked to be one of the snowiest in years.

"What are we going to do with the body?" Mesa asked. "We can't leave it here."

"I know that," Aquino snapped. "Grab an arm or a leg. Let's haul him up to my truck."

Half dragging, half carrying the body through the underbrush, getting Salazar to the highway was more difficult than they had imagined. Their progress was impeded by the water-soaked clothing. It took fifteen minutes to cover the hundred yards to the bridge and up the bank. Aquino closed the truck's gate once Salazar was deposited in the bed.

"What now?" Mesa asked.

"I'll take him to the Police Station."

"You can't keep him there till the funeral."

"I don't plan to. I'm treating this death as suspicious. I need to talk to the county sheriff's office. See if they can arrange for an autopsy."

"Why? We know how he died," Juan El Tano protested. "He drowned."

"How do you know?" Aquino snarked. "Did you drown him?"

"Course not!"

"You can't make a decision like that," Mesa argued. "You don't have that kind of authority."

Aquino glared at the new sheriff. "I'll talk to President Kata . . . Let him know what I'm doing. Is that authority enough?"

"I suppose," Mesa caved.

"Why do you think Diego's death is suspicious?" Pauline asked.

"He's not wearing a coat or a jacket. Just a long-sleeved shirt. I don't know about you, but I wouldn't be out in this weather without a coat."

"I think he lived on Kennedy Loop," El Tano offered. "Somebody should tell his family."

"Yeah," Aquino agreed. "I'll handle that. Maybe Father Iglesias can come with me." He started toward the cab of his truck. "I appreciate all the help."

Chapter Two

Sheriff Cliff Lansing stomped the snow off his boots when he stepped into the barn. He was getting a late start. He'd been out clearing a traffic accident until two in the morning. It was already 8:00 am. Being late into the office was one thing. Being late for feeding the horses was a whole different matter.

Cement Head, Paladin and Little Orphan Annie glared at him from their stalls. They were used to getting their oats before 7:00 and their hay cradles were almost empty. Always the ringleader, Cement Head gave an admonishing snort.

"You three don't have it that bad," Lansing remarked flatly. "You could be standing out in a foot of snow right now."

It was well below freezing outside. The two space heaters at either end of the stable kept the interior at an acceptable 50°. For added protection, each horse had a quilted blanket with a strap across the chest that held it in place.

It took thirty minutes for the rancher to water and feed his animals.

The stalls needed cleaning daily. Oscar Vega, Lansing's seventeen-year-old neighbor, was the part-time ranch hand. He worked two to three hours every afternoon after school. The young man was reliable and thorough. Lansing knew the horses would be well looked after while he handled the security of San Phillipe County.

As he reached for the door to leave, his cell phone rang. "Lansing."

"Good morning, Sheriff." It was Marilyn from dispatch. "I'm not interrupting anything, am I?"

"No, I was on my way in."

"Before you come this way, you might want to head south . . . San Juan Pueblo's police chief found a body in the Rio Grande."

"Was it on the reservation?"

"I suppose."

"What does he need from us?"

"He said the death is suspicious. But he doesn't want to call the FBI if he doesn't have to. He needs our help arranging for an autopsy."

"Contact the state Medical Investigator's office. Tell them we have a DB . . . suspicious cause of death." On January 1st, all deaths not attributed to natural causes were now routed through the State Medical Investigator's office in Albuquerque. "I'll head down to the Pueblo. See what they have . . . Anything else?"

"Yes. Road crews found an abandoned vehicle in a snow drift on Route one-eighty-two when they were plowing. Jack Rivera's on his way up there."

"Is that it?"

"One more thing. We got a 'Be On The Look Out' request for an escaped prisoner. A Ralph Miera was being transferred from Albuquerque to Denver. Some private prisoner transport company. He overcame the guards, took their guns and locked them in the cage."

"Where was this?"

"I-twenty-five, just outside Santa Fe. They have no idea where he went."

"Isn't that a great start for the New Year?" he sighed. "I'll be in my Jeep in a minute. From here on out, you can contact me on the radio."

As he drove down the half-mile stretch of ranch road toward the highway, the 8 inches of fresh, powdery snow crunched beneath the tires. Lansing was relieved to find Highway 15, the main north-south route through San Phillipe County, had been cleared.

The 125-man county road department prioritized which roads would be plowed for snow. Highway 15 came first, though it seldom needed plowing south of O'Keeffe Ranch. Highway 64, which ran from San

Juan County in the west to Taos in the east, was the longest and highest in elevation. Three crews were usually assigned to keep that road clear. The smaller county roads came last.

For the most part, the high desert roads were seldom closed because of snow. The wind was usually enough to keep them clean, though the occasional drift might cause a problem. However, the mountain roads needed attention several times during the winter months.

Despite the snowstorm from the night before, the skies were clear now. The reflection of the sunlight off the clean blanket of white was blinding.

After the long New Year's weekend, Lansing found the drive south pleasant. It was a nice break from the previous four days. He wondered how long it would last.

Chapter Three

Located 5 miles north of Segovia, San Juan was one of the 19 Native American Pueblos scattered across New Mexico. It was one of the 7 Tewa speaking Pueblos still in existence. It was not one of the oldest Pueblos. Taos, Zuni and Acoma were considered older by almost 300 years. Still, the Pueblo had been in its location for 700 years and held the distinction of being the first Spanish Capitol of New Mexico. The entire reservation covered 35 square miles, though the Pueblo itself only sat on 16 acres.

Lansing parked his patrol Jeep in front of the police station. The building was single-story, adobe-style, located on the Pueblo's main street, Po'Pay Avenue. It was not very big. Behind it, on the side street, was the much larger Tribal Courthouse. Just to the north was San Juan Bautista Catholic Church. Across the avenue was the San Juan Pueblo Administration building.

As he stepped out of his unit, the sheriff couldn't help but notice how much warmer it was than when he left his ranch. He reminded himself the Pueblo was 2,000 feet lower in elevation than north San Phillipe County. He entered the building.

The office was small, crowded with desks for the police commander and his three officers. The office secretary/receptionist looked up when Lansing entered. Before she could say anything, the Police Chief greeted their visitor.

"Sheriff Lansing," Aquino said, acknowledging his counterpart. "I didn't expect you to show up."

"It's been a while since I've been to the Pueblo. I was curious what you had," he replied, shaking the extended hand. Over the years the two men had met professionally a dozen times. "Congratulations on your promotion."

"Thank you, Sheriff. Can I offer you some coffee?"

"I'm fine, thanks. Call me Cliff. We're equals now. I understand you have a corpse on your hands."

"I do, and please, call me Joe." The police chief motioned Lansing to follow him. "I'll show you what we found."

Diego Salazar's body, now covered with a blanket, had been placed in a holding cell. A window was open to keep the body cool.

Lansing lifted the blanket to examine the corpse. Salazar was face up, his arms at his sides. The clothing was damp. Looking closely, there was no obvious damage to the body.

"He was a member of the Pueblo?"

Aquino nodded. "His name is Diego Salazar."

"Who found the body?"

"Pauline Dominguez, the elementary school nurse, saw his body from the Highway Seventy-four bridge. She reported it to me. Four other men helped me retrieve him."

"Do you think he drowned?"

"Probably. I hope it will turn out to be an accident."

"Why do you think the death was suspicious?"

"He was wearing just what you see there. We didn't see a jacket anywhere and it's been too damned cold to wander around without a coat."

"So, what are you thinking?"

"That he died somewhere else and someone dumped his body in the river." He was quiet for a moment. "I still need to notify Mr. Salazar's family . . . but knowing the *Ohkay Owingeh* people, I'm sure they know by now. It's a small community."

Lansing nodded. "The Medical Investigator's Office said they would retrieve the body before noon. I'll let them know where to come. You'll have someone here, won't you?"

"The receptionist will be here."

A man was waiting for them when they returned to the front office. "I'm Raymond Mesa," he announced. "I'm the new Pueblo Sheriff." He nodded toward Lansing. "You are?"

"Sheriff Clifford Lansing, San Phillipe County."

Mesa's introduction was icy. Lansing chose not to offer his hand. The "new" Pueblo Sheriff appeared to be in his mid-forties and very proud of himself. The county sheriff didn't understand the exact relationship between Police Chief and Sheriff.

Segovia had a Police Department with a Police Chief. Their jurisdiction was well defined, and Lansing went out of his way not to interfere. He was unsure how the Pueblo law enforcement worked.

"Sheriff Mesa was appointed last Friday," Aquino explained. "His job is to advise the Tribal Council."

Mesa shot him a dirty look. "The position of Sheriff is important."

"Yes," the police commander said, almost condescendingly. "Yes, it is."

Lansing felt like he had been dropped into the middle of a turf war. "I was curious. Is the new casino going to be far from here?"

"It's a mile and a half away. You passed the construction site on Highway Sixty-eight."

"I came in from the north on Seventy-four. I'm heading for Segovia from here. I'm sure I'll see it then."

Before leaving, he pulled a business card from his wallet. He jotted down something on the back and handed it to Aquino. "That's my new cell number. I know I don't have any jurisdiction around here, but if you

9

ever need help, let me know." He excused himself, insisting he had important things to attend to.

Chapter Four

The first day of school after Christmas Break didn't crackle with the same level of excitement as the first day of the school year. In fact, the resentment Tina Morales sensed among the students was almost palpable. It would take most of them a week before they were completely settled in.

Chemistry I was a core requirement for graduation, as was Biology. (Chem II, a senior course, was an elective.) Most of Morales' Junior students started the year scared to death of taking a "hard" science. Within a month she had won them over. She had convinced them chemistry was not only interesting but applicable to daily life.

For the female students who grew up watching their mothers and grandmothers in the kitchen, they discovered cooking and baking was nothing more than applied chemistry.

For the males, especially those on farms and ranches, chemistry was used daily for fertilizing plants or inoculating herds. For the others, chemistry was what made paint colorful, glue sticky and explosives go "boom."

"Don't look so gloomy," the teacher chirped from the front of the room. "You get a three-day weekend in two weeks and President's Day a month after that."

"But it's five months till summer vacation!" a boy in the back complained.

"Then again," Tina countered, "Spring Break is in three months . . . so there's that . . . Did everyone review Chapters Eleven through Thirteen over the holiday, like I suggested?"

Out of twenty-five students, less than half nodded.

"It's a shame if you didn't." Morales retrieved a small stack of papers from her desk drawer. "Let's try a quiz to find out what everyone remembers."

She was greeted with a chorus of "Aws!"

"That's all right," she said, passing out copies. "Keep it up and I'll make the quiz count for your final grade."

The sighs of relief were audible.

"You have fifteen minutes."

Morales stood at the front of the class, monitoring. Since the students had been assured the results didn't count, there was less glancing at a neighbor's paper than usual.

From the corner of her eye, Tina thought she saw movement. She turned her head toward the window of the classroom door. She could see nothing in the hallway.

Observing her students again, a dark shadow once more hovered in the periphery of her gaze. She shot the door a quick glance. Again . . . nothing.

This time she wanted to make sure. She hurried over and jerked the door open.

There was no one outside the door. Poking her head beyond the jamb, the hallway was completely empty.

"Is anything wrong, Miss Morales?" Maria Alba asked from her seat on the front row.

"No," the teacher said, shaking her head as she quickly closed the door. "I thought I saw something."

She went to her desk and sat. "Ten minutes left. When you're finished, put your pencils down."

Tina glanced at the door, truly wishing someone had been on the other side.

She couldn't help but be worried. She had seen those shadows before. A long time ago. If they were back, that wasn't a good thing.

Chapter Five

Lansing eased onto State Highway 68 from the Pueblo proper, heading south. The construction site was only a half mile further down. Driven by nothing more than plain curiosity, he turned left, onto the access road and parked.

The soon-to-be hotel/casino looked like it would be larger than he had expected.

The Ohkay Casino Resort would be a first for San Phillipe County. The two-story hotel would have 100 rooms. The casino would be for slot machines only . . . several hundred, Lansing had heard. Opening day was July 1st.

Although the operation was on reservation land, there still had to be coordination with outside agencies: Bureau of Indian Affairs, State Gambling Board, State Utilities Commission, plus the county sanitation services.

The new resort was supposed to be a boon for the jobless. When it was fully operational, it would employ 400 people. Not only Pueblo Indians but residents of Segovia just a quarter mile away could find work.

But there was also the security aspect. He wondered if the casino would have its own security or would it be folded into the San Juan Pueblo Police Department.

Lansing knew the casino's presence would bring in more traffic and impact every law enforcement agency in the area. The State Police District 7 office was three miles away. Headquarters for the Segovia Police Department was a mile beyond that. Whatever affected those two agencies affected the county sheriff's office, as well.

For Lansing, the big concern was drunks on the road. Ohkay Casino provided one more source for alcohol on the highway, on top of the other seven restaurant/bars county wide. As far as he was concerned, the one saving grace was, by state law, alcohol could not be served on the gaming floor. Drinking had to be done in the bar. A patron could not sit at a slot machine for hours on end, getting plastered, while gambling away their paycheck. They would have to do that semi-sober.

Some county residents voiced concern about an Indian Casino serving alcohol. After all, didn't "those people" have a problem with booze?

Lansing knew alcohol had been a part of Southwest Native American culture long before the Spaniards ever showed up. The Apache ferment-ed corn to make *tiswin* and *tula-pah*. *Haran a pitahaya* was a wine made from saguaro cactus. The yucca and agave plants were both used for such purposes. Hard liquor was another matter. It might have done-in a lot of Native Americans, but probably no more than it did the average white settler.

The sheriff turned his Jeep around and headed back to the highway. He was beginning to wonder if his department needed a satellite office in the area. Since he was on the south side of the county, he would give the Segovia Police Department a courtesy call . . . maybe broach the topic with the police chief. He didn't want to make a proposal to the county commissioners unless he had full cooperation with the Segovia folks.

"Patrol One, Dispatch," Marilyn called over the radio.

Lansing picked up the unit's mic. "This is Patrol One."

"We have an update on that earlier BOLO. Miera carjacked a Ford Explorer in Santa Fe. Pistol whipped the owner."

"I expect he'll avoid the main roads," Lansing said, thinking out loud. "Make sure everyone knows. I'm making a stop at Segovia PD, but I won't be long."

"Dispatch copies."

Chapter Six

"I know," Tomasita Salazar said. "Juan El Tano's wife called me."

When she opened the door, Salazar's eyes were red. Aquino couldn't tell if she had been crying or trying not to. He offered his condolences, half relieved he didn't have to break the bad news. This was especially true since Father Iglesias wasn't available. It wasn't surprising she knew already.

The Police Chief stood inside the now closed front door. The house was a bit more upscale than most of the reservation homes . . . and warm. "Do you mind if I ask you a few questions?"

"No . . . Would you like some coffee?"

Aquino shrugged. "Sure." He followed her into the roomy kitchen.

Tomasita Salazar was short . . . barely 5-foot tall . . . and roundish, though not fat. Aquino guessed she was in her mid-thirties. She wore a blue top embroidered with a Native American motif and blue jeans. Her black hair was short, barely down to her shoulders. She indicated for Aquino to sit at the kitchen table.

"I'm sorry. I don't have any milk," she said, filling a mug with the fresh brew. "The kids finished it with breakfast." She set the mug in front of the policeman along with a spoon.

He noticed the bruises on her arm. Salazar quickly pulled her sleeve down to cover them. "Sugar's on the table."

"Thanks." Aquino sweetened his coffee.

Tomasita sat across the table from him. "Eva didn't say when you found Diego."

"This morning . . . before seven-thirty. Pauline Dominguez saw him on her way to school." He hesitated before taking a sip from his mug. "When did you see him last?"

"Yesterday. He left the house after lunch."

"Oh, really?" Aquino wasn't ready for that answer. After his conversation with Dominguez, the scenario of Salazar getting drunk on New Year's Eve and falling into the river had been etched into his brain. "Is that your car in the driveway?"

"Yes."

"Do you have a second vehicle? Is that how he left?"

"No. Someone picked him up."

"Who?"

"I don't know. I think it had to do with the Northern Pueblo Council."

"Diego worked there, right?"

Tomasita nodded. "He was the Director of the Arts Council."

"What does that mean?"

"He worked with the local artists and craftsmen of the Eight Northern Pueblos. They would come to him with their projects. He arranged for their display and sales in Santa Fe."

"Sounds like an important job."

"I guess so."

Aquino thought for a moment. "Do you have any idea why he ended up at the river?"

Salazar shook her head.

"Was he wearing a coat when he left?"

"Of course!" The question surprised her. "Why wouldn't he wear a coat?"

"It's just that when we found him, he wasn't wearing one."

"It was his winter coat. Heavy wool, with brown and white patterns."

She started looking around the kitchen, distracted. "I need to start cleaning. People will be coming over . . . and I need to talk to Father Iglesias about the funeral."

17

She looked at the policeman, frantic. "Does the Summer Chief know? And the Bear Chief . . . Diego belonged to the Medicine Society."

"Calm down, Tomasita," Aquino said. "We have plenty of time."

"We only have four days!"

"That time won't start until we get Diego's body back."

"What do you mean?"

"The Medical Investigator's office out of Albuquerque is picking up your husband this morning. I've asked them to do an autopsy."

"Why?"

"To find out how he died."

"Eva El Tano said he drowned."

"We don't know that for sure."

"But he must have drowned . . . He was in the river."

For the moment, Aquino kept his alternate theory about Diego's death to himself—that the man died somewhere else and the body was dumped in the river. "Is there anyone who can be with you?"

"I called my sister. She's coming over." She shook her head. "I don't know what to tell the kids."

"If you want, I'll make arrangements for your children to be excused from school. They should be with you."

"That would be good." Tomasita nodded. The tears started to stream down her face. The impact of her husband's death was hitting her. "That would be good."

There were three children: a daughter and two sons at *Ohkay Owingeh* Community School. Aquino got the names and assured their mother they would be home within an hour.

The Police Chief stood. He wanted to ask about her bruises. At the moment, that didn't seem appropriate. "If it's all right, I may have to ask you more questions later."

"I'm not going anywhere." The response was flat, her voice hollow.

He excused himself and left. His next stop was obvious. The Eight Northern Pueblo Indians Council on Eagle Drive, barely a mile away. He wanted to know what council business Diego Salazar was doing on a Sunday afternoon. Especially on a long, holiday weekend.

Chapter Seven

The hallway of Las Palmas Middle/High School was bustling. Middle School students were rushing to their lockers after lunch, grabbing books and heading to afternoon classes. The high schoolers were going to lunch. Their pace was less panicked.

It was time for Tina Morales to eat, as well. As she made her way to the teachers' lounge, she couldn't help but pick up bits and pieces of teenage conversation.

"I could see through her window!" one tenth grader claimed. "I swear I could see everything!"

"Shut up, Jose," his companion commanded in a loud whisper. "Here comes a teacher."

A few lockers further down, a great confidence was being betrayed.

"Linda told me not to tell anyone, but she said that he said it was a big secret and nobody was supposed to know . . . Sh-h . . . Here comes Miss Morales."

The two juniors turned their heads toward the wall so the teacher wouldn't recognize them.

Tina suspected they forgot she'd had them in class two hours earlier. She had no idea what the great secret was. She was, however, confident it would be common knowledge in the entire building by the end of the school day.

In the short hallway leading to the cafeteria, Maria Alba's boyfriend, a senior named James, pleaded, "Come on, Maria . . . Skip the bus. I'll give you a ride."

"My mom said I had to go straight home."

"Tell her you missed the bus . . . We can go to the Dixie Queen. Maybe we'll take a ride."

"Yeah and get stuck somewhere! Forget it, James." She pulled away from his grasp and pushed past him.

The teacher slowed slightly to make sure the situation defused.

James noticed Morales' scowl. He quickly turned and followed Maria into the cafeteria.

Three other teachers were in the lounge when Tina arrived.

"I see you survived the holidays," Howard Duran, the history teacher observed.

"The holidays were a piece of *Tres Leche*," Tina said, referring to her favorite Mexican cake. "Wading through a hall filled with adolescent angst . . . that's the challenge!"

"You forget what it's like to be young," Susan Bustillo said. Bustillo had been teaching English for twenty years. She was fed up with her job and even more so with students that didn't care. She was threatening to retire. The rest of the teaching staff hoped she would follow through.

"How could she forget? She's still young," Duran snorted.

"Go anywhere?" Coach Moran asked.

"I visited my folks in Phoenix. My grandparents drove up from Nogales."

"Did you take the sheriff with you?" Bustillo asked. There was an air of snotty-ness to the question.

"No . . . not that it would be any of your business, Susan." Tina didn't want to sound harsh with her reply, but Bustillo brought out the worst in people.

***

At the end of the previous school year, something had happened in Rio Cohino Canyon, near *St. Anthony's Monastery*. Rumor had it some bad men had been killed. It involved Sheriff Lansing and, somehow,

21

Tina Morales. Neither one of them would talk about it. But they were an item now.

Over the summer, Morales spent more and more time at the Lansing Ranch.

That wasn't a rumor. That was a fact. There was even a witness— Oscar Vega. He had worked at the ranch for three months. He even slept there most of the time . . . in the bunk house.

When the schoolyear started, Oscar was asked about the romance.

He didn't supply any lurid details about the affair, though, mostly because he didn't know of any. Sure, he had seen them kiss a couple of times. But he certainly couldn't vouch for anything more serious. If she ever spent an entire night there, he either didn't know or refused to talk. He knew Sheriff Lansing trusted him and he would never betray that trust.

Most importantly, Oscar kept the promise he made to Lansing. He had told no one that Tina Morales was a *curandera* . . . a witch.

Chapter Eight

The Eight Northern Pueblo Indians Council headquarters was located on Eagle Drive, just off Highway 68. The construction site for the Ohkay Hotel/Casino Resort was just a quarter mile to the south.

Police Chief Joseph Aquino knew the primary reason for the council being located at San Juan Pueblo was its central location. Five other Tewa speaking pueblos, Santa Clara, San Ildefonso, Nambe, Pojoaque and Tesuque, belonged to the council. They were just to the south, in the Rio Grande valley. To the north, also in the river valley, were Taos and Picuris Pueblos, the other two members.

The council was first created in 1962. The Pueblo leaders knew they had problems: too much poverty, too little education, rampant unemployment that manifested itself in rampant domestic abuse. They realized through combining resources each Pueblo had a better chance of combating those problems than if they stood alone.

PeaceKeepers was one of the first efforts. It was created to combat domestic violence and to protect victims and their children. Over the years, services had expanded to provide shelters for abused women. Support groups met weekly in Segovia and Taos.

Aquino knew the program's endeavors didn't reach everyone. He was afraid he had seen a victim that morning.

The Pueblo Governors met monthly to address issues. Programs expanded over the years. They ranged from Head Start to Adult Vocation Training to Elder Care. Education and employment were high priorities, as was the need to preserve their heritage, religion and arts.

Aquino was in his late thirties. The council had always been there, a presence in his life. But so were the Bureau of Indian Affairs, the State of New Mexico and the Federal Government. He tried to give none of them much thought. His concern was the protection of the people of San Juan Pueblo . . . something that would get much more complicated when the new casino opened.

He parked his patrol car in front of the Council building. It was a large, adobe-style structure with a round, two-story council chamber to the right. The rest of the building started off as a single story, expanding to two-stories with offices in the back. The parking lot accommodated two dozen cars. Six were parked there.

Once inside, Aquino realized he knew the receptionist. Karen Kata was the granddaughter of Manuel Kata, President of the San Juan Pueblo Tribal Council and, essentially, his boss.

"Hi, Joseph!" she chimed. "What are you doing here?"

"I need to talk to someone, but I'm not sure who."

"What about?"

"Diego Salazar."

"I haven't seen him today."

"You won't be seeing him, I'm afraid." He saw the confused look on the receptionist's face. "We found his body this morning . . . in the Rio Grande."

"Oh, no!" The response was almost a squeak. Kata covered her mouth with her hand. "Did he drown?"

"We're looking into that . . . I need to speak to whoever he worked with."

"He works . . ." She corrected herself. ". . . worked under the Executive Director, Isaac Yope. But he's still down at San Ildefonso. He won't be in until this afternoon." The receptionist was visibly shaken. "His, uh . . . Diego's assistant is in, if you want to speak to her."

Kata directed him to the second floor.

The office for the Council Director for the Arts was in the back of the building. Aquino got the impression education, employment and social services held higher priorities than arts and crafts. Still, Salazar's outer office was tastefully decorated with photos and paintings on the walls along with glass encased displays of embroidery work, carvings and sand paintings.

Constance Gomez, the secretary/assistant, sat at her desk. She was upset, fighting back tears. "Karen just told me about Diego . . . I'm sorry, Officer. I don't know what to say."

"That's all right," he noticed the name plate on her desk, "Constance."

"Connie," she offered. "I go by Connie." She realized he didn't recognize her. "I'm from Santa Clara Pueblo."

Connie was in her early twenties. She was dressed in "Pueblo casual." A brightly embroidered white cotton shirt, beaded necklace, hair done up in a bun. Aquino guessed she wore an ankle length skirt.

"Okay, Connie. I needed to ask a couple of questions about Mr. Salazar's work."

"I'll help, if I can."

"I was told it was his job to help get Pueblo artwork displayed at Santa Fe galleries. Is that right?"

"As far as I know, the council dealt with only one Santa Fe Gallery. But our office helped put on three major Arts and Crafts fairs every year." She sounded proud of their work.

"Very impressive. How long had he been Director for the Council of the Arts?"

"Five years. He started January of ninety-four."

"Was he going to leave?"

"What do you mean?"

"Was he going to leave his position? I know some of the Council positions rotate through the Pueblos, so everyone gets a shot at being in charge."

"I—I don't know about the Arts Council. I haven't heard anything."

"How long have you been secretary?"

"About two years."

"Did you take care of his schedule?"

"You mean like meetings and stuff?"

"Yes."

"I kept his calendar. Reminded him about his meetings. But he usually set his own schedule. He would let me know so I could keep track."

"Was there anything on his calendar about a meeting he had yesterday?"

Connie held up his schedule ledger. The first annotation was for Tuesday the fifth.

"When was the last time you spoke with him?"

"Last Thursday. New Year's Eve."

"He didn't say he was meeting anyone over the weekend?"

"Not to me."

Aquino nodded thoughtfully. "Thank you for your help." He turned to leave.

"When is the funeral?" the secretary quickly asked before the policeman was out the door.

Aquino shrugged. "I'm sure somebody will let you know."

Chapter Nine

Agustina Jacona sat in her two-room apartment wrapped in a blanket, fighting the chill. Her home was part of *Owe'neh Bupingeh*, the 700-year-old core of the San Juan Pueblo. Despite the fact that the adobe building she lived in was crumbling around her, Agustina refused to leave. The rest of her family had moved to government subsidized housing just outside the Pueblo, but still on reservation land.

The 16-acre Pueblo and its three plazas were in constant use for the many "dances" and ceremonies throughout the year. The kiva, the religious heart of the Tewa traditions, was located in an adobe building on the south side of Plaza One. It was in constant use and had to be repaired and maintained. Unfortunately, the rest of the historic Pueblo was in decay, the victim of a "good idea" someone had in the 1960s.

The traditional adobe home was built using sun-dried bricks made of clay, aggregate (usually sand) and straw. A similar mixture was plastered over the brick to give a clean, smooth look. Pigment mixed into the plaster provided the color. Naturally, the elements took their toll and the adobe plaster was in constant need of repair. The "good idea" was to use cement instead of adobe plaster. The cement would harden, be water-proof and last for years, negating the need for constant repair.

No one suspected the adobe plaster actually allowed the underlying bricks to "breath." The cement plaster did indeed last for years, but cracks developed, and water eventually seeped into the adobe bricks, dissolving them. One by one, the adobe building melted away, leaving the cement shells. The occupants had no choice but to move.

There were once over 400 dwellings. Now, only 35 families still lived in the Pueblo.

There were two reasons Agustina Jacona refused to leave. The first was she had lived in that home for fifty years, since she was first married at the age of fifteen. Pardo had died years earlier. But she remained there with her children and, eventually, her grandchildren. At one time, ten family members occupied the two rooms. She couldn't imagine living anywhere else.

The second reason for remaining in the heart of the Pueblo was she had finally become *Apienu,* the cacique, the head of the Women's Society. Her parents had pledged her to the Society when she was a baby. At age eight, when she was initiated into the tribe as one of the "Dry Food People," she began her apprenticeship.

At age 25, she became one of the "Made People," a member of the Women's Society. She was given an elaborately decorated ceramic bowl, the symbol of her position. At age 30, she was selected to become one of two Blue Corn Women. That was when she became privy to the inner secrets of the moiety.

Agustina had waited 35 years. The old *Apienu* and her successor had to pass on before Jacona could assume her new position. Her time of pain and frustration had come to an end. She could now use the sacred knowledge she had garnered over the many years. She felt in her heart, if she left the Pueblo, her abilities would be diminished.

Someone knocked on her door.

"Come in . . . quickly," Jacona called.

A rush of cold air accompanied the visitor when she entered. She immediately shut the door. "Mama Agustina, I thought you should know . . ." Carla Naranjo said. "They found Diego Salazar in the river this morning."

"Yes, I heard," the *Apienu* nodded.

"Do you think we should go to Tomasita? I'm sure she could use our support."

"Maybe tomorrow," Jacona said, thoughtfully. "She has family. She has friends. I'm sure Father Iglesias will be there. We certainly don't want to get in the way."

Of the eight Tewa societies at the Pueblo, the Women's Society was on the lowest rung. Women could join the other societies, but they could never rise to Chief. Only women could belong to the Women's moiety. Because of this, Agustina Jacona was held in high esteem by the other females of *Ohkay Owingeh*. Out of respect, she held the unofficial title of *La Madre de San Juan*. Her followers affectionately called her "Mama."

Naranjo looked around the darkening room. Jacona's apartment faced east. The morning sun would have streamed in through the only window, brightening and warming the space. It was past noon. The sun had moved on. The deepening shadows and a breeze from the north helped the cold seep into the ancient home. The only heat came from a burner on the gas stove in the other room.

"Mama, can I get you anything?" the younger woman asked. "Or maybe I can take you to your son's place. I'm sure it's warmer there."

"I'm fine, Carla."

"I worry about you."

"Thank you for stopping by," the old woman said dismissively, ending the conversation.

Chapter Ten

Galeria de Magdalena was snuggled amongst other art galleries, jewelry stores and boutiques on West Palace Avenue, a block from Santa Fe Plaza. All the retail businesses in Old Santa Fe that depended on tourists were preparing for the doldrums. January through March was the slim time of year. Sure, a few visitors on their way to Ski Santa Fe might wander through. But for the most part, during the Winter months, sales were down to a trickle.

Gallery owner William Bryce checked his watch. It was already 2:15 and he hadn't had lunch. Murdock said he would be there by noon.

Bryce's contacts in Boston and New York were impatient. The Christmas Holidays had been a huge success for them. The mania for Pueblo Indian art had been phenomenal and it looked like that demand would not subside any time soon. The *Galeria* got some pieces from Hopi and Zuni artisans, but its primary source for Native American craftwork came from the Eight Northern Pueblo Indians Art Council.

The day after Christmas, Bryce's buyers started making their demands. The galleries had to be restocked. He had guaranteed that he could fulfill their requests. If he couldn't, they assured him they would find other suppliers. If they did, he would be ruined.

That's why Edmund Murdock had been dispatched to San Juan Pueblo. Diego Salazar was dissatisfied with the current arrangements. He thought he could take the Pueblo's business elsewhere and get a better deal. Salazar had made the mistake of signing an agreement making *Galeria de Magdalena* the exclusive representative for Pueblo artwork. (Bryce knew the contract was worthless. He had been counting on Salazar not coming to the same realization.)

The other thing Bryce didn't need the Pueblo Art Council to know was the fact that he maintained two sets of books. Bryce and Salazar agreed ahead of time what the artwork would sell for. Bryce took a 25% commission on all sales to cover his overhead. The rest of the money went to Salazar and his artisans.

What Salazar didn't know was 95% of all sales were bogus. Bryce and his cohorts purchased the works from the gallery on the agreed upon prices, with the gallery keeping its commission. Then *Magdalena* would jack up the prices by up to 400% and sell the same artworks to eastern dealers.

Bryce didn't seem to think there was anything wrong with his operation. The Pueblo Indian artisans were getting paid what they asked. The art dealers on the East Coast were getting what they demanded. If he happened to make a tidy profit in between, what difference did it make?

Bryce hurried into the front display room when he heard the entry door chime.

"It's about time Edmund," the gallery owner groused. "What did Salazar have to say?"

Edmund Murdock was a big man. Some people considered him intimidating. That worked to his advantage. When he made a suggestion, most people complied without him having to do anything further. "You're not going to like it, Mr. Bryce."

"Why? What? What did he say?" Bryce asked impatiently.

"He said his office got a call from The Adams Gallery in Boston last week."

"Oh, God!" the art dealer gasped. He had been dealing with The Adams Gallery for years. Adams was one of the galleries that threatened to find "another supplier." "What did they say?"

"They wanted to know if they could represent the Pueblo Art Council in the Boston area. If things worked out, Adams said they could expand into the New York City/Washington D.C. corridor."

Bryce began to tremble. "What did he tell them?"

"He said he wanted to talk to you first."

"About what?"

"Something about revisiting a contract you had with him."

"Oh." The word was no more than a whisper.

"I don't think you have anything to worry about."

"What do you mean?"

"Have you heard from him?"

"No," Bryce said. He could see his world crumbling around him. "No, not yet."

"I don't think you will."

Bryce gave him a quizzical look.

"Let's just say, we had a talk." Murdock shoved his hands into his coat pockets. "If that's it, Mr. Bryce, I'll be going."

The gallery owner could only blink in response.

Assuming his employer was satisfied, the big man turned and left.

Chapter Eleven

"Joey Lopez!" his mother, Elena, scolded. "You're soaked."

"We had a snowball fight," the nine-year old explained. He pulled off his gloves and stocking cap. His mother unzipped his coat.

It was almost dark outside, even though it was only 4:30 in the afternoon.

"I want you to take those wet things off. You need a hot bath."

"It's not bedtime."

"No, but it will warm you up. By the time you're done, your dad will be home and we can eat."

"Aw," the fourth-grader complained, stomping out of the kitchen and heading for his bedroom.

"By the way," Elena called after him, "do you have any homework?"

"A little," he answered back.

She shook her head. The rule was homework had to be done before he went out to play. Since it got dark so early, Mrs. Lopez didn't press the issue. There was plenty of time for his school assignments after the evening meal.

She listened for the bath water to run. Soon after, she heard the splashing. Joey was an only child . . . and her baby. She couldn't help but coddle him. She knew he would need help shampooing, so she joined him in the bathroom.

As usual, he was doing more playing than scrubbing. When he saw his mom, he knew it was time to get serious. He grabbed a washcloth and began rubbing his arms, as if that was where all the dirt accumulated.

Elena knelt with shampoo in hand and helped her son finish his bathing. When the job was done, she reached for a towel. He stood. When she turned back, she almost screamed.

"My god! What happened to your legs?"

Joey had scratches that started above his knees and went down to his ankles. In some spots the scratches were deep enough to draw blood. Scabs had formed. It looked like he was clawed by some animal . . . or a human hand with long nails.

"I don't know," he whimpered, afraid he was in trouble.

"*Mejo*, when did this happen?"

"Last night." His voice was small, trembling.

"Who did this?" Elena tried not to sound alarmed.

"The ghost."

"What ghost?"

"The one in my room. It was in the corner . . . It came to my bed . . ." He started crying. "I tried to call you, but I couldn't move!"

"What did it do?"

"She hurt me . . . She said if I told you she would come back!"

"This ghost . . . what did it look like?"

"I don't know. My room was dark, but she was even darker."

"How do you know it was a 'she' ghost?"

"It sounded like an old woman." He started crying even more.

Elena wrapped him in the towel and picked him up. She carried him to her room, then sat on the bed with Joey on her lap. "It's all right, baby. It's all right."

She held him and rocked back and forth. They stayed like that until Jonah Lopez got home from work.

Chapter Twelve

Tina Morales opened her front door.

"Sorry I'm late!" Lansing said, pulling the teacher close and giving her a long, hard kiss. They hadn't seen each other since before Christmas. Even though she was in Phoenix, they talked every day. They had been dating for six months. The sheriff was afraid their summer romance wouldn't last. Once school started, he figured she would go back to teaching and have no time for the two of them.

Instead, she would drive down to the ranch in the evenings dragging along lesson plans and papers to grade. They took turns fixing meals. Sometimes Oscar would eat with them if his work kept him late. Weeknights, she drove back into town for school the next day. Weekends, she stayed at the ranch, exclusively.

In the evenings, if the sheriff was called away on business, Morales would make sure the kitchen was clean before she headed home. She was never upset if he had to leave. That was his job and she understood.

Tina had gotten back late Saturday evening. Sunday, she spent doing laundry and preparing for the first day of school in the new year. Monday evening was their first chance to get together. Lansing promised to take her to dinner.

"I should go away more often!" Tina purred. "I think that was your best kiss ever."

Lansing tightened his hug. "I've been practicing . . . Little Orphan Annie really surprises me sometimes."

The teacher pulled away and gave him a gentle punch in the chest. "And another load of horse manure from my favorite cowboy."

She turned and grabbed her coat from the arm of the sofa. Lansing helped her slip it on.

"So, what kept you tonight? Bank robbers?" she asked after they were in his Jeep.

"Naw. I was on the other side of town. I was checking on a possible break-in . . . at a residence." He sounded serious. "They think their son was attacked."

"You're kidding!" Morales was especially concerned where children were involved.

"I wish I were. They showed me the scratches on the boy's legs. But they said their house was locked last night. His window, too. I checked the yard leading up to the boy's window . . . No tracks in the snow. So, I don't know."

"How old is he?"

"Nine. He goes to Las Palmas Elementary."

They had already turned onto Highway 15. Instead of slowing to turn into the parking lot, they proceeded past *Paco's Cantina*, heading north.

"We're not eating at *Paco's*?" she asked, surprised.

"I was there almost every night for two weeks. We're going to Cohino."

They drove in silence for a few miles. "This boy with the scratches . . . Do you think he did it to himself?" the teacher finally asked. "You know, sometimes kids act out for attention."

"I looked at his nails. They weren't long enough to do that kind of damage."

"Where did he say they came from?"

"He said there was a ghost in his room. That's who scratched him."

"I don't know, Cliff. If the house was locked and nobody could get in, one of the parents probably did it. He just made up the ghost story to protect them."

"I could see that happening if the scratches had been found by a doctor or a school counselor," the sheriff agreed. "But in this case, the parents found the scratches and reported them."

"Who saw them first?"

"Evidently, the mother, when the boy took a bath."

"Why didn't he tell his parents about the attack?"

"The ghost told him, if he said anything, she would come back."

"Yeah, and his father could have told him the same thing."

"You certainly have a jaded opinion of parents," Lansing observed.

"I've been teaching for seven years and for seven years, when a kid fails in school and, ultimately, in life, teachers usually get the blame. The thing is, we only have them in classrooms for six hours a day. If a child has problems, it's usually the parents' fault."

"If it's so bad, why don't you quit?"

"Dammit, Lansing! Don't you dare try to use logic on me," she snapped. "I teach because I love it and I love the students I teach . . . and you know that!"

"Okay! Okay!"

Tina stared out the window watching the darkened country side roll past. "I still think you're going to find out it was one of the parents," she harrumphed.

Neither said anything until they pulled into the restaurant parking lot.

Chapter Thirteen

Cohino, 13 miles from the Colorado State Line, had only 1200 permanent residents. Most of the dwellings were either single-story, frame houses or manufactured homes. Surprisingly, after the O'Keeffe Ranch and the Jicarilla Apache Indian Reservation, it was the third most popular tourist destination in San Phillipe County. That was because of the Chisum and Aztec Scenic Railroad.

Originally built as a spur for the Denver and Rio Grande Western Railroad in 1881, the narrow-gauge line supported mining operation in the Colorado San Juan Mountains. Traffic dwindled over the years until, finally, in 1968 the spur was scheduled to close. Colorado and New Mexico jointly purchased the portion of the railroad that ran from Cohino to Antonito, Colorado in 1970 to encourage tourism. It worked.

The coal-driven, steam locomotives operated the 64 mile stretch of rail line from the end of May until the end of October. Passengers packed the rail cars and enjoyed daily, round-trip excursions. In the summer months, Cohino swelled to three times its normal size. To accommodate the visitors, the town boasted two RV parks, two bed-and-breakfasts, four motels, a lodge with cabins, and eight places to eat.

During hunting season, the town also saw business from hunters that used the Quincy Game Ranch 5 miles outside of town. That kept the tourist traffic trickling through, even in the Fall and Winter.

As far as Sheriff Cliff Lansing was concerned, the *High Desert Restaurant* in Cohino was the best steak house north of Albuquerque. That was their destination this Monday evening.

The parking lot was nearly empty, not unusual for a weekday night in the middle of Winter. A rush of warm air greeted them as they entered. A large blaze crackled in the stone fireplace at one end of the large room.

"Oh, hi, Miss Morales!" Maria Alba bubbled. "Welcome to the *High Desert*."

"Well, hello, Maria!" Tina exclaimed. "I didn't know you worked here."

"I do. Since last Summer." Alba had swapped a green, pullover sweater for a long-sleeved, white shirt with a silver name tag. She wore the same dark slacks.

Morales turned to her date. "Cliff, this is Maria Alba, one of my chemistry students." Then back to Alba. "Maria, this is Sheriff Lansing."

The student blushed. "Everybody knows the sheriff."

"Pleased to meet you, Maria," Lansing said, removing his hat and nodding to the young lady.

Alba grabbed a couple of menus. "I'm going to be your waitress this evening. Where would you like to sit?"

"Close to the fireplace?" He asked the teacher.

"You don't want to get too close," the student warned. "You'll get roasted."

"Okay, Maria," Morales said. "Why don't you seat us where we'll be safe?"

"Follow me."

The couple draped their coats on an empty chair at their table. They both ordered warm cups of apple cider to sip while they looked over the menus. Nearby, another waitress handled the other two diners in the restaurant.

Maria delivered their drinks. Morales stopped her before she walked away. "Is this why you didn't go joy riding with James Cooper this afternoon?"

"You heard us?"

The teacher nodded.

"I come here straight after school. If we're not busy, I study in the back. James just doesn't understand."

"That you're working? Are you saving for college?"

"I wish. My dad's an engineer on the railroad, which means he only works six months a year. The whole family has to chip in, especially over the winter."

"Your dad doesn't work at all this time of year?" Lansing asked.

"He runs a snowplow . . . does a lot of the back roads and the streets here in town. We're lucky. He's been busy this year."

"How late do you work?" The teacher was sincerely worried.

"Till closing, at Ten. Then I walk home." She saw Lansing scowl. "It's okay, Sheriff. It's only a mile."

After the chitchat, it was time to order. Tina got the brook trout. Lansing opted for the 12-ounce T-bone, medium-rare. With no kitchen traffic, they didn't wait long for their meals.

Even though they had spoken daily over the holiday, there were plenty of gaps they could fill in. The twosome talked through the meal and during the coffee after they ate.

The couple was engrossed in conversation. When not attending the table, the waitress tried to study. No one noticed the shadow hovering outside, beyond the plate-glass windows.

It was half-past nine before the lawman and his lady finished.

The tip was generous, and Maria gratefully thanked them.

Back in Las Palmas, Tina's goodnight kiss took longer than Lansing planned. It was nearly midnight before he got back to the ranch.

Chapter Fourteen

"You sure you don't want to wait for a ride?" Poncho, the chef, asked. "We'll be done by ten-thirty."

"I'll be home before you're finished," Maria said. She was already back in her green sweater and slipping on her coat. She knew the kitchen cleanup would take until at least eleven. "All I want to do is take a shower and slide into a nice warm bed." She pulled the stocking cap over her ears, slid on her gloves and slung her backpack over her shoulder.

When Alba stepped out the back of the restaurant, she was enveloped by a cocoon of icy mountain air. There was no breeze. She was glad for that.

The single light over the back door lit an area 20-feet by 20-feet. It took the waitress only a couple of steps before she was in the dark. She had to walk 500 feet along Highway 15 to the north, past the drug store, before she got to the cross street that took her to Oak Drive.

The few street lights in Cohino were positioned along Highway 15. The rest of the hamlet was dark. The only sidewalk was a thousand-foot stretch near the train depot, over a mile from where Alba was. She had to satisfy herself with walking down the middle of the road, or on the gravel shoulder when a car passed. The moon was a sliver. What little light she had along her way came from porches, the few that were lit-up.

Marie wasn't worried. She had made the walk hundreds of times. Probably could do it with her eyes closed. She would have been wearing her Walkman, if the batteries hadn't died. She had to satisfy herself with humming her most recently favorite song, THIS KISS by Faith Hill.

Her trek would take her a half mile up Oak Drive. Then she would zig-zag over a couple of streets until she reached Cedar and home.

From the corner of her eye, she thought she saw movement. A shadow, maybe? She turned her head and quit humming.

If someone was there, she surely would have heard the crunch of steps on snow.

She didn't stop. She kept moving down the street. She heard a truck speeding down the highway two blocks away and her own footsteps.

She stared straight ahead. She had one thought: Get home.

The movement came again. The silent shadow.

She picked up her pace. Before she knew it, she was running.

The only sound was her labored breathing and the soles of her shoes scraping the pavement.

If the shadow was keeping pace, she didn't want to know.

She was running as fast as she could now.

The light on her porch was a half block away. If only she could reach the front door, everything would be fine.

If only she could reach the porch . . .

If only . . .

Chapter Fifteen

It was another cloudless day in the high desert. The forecast called for temperatures in the high thirties. To Lansing, that meant he could turn the horses loose in the corral for most of the day. It also meant melting snow and sloppy roads. This time of year, his fleet of vehicles had to hit the car washes twice a week at a minimum.

"There's a fresh pot of coffee in the day room," Peters said when Lansing entered the offices. Deputy Phil Peters still manned his night dispatch post. Marilyn Bea, the day dispatch, and Clem Montoya, the Desk Sergeant, hadn't arrived yet.

"Thanks." Lansing put his hat and coat in his office, then hit the day room to fill his mug. His next stop was the overnight logs. He needed to keep track of what went on in San Phillippe County.

A dispatch, logged at 11:30 pm, jumped out at him: Cohino. 16-year-old female failed to come home after work. Deputy W. Estrada took the call.

"Phil," Lansing asked, "what can you tell me about this missing girl in Cohino?"

"Just a minute." He looked around his desk. "The nine-one-one operator gave me a name." He found the piece of paper he was looking for. "The call came from a Klara Alba on Cedar Street."

"Is Willie still on the road, or has she signed off?"

"No, she hasn't signed off."

"Contact her. Tell her I'd like to hear her report."

"What's going on?"

"I think I know the young lady who went missing."

As Peters contacted Willie Estrada, Chief Deputy Jack Rivera came in. He usually grabbed a cup of coffee before hitting the highways.

"Morning, Sheriff."

"Hey, Jack," Lansing said. He was obviously distracted.

"Anything wrong?"

"Missing teenage girl . . . One of Tina's students. She waited on us at *The High Desert Restaurant* last night."

"When did she go missing?"

"She got off work at ten, so, sometime after that."

"Sheriff!" Peters called. "Estrada said she'll be here in fifteen minutes."

"Good." He thought for a moment. "Phil . . . that escaped prisoner, Miera . . . Have there been any more updates?"

"No, sir."

Deputies Danny Cortez and Jerry Lopez came in the front door, laughing about something.

"Hey, Jerry," Lansing interrupted.

"Yeah?"

"Could you come back to my office?"

Lopez gave Deputy Cortez a shrug that said, "I don't know." He followed Lansing to the Sheriff's private office.

Once they were in the room, Lansing motioned for the door to be closed. Lopez stood in front of the sheriff's desk, concerned. "What's wrong, boss?"

"Did you talk to Jonah about your nephew yesterday evening?" Jonah was Jerry's brother and Lansing knew they were close.

"No. Was I supposed to?"

Lansing shook his head. "I went over there right after work last night. They had reported a break-in. I was curious why he didn't call you?"

"He's not allowed to, unless somebody's getting killed."

"What's that all about?"

44

"When Joey was born, Elena became a pain in the butt. She was just a little overprotective," he said sarcastically. "She thought I was their personal bodyguard. I would get called four times a week, day and night, because she heard a noise outside, or she thought someone was breaking in, or someone was getting ready to kidnap her baby."

"I remember you complaining about that back when I was still a deputy."

"After nearly two years of that BS, I finally had enough. I told Jonah, if they needed someone from our office, they had to call nine-one-one, just like everybody else."

He paused his rant. "Did somebody break in?"

"I don't think so." Lansing wanted to make sure he used the right words. "The reason they called was because your nephew's legs were covered with scratches. They thought a stranger broke in and did it. But the house was locked. So was the boy's window . . . and no tracks outside."

"So, what are you driving at?"

"The scratches were pretty serious. Do you think Jonah, or your sister-in-law could have done something like that?"

"To their own son?" Lopez exploded. "That's insane! Did Joey say who scratched him?"

"Yes." Lansing nodded. "A ghost."

"That's insane, too!" Lopez said.

The sheriff shrugged. "I'm just telling you what your brother said."

"Do you think I need to talk to them about what really happened?"

"That wouldn't hurt." He paused before his next statement. "We want to make sure we're not looking at child abuse."

Lopez considered the situation for a moment. "My daughter, Melanie, is twelve. Maybe she should talk to Joey. They get along okay. She could find out what's really going on."

"It's your family, Jerry. Do what you think is best. I'd like to keep the office out of your business, if I can."

"I appreciate that, Sheriff." Lopez hesitated. "Anything else?"

"Just be careful out there today."

Chapter Sixteen

"Mrs. Alba got concerned when Maria hadn't gotten home by ten-thirty," Deputy Wilma (Willie) Estrada said, reading from her notes. "She called the restaurant first. The cook said she left at ten. She called her daughter's friends to see if she stopped off, but no one had seen her. That's when she called nine-one-one."

The night before, Lansing had been concerned when Maria said she walked home after work. His worries had become justified. "You got the call from dispatch at eleven-thirty. What time did you get to the house?"

"A quarter to twelve. Something like that."

"So, no one had seen her for almost two hours," he said, thinking out loud. "How far is it from the restaurant to her house?"

"I drove it to see," Estrada replied. "It's right at a mile."

"I take it you didn't see anything along the way?"

"No, sir."

"We'll canvass the neighborhood. Hopefully someone saw or heard something."

"Is that all, Sheriff?"

"Yeah, Willie. Thanks for coming in . . . Go home and get some rest."

As Deputy Estrada left, Jack Rivera stuck his head in the door. "I'm getting ready to head out, Cliff. I just wanted to give you an update on that abandoned car up on Route one-eighty-two."

"What did you find out?"

"It belongs to a guy by the name of Robert Paul. Lives out in the country near Estrella. He was driving in that snowstorm we had last Friday night. He thought he saw an old woman standing in the middle of the road, swerved to miss her and ended up in a snowbank.

"He got out and looked for the lady, but nobody was there. He had to call a friend to pick him and his wife up."

"This wasn't a case of too much News Year's Day partying, was it?"

"I don't think so. They're a couple in their fifties. They had dinner at *Paco's* and I think they were just trying to get home. At any rate, a tow truck pulled their car out of the drift yesterday. There wasn't any damage."

"Okay," Lansing nodded. "Thanks for the update."

The sheriff leaned back in his seat and looked out the window. He had a meeting with the county commissioners at 10:00. A budget discussion. He wondered how much more belt tightening they were going to ask for.

His office had finished the 1997-98 annual budget with a surplus. Instead of being praised, the county commissioners cut his current budget by the amount of the previous year's surplus. (He had been warned that could happen, but he didn't listen hard enough. Lesson learned. No more surpluses, although he didn't know who benefited from money being spent for the sake of spending money.)

He would have preferred being on patrol. Even going door-to-door in Cohino looking for information about Maria Alba would beat sitting in a meeting with the commissioners.

He let out a heavy sign, then headed for the Day Room for another mug of coffee.

Chapter Seventeen

Tribal Police Chief Aquino stood outside a holding cell in his small jail. Carlos Dominguez sat on a cot with his head in his hands. Aquino knew the problem was that the man was hung over. He hoped some regret was mixed in with the evaporating alcohol.

Aquino got a call at 9:30 the night before. A neighbor had reported a disturbance at the Dominguez house. When the officer got there, he found a drunken Carlos standing over his wife, Pauline. She was cowering in a corner, a paring knife in her hand, trying to fend off another assault.

The school nurse had been smacked around. Her hair was mussed, her face streaked with tears. Aquino could see the fear in her eyes.

Two children, four and five, stood in a nearby doorway, holding each other, crying.

"That's enough, Carlos!" Aquino ordered.

Dominguez wheeled around to confront the intruder. The man was so drunk, he lost his balance and fell against the wall. Before he could recover, Aquino was on him. The officer threw him to the ground, face down. It took only a moment to yank the hands behind his back and cuff him.

As he was being dragged to the patrol car, Dominguez kept demanding to know, "Why are you doing this? Why are you doing this?"

Once Carlos was secure in the back seat, Aquino went back inside. Pauline was on her knees, hugging her children. They were all crying.

"Are you all right, Pauline? Do you need to go to the hospital?" The nearest medical unit was the Five Pueblo Health Clinic in Segovia, nearly 6 miles away.

"I don't think so . . ." she said between sobs. "Thank you for coming, Joseph."

"Of course. It's my job." He waited for her to calm down. "Should I ask one of your neighbors to sit with you?"

Pauline nodded. "Isabel . . . next door. Could you ask her to come over?"

Isabel watched the Dominguez children during the afternoons, after they finished the half-day at Head Start. She took them to the bedroom while the police chief asked some questions.

"How long has Carlos been beating you?"

"Tonight was the first time . . . I mean that it was this bad."

"He never hit you before?"

"I guess there were times he slapped me," she said, sadly.

Aquino didn't push the issue of her pressing charges. The Tribal Council would do that for her. Over the years, the Council had been proactive about addressing domestic violence, though some people felt they hadn't been proactive enough. Especially over the last six months. It seemed like domestic abuse calls had gone up from a couple a month to a couple a week. The police chief didn't know why. Maybe it was just his perception.

"You need to speak to the PeaceKeepers. They can get you into a shelter if you want."

"That's okay. I know who I need to talk to."

Carlos was passed out in the back of the car by the time they reached the police station. Aquino literally dragged him to the cell. He wondered if the night in the clink had any affect.

"Do you know why you're in here?" the officer asked.

"'Cause I got drunk," Dominguez mumbled.

"Do you remember what else got you here?"

Carlos thought hard for a moment, then lifted his head and squinted at the police chief. "Pauline?"

"Yeah," a tinge of anger in Aquino's reply. "Pauline." He turned away without elaborating.

The tribal cop stepped outside of his headquarters. It would be relatively warm that day. The mid-forties. They would have blue skies and about the same temperatures for tomorrow, January 6th, Kings Day. In Catholic tradition, this was the day the Three Wise Men arrived in Bethlehem.

For San Juan Pueblo, this was the day for the Buffalo Dances. First, the Winter Society would perform theirs, followed by the Summer Society. People outside the seven Tewa speaking pueblos had no real concept of the Tewa social/political/religious structure.

***

San Juan Pueblo had two chiefs: The head of the Summer Moiety and the head of the Winter Moiety. They were in charge of Pueblo activities from the Spring Equinox to the Fall Equinox, and vice versa. All persons born into the tribe belonged to one or the other, based on their father's lineage. However, children weren't officially inducted into their society until at least the age of six. At that point they became Dry Food People.

Within this structure, a Dry Food Person could graduate to a higher, more important position by becoming a *Towa e*, a protector of tribal traditions, or becoming a Made Person. To become a Made Person, an individual had to belong to one of the six lesser societies: Medicine, Kwirana, Kossa, Hunt, Scalp, and Women. Kwirana and Kossa were the Sacred Clown Societies and had special functions during the many festivals throughout the year. The other four functioned as their names implied, though since the beginning of the Twentieth Century, the Hunt and Scalp Societies importance had diminished.

The Women's Society had been created to assist the Scalp Society to take care of the "scalps" or prisoners captured during war. With no more war, the Women's Society's importance had receded, as well.

The Spanish moved into northern New Mexico in 1598. The *Ohkay Owingeh* people occupied Pueblos on both sides of the Rio Grande. Juan de Onate and his men were "invited" to move into the western Pueblo, establishing the first Spanish capitol of New Mexico. The previous occupants were escorted across the river to live in the eastern Pueblo. This new capitol was named San Gabriel de Yunge, and the *Ohkay Owingeh* was christened San Juan de los Caballeros. (Because of mismanagement, Onate was replaced after ten years and the capitol moved to its present location in Santa Fe in 1608.)

Under the dictates of Madrid, 4,000 miles away, the foreign rulers imposed a new, more secular, layer of bureaucracy on top of the existing traditions. This gave the Pueblos a governor, two lieutenant governors and a sheriff, as well as six *Towa e* to manage native religious affairs and four *fiscales* for Catholic church functions. These 14 officials held office for a single year, beginning on New Year's Day. An effective leader may hold the same post for multiple years.

The two moiety chiefs alternated years naming these office holders.

The complexities of a modern world led the Pueblos to adopt more conventional ways to manage their affairs. The older societies and the newer "Spanish Offices" remained in place. But a Tribal Council, comprised of the governor, the lieutenants, the sheriff and eight society chiefs ran the Pueblo. The council had a Chief, called the President, who presided. He was a former governor and held the position for the rest of his life.

At San Juan, President Manuel Kata managed the day to day affairs with a staff of seventy personnel, which included the Chief of Tribal Police and his three officers.

For King's Day, Aquino and his men would be positioned around the Pueblo to manage the many outsiders that gathered to watch the Buffalo Dances. The *Towa e* assisted in handling the crowds. Most visitors wouldn't know this first ceremony of the year beseeched the ancient deities for bountiful rain for the annual crops. In the high desert, rain was everything. In a culture that needed that gift from the gods for mere survival, almost every ceremony addressed the importance of rain.

Every member of the Pueblo was raised Catholic. There was no hypocrisy. In the Tewa Universe, Catholic Saints were folded into the pantheon of traditional deities. The duality of Catholic and Tewa religions matched perfectly with the duality of ruling moiety chiefs and the duality of traditional tribal societies sharing power with a Spanish system.

Over the years it had been tweaked and refined, but it was a system that worked. It had been in place for 400 years and it made no sense to change it.

Chapter Eighteen

For the Juniors at San Phillipe Middle/High School, second period was for Chemistry I. Among the students, since Home Room, the big discussion had been Maria Alba's disappearance.

Speculation about what happened started on the school bus. The two Cohino girls in Maria's class had gotten calls from Klara Alba . . . late. Had they seen her daughter? Did they know where she could have gone? Had she said anything to them?

Mrs. Alba sounded frantic.

The discussion of the mystery became disruptive. It spread from the Junior class to all the other grades. With a school of less than 200 students, everyone knew everyone else.

Tina Morales noticed the empty seat on the front row. She too asked questions. That she had seen Maria the evening before was information she kept to herself.

James Cooper got a lot of hard stares. He insisted he was at home in Las Palmas all night. He wasn't anywhere near Maria.

A rumor started that a strange van had been seen prowling the Cohino streets after dark. A ninth grader even claimed he had witnessed the van's driver jump out and grab a girl from Cohino Elementary. His claim didn't stand up to intense cross examination from his fellow students: no other witnesses, no reports to the sheriff's office, and no corroborating rumors.

Tina had lunch after fourth period. It was warm enough she could step outside and make a quick call to Lansing.

"It's ongoing, Tina," Lansing reported. "Deputy Cortez is up there asking around. He only has a couple dozen houses to cover, so it shouldn't take long."

"What if no one saw anything?"

"We've started a search. I got as many men together as I could. They'll go building to building if they have to. People are driving the roads. They're looking for tracks in the snow. Anything suspicious. I promised her mother, we'll do everything we can."

"Is there anything I can do?"

"Have your students said anything?"

"Maria's disappearance is all they've talked about. Evidently they know as much as you do . . . which means they don't know anything."

"Thanks, I appreciate the vote of confidence."

"I'm just saying . . ."

"I know what you're saying. You're right. We don't know anything, yet. Hopefully, we will have an answer before dark."

"I hope you're right. I'll give you a call after school's out."

"Okay. Talk to you then, Tina. Bye."

"Goodbye, Cliff."

The afternoon classes dragged by.

Morales had bus duty, so she wasn't free until 4:30. By then it was almost dark. Instead of calling, she went straight to the Sheriff's Department. She needed to know what happened to her student.

Chapter Nineteen

The San Juan Pueblo Tribal Court had to follow the U.S. Constitution and the State Laws of New Mexico. From the time of arrest, Aquino had 48 hours to get Carlos Dominguez in front of a judge for a preliminary hearing. Wednesday, the 6th, everything in the Pueblo would be shut down for the Buffalo Dances. So, that afternoon the police chief had to drag Dominguez from his cell to the Tribal Court building next door.

There was only one presiding judge, Paul Lovato. He handled preliminary hearings and misdemeanor offenses. Capital crimes were overseen by the Tribal Council.

Once inside the courtroom, Aquino explained their visit.

"Carlos, I'm not happy about you being here," Lovato said, frowning.

"I didn't do nothin'." Dominguez's response was surly.

"You've been here before . . . public intoxication."

"I wasn't in public. I was at home . . ."

"Chief Aquino said you were beating your wife."

"She hit me . . . And she had a knife . . . And nobody saw me hit her!"

"Your neighbors heard you beating her," Aquino interrupted. "That's why I was called."

Lovato pounded his gavel. "That's enough!" He looked at Dominguez. "Carlos, are you currently working?"

"No, I got laid off."

"You are being arraigned on domestic violence. Since you are currently unemployed, being locked up won't prevent you from making a living. I'm going to keep you locked up until you can be formally charged."

"How long is that?"

The judged studied an appointments calendar on his desk. "Today is Tuesday. We have till next Friday to bring you up on charges. That's ten days."

"That's bull!" Dominguez shouted.

The judged pounded his gavel again. "Careful, Carlos. You don't want an extra thirty days for contempt."

Lovato addressed the police officer. "Chief, put him back in his cell. He needs to cool off . . . a lot."

Rebecca Luna, the police department's receptionist/secretary, greeted Aquino when he returned. "We got a call from the county sheriff's office."

"Just a minute, Rebecca. I need to finish my escort service here."

The officer lead Dominguez to his cell. Back in his office, he asked, "What did they have to say?"

"The Medical Investigator's office has the preliminary autopsy results on Diego Salazar. It was faxed to the county by mistake. They want to know what they should do?"

"I'll talk to them."

There was little privacy in the crowded office. He sat at his desk a few feet away and called Las Palmas.

"San Phillipe Sheriff's Department, Sergeant Montoya speaking."

"Yes, Sergeant, this is Police Chief Aquino, San Juan Pueblo. Is Sheriff Lansing available?"

"I'm sorry. He's out on an investigation. Can I help?"

"I think so. You called my office about a coroner's report."

"Yes, just a moment." There was a pause at the other end, then. "I have it here. We got it by mistake, I think. I have the number for the Albuquerque office. I'm sure you need a copy for your files."

Aquino copied down the number. "Can you tell me what they found?"

57

"It says here he drowned."

"Was he injured in some way? Does it say anything about a struggle?"

"No."

"Did they test him for drugs?"

"It said they did a Standard Panel. There's a list. Alcohol, Antipsychotics, Benzodiazepines, THC, Cocaine, Opioids, Stimulants to include Amphetamines, Methamphetamines and Ecstasy . . . All negative."

"Okay. Thanks."

The Tribal Police Chief hung up his phone. He could accept the fact that Salazar drowned. After all, he found the man face down on the bank of the river. What he couldn't understand was why Salazar was in the river to begin with.

He wasn't drunk. He wasn't on dope. He wasn't physically harmed and dumped into the river. But he had gone out in the middle of winter without his coat and ended up in the Rio Grande.

Maybe when he saw the actual report, he would learn something, but Aquino had his doubts.

Chapter Twenty

The brief meeting with Edmund Murdock the day before had left Bryce unnerved. The Gallery owner spent most of Monday night wondering if he should call Diego Salazar . . . try to feel him out about what Murdock said.

Late Tuesday, he finally worked up the nerve to call the Northern Pueblo Arts Council.

"This is William Bryce with the *Galeria de Magdalena* in Santa Fe. I'd like to speak to Mr. Salazar."

"I'm sorry," Constance Gomez replied. Her voice was a whimper. "Mr. Salazar is dead!"

"What?" The response reflected genuine shock.

"What the hell did Murdock do?" ripped through Bryce's thoughts. He calmed himself down. "My God," he said, now under control. "What happened?"

"It looks like he fell in the river. They found his body yesterday morning."

"Was it an accident?" The art dealer didn't want to sound too hopeful.

"I don't know," Gomez confessed. "I guess so." She paused. "I'm sorry. Is there anything I can help you with?"

"No. That's all right. I'll call back another time."

Bryce hung up. Sitting in his office chair he could only stare at the phone. He appeared calm on the outside. Inside, a debate raged. Should he call his fixer . . . find out what happened? Or should he keep his distance?

If it wasn't an accident . . . If Murdock was involved . . . It would be better if he didn't ask questions. That way he had plausible deniability.

If the police asked, he could honestly say: Yes, I sent Murdock to talk to Salazar, but just to talk. I have no idea what happened at the meeting.

A wave of relief washed over Bryce.

If Salazar's death wasn't an accident, he was sure it couldn't be traced to him. On top of that, as far as he knew, the Adams Gallery just lost their only connection with the Pueblo Arts Council.

Bryce had others he could approach . . . individual artists. If he had to, he could deal with them directly until a new director could be named.

That a man had died didn't bother him.

The important thing was he was still in business.

Chapter Twenty-One

It was after 6:00 before Lansing got back to his offices. He found Tina waiting for him in the day room. She was nursing a half-finished cup of coffee. The teacher jumped up when she saw the sheriff.

"Did you find her?"

The look on his face told her they hadn't.

"Cohino's not that big," Lansing complained. He sounded tired. He sat in one of the chairs. "Danny Cortez found her book bag in a yard two houses down from the Alba's place. We're guessing she made it that far. After that, we don't have a clue. We talked to all the neighbors. Checked every vacant building we could find. I had people driving the back roads, looking for anything."

Tina's brow knitted as she tried to think of a new place to look. Her face brightened. "How about the train depot . . . the locomotives and cars? You could look there!"

"Maria's dad thought of that. He went down there with as many of the Summer workers as he could round up. He said they searched every inch of that place."

"So, you're going to quit?"

"No, we're not going to quit." He pondered the situation for a moment. "State Police put out an alert yesterday. An escaped prisoner. They were taking him to Denver to stand trial for rape and murder. I don't like the scenario, but there's a remote chance this escaped prisoner abducted Maria."

"How would he get here?"

"He carjacked an SUV in Santa Fe."

"If this guy's trying to get away, why would he abduct some teen off the street?"

"Target of opportunity. No telling how long he's been locked up. He probably has urges we could never imagine."

"Well, we can't just sit here. She could be out there freezing to death!"

"I know that, Tina!" He immediately regretted snapping at her. "I'm sorry. Everybody's nerves are frayed . . . I'll talk to the State Mounted Police. With their help we can check the back country."

Clem Montoya burst into the room. "Sheriff! The nine-one-one operators just got a call. A teenage girl was found walking along the road not far from Estrella. They think it's her. They think it's Maria!"

"Do you have a twenty on where she is?"

"A rancher picked her up. He told the operator he's bringing her to the clinic here in town. Evidently, the girl's in pretty bad shape."

Lansing looked at the teacher. "Come on. Let's go."

"Should I call the Albas?" the Desk Sergeant asked.

"No, not yet. If it's not her, they'll be crushed. Let me find out who it is first."

***

The Las Palmas Medical Clinic was less than a half mile from the Courthouse, the Sheriff's Offices and the nine-one-one Call Center.

The clinic had a new physician in charge: Nicholas Picado. In his late thirties, he replaced the county heart throb, John Tanner. Tanner had been indentured for five years, paying off his Med-School loan. Tanner, now free, headed for Texas. Picado hailed from Texas.

Much to the disappointment of the single women of Las Palmas, Dr. Picado showed up in town with a wife, Fabiana, and two children.

Picado relished his new position. Big cities and their huge hospital complexes smothered him. He loved the small town and the intimacy of the rural clinic.

"Sheriff Lansing," the receptionist said. "What are you doing here?"

"Someone found a teenage girl out on the highway. They're bringing her here."

"Maria Alba!" the woman exclaimed. "Did they find her?"

The sheriff wasn't surprised the story about the missing girl had spread. "We're not sure." If it was Maria, that would be great. If it wasn't, Lansing still had to find out who the girl was.

The sheriff and the teacher stationed themselves near the front doors. They could see the parking lot and any car pulling in. A couple of cars did. The clinic was normally open until 7:00 in the evening.

After twenty minutes, a pickup truck parked near the entrance. The driver got out and ran around to the passenger door. A moment later, he was escorting a young lady to the building.

Lansing ran to the door and held it open for the two. As they entered, he could tell, it was Maria Alba.

Chapter Twenty-Two

Both Lansing and Morales were shocked at the young woman's appearance. Maria wore her coat, but no hat or gloves. Both feet were bare. She looked like she hadn't slept in days. Her eyes were sunken and red. Her black hair was disheveled. She barely resembled the perky waitress from the night before.

The teacher grabbed the girl by both shoulders. "Maria, are you all right?"

The girl said nothing. She only stared ahead, shivering.

"She was like that when I found her," Maria's rescuer, David Robles, said. "She didn't say anything all the way into town."

Dr. Picado and Jan Silver, one of the clinic's nurse practitioners, entered the reception area.

"What's going on?" the physician asked.

"We have a girl here who went missing last night," Lansing explained. "This man just brought her in . . . She needs your attention."

Tina moved aside when the doctor approached. "What's her name?"

"Maria," Morales said. "Maria Alba."

Picado took one look. "The girl's in shock . . . Jan, we need to get her into an exam room." He noticed the shivering. "She probably has hypothermia, as well. Get her into a gown and break out one of the emergency thermal blankets."

The nurse put her arm around the student's shoulders and led her to an exam room down the hall.

"How old is she?" the doctor asked.

"She's sixteen," Morales said. "She's one of my students. I teach at the high school."

"Do her parents know she's here?"

"I was getting ready to call them," the sheriff explained. "They live in Cohino."

"We can get her comfortable, but if she needs further treatment, I'll need their consent."

"They should be here in thirty minutes," the sheriff assured him. "I'll call my office now."

Lansing and Morales couldn't force themselves to sit. They hovered near the reception counter, continually peering down the hallway, hoping for word about Maria. The sheriff instructed his office to call the Albas. They arrived quicker than he would have predicted.

Robles had waited to see how she was doing. The parents thanked him profusely for finding their daughter, then hurried to the exam room.

As grateful as Lansing was for Maria's recovery, everyone was a suspect in her abduction . . . even Robles. The sheriff pulled the man aside and peppered him with questions: How did he first discover the girl? Why was he on the road to begin with? Where had he been the last twenty-four hours? Can people vouch for his whereabouts?

The rancher calmly answered every question. If he was annoyed about the impromptu interrogation, it didn't show. For the moment, Lansing was satisfied Robles' involvement was just as he described.

The Albas, Picado and the nurse remained sequestered with the patient for thirty minutes. Ron Alba eventually emerged, a grim look on his face. He slowly walked to the reception/waiting area.

"How is she doing?" Morales asked anxiously.

Alba shook his head. "Her whole body is covered in cuts and scratches. The doctor's doing a rape kit."

"Did she say anything?" Lansing asked. "Does she know who attacked her?"

"She's in shock . . . The doctor said she has cata . . ." He couldn't remember the term.

"Catatonic?" The teacher completed.

"Yeah. Catatonic. She has catatonic symptoms. But that could be part of the hypothermia. The doctor said her core temperature was ninety degrees when she was brought in. She must have been out in the cold since last night."

"Are they going to admit her?" Robles asked.

"Yes. They're getting a room ready."

"I need to get home," the rancher said. He gave Lansing his phone number and asked if he could get an update on Maria's condition. Lansing told him that wouldn't be a problem.

Ron Alba was a big man. He looked like a railroad engineer. He was also antsy. Unable to sit, he constantly changed location: to the exam room, back to the waiting area, then to Maria's hospital room once she was there, back to the waiting area. His actions were annoying, but no one felt they had the right to complain.

It was 9:00 before Dr. Picado returned to the waiting area. He saw the anticipation on the faces of the father, the teacher and the lawman. "Maria's resting. We need to get her temperature a lot higher before she's out of danger."

"Has she said anything?" Lansing asked.

"No. I don't anticipate she'll say anything tonight. I gave her diazepam to help her sleep."

"Is it all right if my wife and I stay with her tonight?" Alba asked.

"Sure."

Morales was careful how she asked her next question. "Was she . . . molested?"

"No. The young lady is still a virgin."

Alba had already heard, so he wasn't as relieved over the news as the other two in the waiting room.

66

The idea that she had been abducted by an escaped prisoner was becoming more remote.

Lansing waited for Maria's father to return to his daughter's room before he asked the doctor, "What did happen to her?"

"Someone stripped her, then she was lacerated. Someone with long fingernails. It was viscous. They drew blood. We cleaned all the wounds and I put her on antibiotics.

"Also, her fingernails were chipped and broken. The fingertips were raw. It looked like she clawed her way out of a closed door . . . a box . . . something. Hopefully, she'll be recovered enough tomorrow that she can talk."

Lansing and Morales thanked him, then left.

They stood outside the clinic, breathing in the cold, crisp air.

"Are you hungry?"

"I am, but I haven't gotten to the IGA since I got back from Phoenix. You're going to have to feed me."

"I didn't say I was going to feed you," Lansing snorted. "I just asked if you were hungry."

The punch he got on his arm was not gentle. Fortunately for him, the diner was open until 11:00.

Chapter Twenty-Three

"Mama Agustina, what are you doing here?" Tomasita was surprised at her elder visitor.

"I guessed you wouldn't go to the Buffalo Dance today."

Salazar immediately invited the *Apienu* into her home. Mama was followed by Carla Naranjo. Naranjo was second in line to assume the position as head of the Women's Society. As such, she was Jacona's constant companion, assistant and apprentice.

Salazar ushered them into the kitchen, the heart of her home. "Coffee? I can make some."

"That would be good," Jacona said, taking a seat at the table. Naranjo quietly took a chair next to her.

"Was the Pueblo filling up?" the hostess asked.

"Oh, yes," the old woman nodded. "We left early, before the crowds. I would not have gotten out of my place if we hadn't." She watched Salazar busy herself with the coffee. "How are you doing, Tomasita?"

The woman stopped and stared ahead, as if trying to decide. "I'm doing okay, Mama." She continued with her preparation. "They said Diego's body will be back tomorrow. He'll be buried Friday. Father Iglesias said he will do Mass at Eleven."

"I was told the police sent his body to Albuquerque."

"Chief Aquino said they needed to find out how Diego died."

"What did the people in Albuquerque say?"

"That he drowned."

"This is not good." Jacona shook her head. "Diego's spirit must begin his journey to the *Sipofene* from the Pueblo before the fourth day. Tomorrow is the fourth day."

"What does that mean?" Naranjo asked.

"*Ohkay Owingeh* is the navel of the four sacred mountains. Our souls find their way to Sandy Place Lake from here. If Diego's spirit is not here, it will not know how to find the Holy Place of our emergence."

"What will happen to his spirit?" Tomasita was leaning against the counter, a look of fear on her face.

"It could wander the earth. Lost." The *Apienu* noticed the wife's expression. "But if he is back tomorrow, I think Diego's spirit will find its way," she said reassuringly.

It looked like a great burden had been lifted from the woman's shoulders.

The conversation drifted toward more pleasant things. The coffee finished brewing and Tomasita served blackberry filled empanadas.

The morning was almost gone. On this first festival day of the year, the two visitors had other stops to make. Before they left, Jacona had one last item to discuss.

"You know, Tomasita, that you are in my debt."

Salazar's wife hung her head and nodded slightly. "I know, Mama. I know." She hesitated, then looked up. "What do you want?"

"It's not what I want. It's what I need." She reached inside the cloth satchel she always carried and produced a small, linen pouch. "You have a garden. I need these seeds planted."

Tomasita took the seeds. "What are they?"

"It's only a wild grass," the old woman said. "You can plant them along the edge of your patch. If you keep them watered, I can harvest the seeds twice in a season."

"Are they important?"

"Important enough that it will fulfill your debt."

Chapter Twenty-Four

Lansing sat at his desk rubbing his temples. He was getting a headache.

On Memorial Day weekend, Deputy Leroy Ramirez was in a car accident while on duty. It took three operations to put his left leg back together. He was out for six months, on full salary. The sheriff's department had to call up auxiliary deputies to fill in. They had to be paid. Five months of substitute officers' salaries came out of the 1998-99 budget . . . the reduced budget.

The finance meeting the day before with the county commissioners did not go well. They couldn't understand why he was projecting a shortfall for the current budget when he had a surplus the year before. The county was already expecting snow removal expenses to double this year. They simply couldn't afford to pay his department extra monies they didn't have.

Lansing explained he didn't want extra money. All he wanted was the same budget as the previous year. If he didn't get it, he would start furloughing personnel starting in April. If he had to, he would lay off the entire department. The commissioners asked if that was a threat.

"Would you show up to work if you knew you weren't going to get paid?"

The only response he got was a low grumble from the county officials. They would let him know.

He knew he didn't dare ask about opening a satellite office in Segovia.

It was already 10:00. He hadn't heard a thing from the clinic. He needed to talk to Maria Alba, find out what happened to her. He grabbed his hat and his coat.

"Clem, I'm heading over to the clinic," he told his desk sergeant. "I'll be back later."

***

Dr. Picado was with a patient. The sheriff was able to intercept Jan Silver, the Nurse Practitioner, before she saw another visitor.

"I was able to talk to the charge nurse when I first came in," Silver said. "About four this morning, Maria started getting agitated. Very restless. Her mother was in the room when the poor girl sat up and started screaming. Mrs. Alba was terrified. She started yelling for the nurse.

"The doctor left instructions, if something like that happened, the attending nurse could administer another, stronger sedative.

"I just checked. She's still asleep."

"So, she hasn't said anything?"

"Not that I know of."

"Are her parents still here?"

"Mr. Alba is. His wife went home to get some rest. Plus, they have two other kids to take care of."

"I'd like to talk to him."

"He's in Maria's room. I'll go get him."

Lansing stared out the front door while he waited. It would be in the thirties again. More snow would melt. The roads would get sloppy, just in time for another storm from the north. They were in a 3 to 5-day cycle.

The slopes of Taos Ski Valley and Ski Santa Fe already had a snowpack of 75 inches. They were having a banner year with more snow on the way.

"Sheriff, you wanted to see me?"

Lansing turned. "Yes, Mr. Alba. I just needed to ask you a couple of questions."

They found a corner of the waiting area, away from prying ears.

"I know you said you couldn't think of anyone who would harm your daughter. Mr. Robles found her near Estrella. That's twenty miles from Cohino. Do you know anybody who lives out that way?"

Ron Alba could only shake his head. "No, I don't."

"She still hasn't said anything, has she?"

"No."

The man looked tired. He looked worried.

"If there's anything I can do," Lansing said, "let me know."

"Just find the bastard who did this."

"We will, Mr. Alba. We will."

Chapter Twenty-Five

It wasn't unusual for Three King's Day and the Buffalo Dances to draw a respectable crowd. A lot of the visitors were members of the Pueblo who had moved away. They moved looking for better educations, better jobs or just better living conditions. But the naming of the 14 new officials for the next year was always a cause for celebration.

After the dances were completed, San Juan Church would be packed for the Mass that certified the appointments.

The Winter Buffalo Dances started at 1:00. Three dancers, two men, one woman, dressed in traditional outfits began the dance at the kiva. The men wore Buffalo head dresses. A dozen drummers and singers kept the beat and sang the ancient song. The dance was performed in Plaza One. Then, moving clockwise, the entire group moved to Plaza Two and repeated the dance again. Once that round was completed, the ensemble moved to Plaza Three, for the final rendition.

If the weather had been inclement, the Summer moiety might have moved their Buffalo Dance to another day. But for January, this was perfect: blue skies, weather warming to almost 50° in the sun. As soon as the Winter Buffalo Dancers were finished, the Summer Buffalo Dancers took their turn.

All the routines were finished by 4:00.

Police Chief Joseph Aquino and his three officers kept a low profile. They mostly concerned themselves with directing traffic. The narrow streets had a limited number of designated parking spots. Most cars were diverted to an empty, gravel lot in the northeast corner of the Pueblo.

The job of keeping the crowds to the sides of the plazas to accommodate the dancers and musicians was left to the *Towa e*. Because their positions fell under Tewa traditions, they did not require Catholic certification.

As the sun dropped closer to the horizon and the shadows lengthened, the visitors began leaving the Pueblo center, looking for their cars. This is when the fender-benders would start happening. People were tired. Visibility was down. Headlights blinded other drivers. Tribal police officers with whistles and flashlights untangled small knots of cars, trying to keep tempers from flaring.

A chill began to creep into Aquino's bones as a northerly breeze kicked in. He could hardly wait to get home. His wife, Sharon, and fourteen-year-old son, Jacob, had stayed for most of the dances. She and the wives of the other officers were preparing a late meal. She had a pork-butt slow roasting in the *horno*. They would have pulled pork tacos with potato salad and roasted corn.

Raymond Mesa approached.

"Shouldn't you be heading to the church for your Mass?" Aquino attempted to sound friendly.

"I just came from the police station."

"What were you doing there?" The police chief couldn't help but be suspicious.

"I was talking to Carlos Dominguez. He said he didn't want to stay in jail until next Friday."

"That's not my call. It's up to the judge."

"I realize that." Mesa smiled. "I'll talk to Paul in the morning."

"You mean Judge Lovato?"

Mesa waived away the question. "He and I are both lawyers. We speak the same language. Plus, my position as Sheriff will carry weight. Keeping Carlos in jail doesn't help anyone."

"It helps his wife. He was beating her."

"That's for the Tribal Court to decide."

"No, the court decides guilt or innocence. The court decides punishment. No matter what the court says, he was still beating his wife."

Mesa shrugged. "I need to be at the church. You need to be near the jail tomorrow. I'm sure the court will arraign Carlos by lunch time."

Aquino didn't reply. He didn't like Raymond Mesa. He wasn't sure the new sheriff would have enough influence to get him fired, but he didn't want to push the issue. Instead of stewing over what might happen, he concentrated on the current traffic flow. Besides, there were other things on his mind besides the new sheriff and his interference.

Diego Salazar's body would be returned in the morning. The MI's office said he drowned. He would be buried on Friday.

What Aquino wanted to know was why was the man in the river to begin with?

Chapter Twenty-Six

Lansing couldn't force himself to sit and do nothing. After his talk with Ron Alba, he contacted David Robles. If the rancher had time, he wanted to see exactly where Maria was found.

The two men met up at the Robles ranch mid-afternoon. Robles took his truck. Lansing followed in his unit. When the rancher found the spot, he pulled onto the narrow shoulder of Route 182 and got out. They were four miles from Robles' spread.

Lansing parked behind him, then turned on his emergency lights to warn other drivers they were there.

"It was right along here." Robles stood on the opposite side of the road, his arms outstretched to indicate the vague area of his rescue. "She was walking toward my ranch."

The sheriff looked down the road. "You didn't see any other traffic along here, did you?"

"Nope. Nada." He shook his head. "I have no idea how long she had been walking or where she came from." He looked down the road, then back to Lansing. He appeared nervous about something. "Listen, my wife's not doing well. I need to get back to the ranch."

"Oh, I'm sorry to hear that. I appreciate the help. I'm going to take a drive down the road. Maybe I'll see something."

They shook hands. The rancher turned his truck around and headed home.

Lansing got into his Jeep and started the engine. He left his emergency lights on as he drove at a snail's pace, studying the path Maria Alba must have taken. This was a desolate stretch of road. The nearest building was nearly three miles away, and it was nothing more than a run-down, abandoned shack.

Route 182—Jack Rivera found a car in a snow drift somewhere along there. Lansing was curious exactly where.

The blue skies of the past two days were gone. A front was moving in from the northwest. The clouds hung heavy with snow and the temperature was dropping quickly.

He had not traveled more than a mile down the road before he got a call over the radio.

"All available units, this is Dispatch. We have shots fired. Lookout Lodge, north of Estrella. Please, respond."

The sheriff grabbed his mic. "Dispatch, Patrol One. I'm rolling. Less than fifteen minutes out."

"Roger, Patrol One. Dispatch copies."

***

Lookout Lodge was one of the seasonal accommodations. It was a cluster of cabins located in the foothills between Estrella and Cohino. It opened a few days before the Chisum and Aztec Scenic Railroad began its operations in May, then closed in October after the last passengers departed.

While he was en route, Marilyn filled the sheriff in on what she knew. Sam Keller, the owner/operator of the lodge, wanted to take advantage of the break in weather. He took a run into the foothills to check on his property.

A vehicle was parked behind one of the cabins. Of course, no one was supposed to be up there. When he approached, whoever was in the cabin started shooting at him. That's when he called nine-one-one.

As Lansing approached the lodge, he found Keller sitting in his truck on the access road, a quarter mile from the nearest building. He was talking on his cell when the sheriff walked up.

Keller rolled down his window. The man was thin, with white hair. Probably in his late sixties, Lansing guessed.

"What's going on, Mr. Keller?"

"Got an intruder. Nobody's supposed to be up here. Pulled up to find out who was in there, and the son-of-a-gun started shooting at me." He pointed. "Put a hole right through my windshield."

"Did they say anything?"

"Nothing. Just started shooting. Didn't even get a chance to ask who they were."

"When did you first get here?"

"'Bout half-an-hour ago."

Lansing looked toward the cabins. "Which one is he in?"

"Fourth one from the end. Driving up to the Lodge House when I saw a car parked behind the cabin."

"What kind of car?"

"Looks like an SUV. Something big."

Lansing looked up at the sky. With the thickening clouds, it was going to get dark even earlier. "Sit tight. I'll be right back."

The sheriff got in his unit. With the emergency lights off, he slowly edged his Jeep up the road, keeping his eyes trained on the suspect cabin. He hoped he could get a make on the SUV behind the shack.

A hundred feet from the cabin, he saw the muzzle flash from the slightly opened door, immediately followed by the sound of the shot. He was satisfied he had gone far enough. He put the Jeep in reverse and retreated, stopping next to Keller. He would need back up.

"Dispatch, Patrol One," Lansing said over the radio. "I have a situation here at Lookout Lodge. I need at least two more units up here . . . And check with the State Police. If they have any troopers available, I could use their help, as well."

Chapter Twenty-Seven

"This is Lansing."

"Hey, Cliff," Morales said into her cell phone. "I'm heading to the clinic. I was wondering if you made any progress finding Maria's abductor?"

"Tina, this really isn't a good time."

"What's wrong?"

"I'm in a situation, right now. Waiting for back up. I'll talk to you later."

Morales was in her car, still in the school parking lot. She couldn't move until the buses pulled out. She stared at the phone's screen: CALL ENDED.

Obviously, the sheriff was busy, but he had never been that abrupt with her. Of course, she had never called him before when he was in a "situation." That was a reasonable excuse. She didn't let herself get upset.

Tina Morales, Science Teacher Extraordinaire, had no idea how the gossip system in Las Palmas Middle/High School worked. She couldn't fathom how rumors originated, who started them, how they spread like an airborne virus.

When she got to school that morning, the assumption was that she, Lansing, and a few other adults were the only ones who knew about Maria Alba—that she had been found and was resting at the clinic.

Not only did most of the students know she was safe, they knew Morales was at the clinic when she arrived. None of the students she queried could explain how exactly they found out. The blank look on the face of the fourth student she asked led her to one conclusion: rumors were spread by osmosis—the unconscious transmission of knowledge from one organism to another.

It was fifteen minutes before she could make her way out of the lot. Another 10 minutes before she got to the clinic. The number of cars in the clinic parking area ebbed and flowed throughout the day. After school, it filled up quickly due to scheduled appointments, but kids had to get home from school first. Morales was able to find a spot before the rush.

"Maria's sleeping." Klara Alba said. Mother and teacher stood in the hallway, outside the patient's room. "She didn't have a good night. They had to sedate her again around four this morning. She woke up scream-ing and I couldn't calm her down."

Alba talked in hushed tones. The rest of the world didn't need to know her business.

"We thought keeping the room dark would help her rest. She woke up again around ten. The screaming started all over again. One of the nurses came in to give her another shot. When she did, she opened the blinds for more light.

"That calmed Maria down as much as the shot . . . She's terrified of the dark."

"I can't imagine what she went through." Morales stared at the closed door to her student's room. "How long are they going to keep her?"

"I don't know. We can't afford for her stay here long, but I can't take her home like this. Ron talked to the insurance people. Our policy allows for three days of hospitalization for each incident. After that, it comes out of our pocket . . . and there's nothing in our pockets."

"First thing's first, Mrs. Alba," the teacher said, trying to reassure the worried mother. "Let's get Maria healthy. That's the important thing.

"Is there anything I can do?"

"Pray for my daughter."

"I will." Tina gave the woman a hug. "I'm going straight to the church. I'll light a candle for her."

Chapter Twenty-Eight

"You are the one who asked for me to come here, Pauline."

"I know I did, Mama Agustina," Dominguez said. The school nurse had called Carla Naranjo the day before. She explained, Carlos had gotten drunk and beaten her . . . again. She wanted help. Could the *Apienu* see her?

"Did you talk to the PeaceKeepers? Couldn't they help you?"

"They said I should go to a shelter at one of the other Pueblos. Picuris, maybe. But I can't do that. I have to work." She wrung her hands. "Besides, why should I leave my home? I did nothing wrong."

"I know, dear," Jacona said, patting the distraught woman's knee. "How long will the police hold your husband?"

"Chief Aquino said he might not be arraigned until a week from Friday."

"So, you have some time to make a decision."

"I've already made my decision, Mama. I want him gone."

"The Tribal Court has been very good about protecting the *Ohkay Owingeh* women," Naranjo offered. "The children, too."

"Oh, I know. And it is my fault I hadn't talked to the PeaceKeepers sooner. I always threatened Carlos I would call the police if he hit me again. He would say he was sorry. I would forgive him. Things would be fine for a while . . .

"But he hasn't worked since before Christmas. He came home drunk Monday. He was angry at everyone." She started crying. "But why did he have to take it out on me?"

The three women sat in the small living room of the Dominguez house. It was already dark outside. The two children of the household peered from the door of their room, afraid of the two strangers talking to their mother.

Mama Agustina, despite her honorary title, was aloof... and far from motherly. She had suffered for years at the hands of her own abusive husband. This was long before the PeaceKeepers were a force for good in the northern Pueblos. She distrusted men. Even more, she resented the patriarchal nature of the Tewa society.

In their religion, Blue Corn Woman and White Corn Maiden, the mothers of all Tewa, were among the first supernatural beings. They were the spirits who first sent men from the *Sipofene*, the place of origin below Sandy Place Lake, to the above . . . to the world. They were the mothers of the Summer and Winter moieties.

When the first men emerged to the above, they became chiefs of the different societies and they held dominion over the women. When a child of six was inducted into either the Winter or Summer society, it was the moiety of his father. The Water Pouring Ceremony was the last step in final initiation into the society.

If a woman of the Winter society were to wed a man of the Summer society, she had to once again go through the Water Pouring Ceremony to be initiated into her husband's moiety.

Agustina Jacona knew she couldn't change 2,000 years of Catholicism. She couldn't change 10,000 years of Tewa traditions. But she could make her stand. Now that she was the *Apienu*, she would wield her influence where she could.

If other Made People considered what she did was nothing more than revenge, let them think what they will. What she had already done, what she would do, in her own eyes, was retribution. She had earned the right.

Mama Agustina signaled her apprentice to come forward and put her arms around Dominguez. The two women hugged.

"Pauline, don't be mistaken. I do appreciate the favors you have done for me in the past. But you must understand, if I do this, you will owe me a debt."

Pauline looked up from Naranjo's shoulder. "I know, Mama."

"It is time to go, Carla," the old woman said, standing. "There are things we must do."

Pauline Dominguez closed the door after her visitors left. She leaned her head against the frame and closed her eyes. She prayed that she was following the correct path.

Chapter Twenty-Nine

It was nearly 5:30 before Sheriff Lansing was satisfied he had enough men for the task. Two deputies, Jack Rivera and Jerry Lopez, had shown up thirty minutes after he put out the request to dispatch. State Police sent two officers, Marty Hernandez and Rich Hidalgo.

While he waited for reinforcements, Lansing gathered as much information as possible.

Keller described the layout of the cabin. It was a single, great room that combined living and sleeping areas with a kitchen nook in the back. A separate bathroom was set to the side. There were two windows in the front, either side of the door. One window in the back over the sink. One small window in the bath. No electricity was available after the end of October.

Cooking and heating were provided by a propane tank behind the cabin. The gas was shut off at the end of the season, but it took nothing to turn it back on.

To Lansing, it sounded like the shooter fired at him with a handgun as opposed to a rifle. He assumed that they had cornered Ralph Miera, the escaped prisoner. If that was the case, he needed to find out what kind of guns he had escaped with. The State Police provided the answer.

Each transport guard had one Glock 17, 9-millimeter pistol. The Federal Assault Weapons Ban of 1994 limited magazines to 10 rounds. Neither guard had a spare magazine with him. Miera had 20 rounds minus the 3 or 4 he had already fired.

Lansing had his Remington 30-30. His deputies were equipped with AR4s. The State Police had AR-15s. If they could get close enough, the State Police also had hand-tossed, flash-bang grenades to stun the shooter. But that was only if they decided on an all-out assault.

Lansing had one goal: Everyone had to go home safely and in one piece.

A light snowfall had started not long after the sheriff first arrived. As the front grew closer, the snow increased, as had the wind. Lookout Lodge sat at 8,000 feet, almost 500 feet higher than the Rio Cohino Valley below.

All five lawmen were dressed for the weather.

Lansing told Keller there wasn't any point in the owner staying. They would take care of things from here on out.

It was his property, Keller said, and he was staying.

"The biggest problem we have is we can't approach from the front," Lansing observed. "Those Glock Seventeens have a range of about a hundred yards.

"I'll come up between cabins with my bullhorn. See if he's willing to surrender. We don't want to hurt him. We don't want him to hurt us."

"What if he doesn't want to play nice?" Patrolman Hidalgo asked.

"The weather service said we're supposed to get another six to eight inches of snow on top of the foot already on the ground," the sheriff said. "If we don't get down this access road tonight, we might be up here for a few days.

"I don't know about you boys, but I didn't bring any food."

"We could drive back to the valley," Deputy Lopez suggested. "Just wait for him. He's going to get hungry sooner or later."

"I'd like to get things resolved tonight."

"What's the rush?" Marty Hernandez asked.

"There's a sixteen-year-old girl laid up in the clinic in town. I need to find out if this is the SOB who put her there."

"So, what's your plan?" Rivera urged.

In the darkness and the blowing snow, the assault team could get close.

Lansing would position himself on the side of the cabin with the bull-horn. The two State Police officers would deploy to the back of the cabin, equipped with their rifles and two flash-bang grenades. The deputies would bring a patrol unit, with no lights, up the road and get as close to the cabin as they thought safe.

All the players had ten minutes to get into position.

From that point on, what they did next would be in response to the shooter's actions.

Chapter Thirty

"Shooter inside the cabin," Lansing announced through the bullhorn. "We have you surrounded. Throw out your weapons and come out with your hands behind your head."

Lansing's order was almost pure bluff. In the darkness, in the blowing snow, it was impossible to see if the intruder was complying. He was hoping for any kind of response. He didn't have to wait for long.

He heard the door of the cabin open. Then: BANG! BANG! BANG! BANG! The shooter fired four quick shots blindly into the darkness, before slamming the door shut again.

That was the signal for the State Police. One officer broke the window over the sink at the back of the cabin. The other officer lobbed in two flash-bangs in quick succession.

The two explosions would have blinded and deafened anyone inside the small building.

Lansing wanted no heroics. No one was to rush the cabin. Let the shooter inside make the next move. In less than a minute, the cabin door flew open and the gunman started shooting again as he ran forward.

The sheriff was truly sorry that was the man's choice. What happened next was inevitable. With nothing more than muzzle flashes to aim at, Deputies Rivera and Lopez returned fire.

The firefight lasted 10 seconds.

When the sheriff could see the cabin's shooter had stopped shooting, he announced over the bullhorn: "Cease fire! Cease fire!"

Lansing turned on his flashlight and pointed it in the direction of the shooter's last position. Stepping through new and old snow ten inches deep, he approached the dark form of a man sprawled on the ground. The shooter lay still, flat on his back. At least three bullets from the deputies had found their mark.

More lights appeared on his left—the state patrolmen from behind the cabin. On his right, the deputies had turned on the headlights of their patrol unit. Jack Rivera came forward, also with his flashlight in hand.

With the shooter surrounded, Lansing pulled off a glove and felt for a pulse on the neck. He could not find one.

"Can you tell if this is Miera?" He was looking at the State Policemen. If it was the escapee, he had ditched his prison attire and found more suitable civilian clothing, along with a heavy coat and stocking cap.

Officer Hernandez fumbled with a folded paper from his pocket. He produced a faxed photo his office had received. He shone his light on the picture, then the face of the dead man and back to the picture. "I don't think so?" He handed the fax to the sheriff.

Lansing went through the same routine as Hernandez, looking from photo to face, then back. The swirling snow made identification difficult. "Let's drag him into the cabin, out of this blizzard. We can get a better look there."

The patrolmen grabbed the body under the armpits and pulled him into the cabin. Deputy Rivera stayed behind for a few minutes looking for the shooter's pistol. When he found it, he joined the others in the cabin. Deputy Lopez had abandoned his patrol car to see for himself what was going on.

The interior of the cabin was noticeably warmer than outside. The beams of the flashlights trained on the shooter. They were all able to get a better look at the dead man.

Pulling off the stocking cap, Lansing brushed away the snow on the man's face, then compared it to the photo. Instead of a 32-year-old Hispanic, they were looking at a white male in his early 40s. "This is not our escapee," he announced. He was disappointed they hadn't cornered Ralph Miera . . . but who did they flush out?

He put down his own flashlight. "Give me some light here," he requested. He examined the man's finger tips.

"What are you looking for?" Deputy Rivera asked.

"Maria Alva's body was covered with scratches. The doctor said she was attacked by someone with long fingernails. Look at these."

The sheriff held up one hand, then the next. Everyone bent over for a closer examination. The nails were all cut short. There wasn't enough length to open the pull-tab on a beer can.

"I don't think he's the one who attacked Maria."

"Who the hell is he?" This came from Jerry Lopez.

"Let's see if we can find out." With the help of Rivera, Lansing searched the body. They could find no identification.

"Jerry, get the numbers off the license plate from the SUV out back. We'll find out who this guy is." He looked at Rivera. "What kind of weapon did he have?"

"I picked up a forty cal, Smith and Wesson."

Lansing stood, flashlight in hand. Looking around, he spotted a Coleman lantern on the dining table. "We need some light in here. Fire that thing up."

Marty Hernandez found matches on the table. They soon had plenty of light.

"We need to secure any more weapons." The sheriff said, turning off his flashlight.

The remaining four lawmen searched the single room. There were no other weapons. What they did find was revealing. He had been there for a few days. A dozen empty cans had been tossed into a corner. Another stack of canned food sat on the counter, enough for two weeks.

On the floor next to the table was a briefcase. Lansing picked it up and opened it. "What have we here?" Somehow, no one was surprised to find it was full of money. When it was eventually counted, it came to nearly $10,000.

"If he was trying to get away, why didn't he bring this case with him?" Jack Rivera asked.

"Beats me." Lansing said.

Jerry Lopez returned from his task. "That's a GMC Yukon out there. I've got the number, Oklahoma plates."

The sheriff gestured to the body. "We'll put him in the back of my Jeep. We all need to get down to the valley before we get snowed in."

"Don't think I ever saw the man before in my life," Keller said. He knocked the snow from his boots as he climbed into his truck. "Course, he might have stayed here once. Can't remember everyone who comes through. You said you got the heaters all turned off in the cabin?"

"It's all secure." Lansing said. He really didn't want to have a conversation. He wanted to get down the road before it became impassable.

"Guess I'll clean up that mess after the storm. You sure that door's closed?"

"I'm sure, Mr. Keller." Lansing said, heading for his Jeep. "I'm sure."

Chapter Thirty-One

When the snow started the evening before, Lansing didn't realize northern San Phillipe County was in for the worse blizzard in 20 years. When he found out school was cancelled, he arranged for Oscar Vega to stay at the ranch. If the sheriff couldn't get back to his spread, he needed Oscar to look after his horses.

It was a struggle to get back and forth from the Vega Ranch.

Driving into Las Palmas was nearly impossible. It took Lansing an hour to cover the 15 miles from his ranch to his office. He stopped twice to help stranded motorists. He brought three people with him to his office. Friends picked them up from there.

The five, day-shift officers reported to the office. Lansing didn't want them on the roads unless necessary. Emergency calls would be handled on a case-by-case basis. Since Chief Deputy Rivera wasn't on patrol, Lansing put him in charge of coordinating with the road clearing crews. If they got a call and the roads were clear, someone would be dispatched.

It seemed ridiculous to the sheriff, but law enforcement protocol required that both Rivera and Lopez be placed on restricted duty. They would be fully reinstated after the county prosecutor reviewed the shooting the night before. Lansing knew it was only a formality, but cops could get skewered if rules were overlooked.

He already had statements from the two State Police officers. He had written reports from the deputies, plus there was his. He needed Sam Keller to come in and make a statement. Even though he didn't witness the shooting, his 9-1-1 call is what got the ball rolling.

The dead man's body was in cold storage at the Las Palmas funeral home. The Medical Investigator's office would retrieve the body for an autopsy when the roads were open. The cause of death was self-evident, but, once again, protocol required such things in a police-involved shooting.

During a lull in the activity, Lansing asked Lopez to come into his office.

"Jerry, did Melanie talk to your nephew yesterday?"

"You mean about those scratches?"

The sheriff nodded.

"She was going to ask him last night. We were supposed to get together for dinner, but I was out on that call till late. Our wives did talk on the phone, though. Elena told my wife the same thing Jonah told you—Joey was scratched by a ghost. He's sticking to that story."

When he was finished with Deputy Lopez, Lansing called the clinic. Maria Alba was improving. She was awake now and not screaming. But she still couldn't . . . or wouldn't . . . talk. She wasn't eating either.

"Hi, Cliff."

"Hello, Tina." The two were talking on their cells. "I just talked to the clinic. It sounds like Maria might be getting better."

"Yeah, I talked to Klara Alba about half an hour ago. She told me the same thing."

"Listen, I'm sorry about having to cut things short yesterday afternoon. I was in the middle of a situation."

"I kind of thought you were going to call me last night. Fill me in."

"It was after eleven before we wrapped things up. I thought it was too late to call."

"Cliff Lansing, don't you know by now, you can call me any time you want."

"I suppose."

"Okay. So, what was this 'situation?'"

"The other evening, do you remember me mentioning an escaped prisoner?"

"Yes!" She sounded anxious.

"Well, we thought we found him."

It didn't take much prodding from the teacher for him to recount the events from the evening before. He tried to keep it from sounding too harrowing. But stories about shoot-outs with bad guys always had an edge to them.

"So, this man who was killed did not attack Maria?"

"No." There was a finality in the sheriff's one-word answer.

"Who is he then?"

"We don't know, yet. We called the Oklahoma Highway Patrol. We gave them the license plate number of the SUV parked at the lodge. Their DMV will have the owner's name."

"Change of subject," Tina said. "I know it's early, but what are you doing for lunch?"

Lansing looked out his window. "I'll try to walk to the diner."

"Can I join you?"

"You're taking your life in your hands on those streets out there. If you get stuck, I can't send anyone to help you."

"I either go to the diner or the grocery store. I still don't have any food in my house."

"How have you managed to survive so long without me around?"

"By living in places that don't have snow!"

Chapter Thirty-Two

"Carlos Dominguez, you are being charged with domestic violence. How do you plead?"

The gathering in Paul Lovato's courtroom was small. Besides the judge and defendant, there was Police Chief Joseph Aquino, Sheriff Raymond Mesa, a bailiff and a stenographer. Mesa had been true to his word. He talked to Judge Lovato and had the arraignment set for Thursday morning.

Dominguez, handcuffed, turned and looked at Sheriff Mesa, not sure what he should say.

Mesa stood. "Carlos pleads 'not guilty,' Your Honor."

Lovato rapped his gavel. "I need to hear it from him, Raymond. Sit down." The judge addressed the defendant again. "Carlos, you are being charged with domestic violence. Specifically, beating your wife. How do you plead?"

"Not guilty." The man's voice was barely audible.

"What did you say? Speak up."

"Not guilty, Judge." Dominguez was louder. He was more sedate than his first visit to the court. Three nights and two days in jail had dulled his surliness.

"Sheriff Mesa informs me that he got you a job."

"Yes."

Mesa stood, again. "He'll be working with Tsay Construction," the lawyer explained. "At the casino site."

Pueblo Police Chief Joseph Aquino thought about the significance of having a job with Tsay Construction and Services. In the Tewa language, *Ohkay Owingeh* meant the "place of strong people." For 400 years the Pueblo had lived up to that reputation.

When the Spanish first arrived in 1598, their strategies for conquest hadn't evolved much since Cortez first entered Mexico. Pacification was initially peaceful. However, if the native populations didn't cooperate completely, which included abandoning their ancient religions, force was liberally employed.

By 1675, all the Pueblos of New Mexico, which included present day Arizona, suffered under Spanish rule. Subjugation and slavery were the order of the day. Bear Chief Po'Pay, of the San Juan Pueblo *Ohkay Owingeh* Medicine Society, had personally been tortured in Santa Fe under orders of the Spanish Governor. When he was released, he saw only one recourse for the Pueblo Peoples: Revolt.

For the next five years, Po'Pay travelled to every Pueblo under Spanish dominion and preached rebellion. By 1680, they were ready. From the Hopi in the northwest, the Zuni in the southwest and Taos in the northeast, every Pueblo rose up against the foreign overlords. In a matter of weeks, all 46 Pueblo towns revolted. Four hundred Spanish were killed, the remaining 2,000 fled to the safety of El Paso.

A strict fundamentalist, Po'Pay wanted a return to the old ways and a destruction of all things Spanish, including the churches. The confederation didn't last. The Pueblos spoke at least seven different languages and there was no unifying religion.

Because of an ongoing drought, continued attacks by Apache and Navajo marauders and general disunity, Po'Pay's promise of a new Golden Age didn't materialize. The charismatic leader was soon deposed. The man himself disappeared into history.

After an aborted attempt in 1681, the Spanish succeeded in reconquest in 1692. Another threatened rebellion in 1694 brought in a new era of cooperation between the Pueblo people and the Spanish. Indian property and religious rights were recognized. Slavery was abolished.

Boundaries were established. It was the *Ohkay Owingeh* people of San Juan Pueblo who first successfully petitioned the Spanish government to recognize Indian claims over encroaching white settler land grabs.

Many in San Juan felt in their hearts that The Eight Northern Pueblo Indian Council was located on their reservation because of the Pueblo's historic leadership. Indeed, in the latter half of the Twentieth Century, San Juan men had started asserting their presence in the greater world. College graduates from San Juan taught at Yale University, held important technical posts at Los Alamos Labs and would eventually head the National Congress of American Indians.

Tsay Construction and Services was founded in 1995 by Matthew Lovato, a civil engineer and Paul Lovato's brother. Tribally owned, the company had started small. One of its first big projects was the Ohkay Casino Resorts. (It eventually would expand to become nationally recognized as Tsay Federal Contracting Group, but, for the moment, one step at a time.)

"You talked to my brother?" the judge asked.

"Well," Mesa hedged, "I talked to one of the supervisors. He said he could use help on a painting crew."

"Carlos, I am releasing you from custody only because Sheriff Mesa found you a job," Lovato scowled. "But you only remain free under three conditions: You don't drink; you don't beat your wife; and you don't get fired. If you violate any of those conditions, you're back in jail. Do you understand me?"

"Yes, judge."

"When does he start work, Raymond?"

"In the morning."

Lovato studied a calendar on his bench top. "Let's see if we can get Carlos on the Greater Tribal Court Docket for February Fourth. That's four weeks from today." He pounded his gavel. "Court dismissed."

Chapter Thirty-Three

"All I can say is the situation has changed since we talked last week," William Bryce said into his phone. "I only found out day before yesterday that the Art Director for the Northern Pueblos had died. I spent all day Wednesday trying to find out who I should talk to. They don't even know who's in charge now.

"As soon as I learn anything, your gallery will be the first one I call . . .

"Okay . . . I'll talk to you then."

Bryce hung up his phone, then put a checkmark besides the next name on his list. This was the sixth major east coast gallery he had talked to. There were a dozen lesser outlets he needed to call, but they could wait.

The Adams Gallery in Boston had been a threat to his operation. By going directly to Diego Salazar, the *Galeria de Magdalena* would no longer be the supplier for their Pueblo Indian Art. But Salazar was gone now.

Bryce was in a much better position to go to the Northern Pueblo Council offices and find a new contact. He had talked to a Constance Gomez in Salazar's office. He told her he would visit their offices that morning. He needed to talk to someone with authority . . . someone who could speak on behalf of the Pueblo artisans. It was important for their very livelihood.

He was confident the young lady understood the gravity of the situation.

Outside the large windows of his gallery he could see a moderate snow falling. He had heard, further north, the snow was much heavier.

He hoped he wouldn't have trouble getting back and forth from San Juan Pueblo.

Chapter Thirty-Four

For the time being, Carlos Dominguez was no longer Joseph Aquino's concern . . . unless he messed up. The Police Chief had other things on his mind.

Tomasita Salazar said Diego had left the house Sunday afternoon. It had to do with Art Council business. Someone picked him up at home.

Aquino found himself back at the Eight Northern Pueblo Indian Council offices. Just because Connie Gomez didn't have an appointment jotted down didn't mean she didn't know who Salazar might have met.

"You saw him last Thursday, New Year's Eve. Can you remember if he had any visitors earlier last week?"

"Yes. He did. Wednesday. One of the artists from Taos Pueblo came to see him."

"What happened?"

"They were in Diego's office with the door closed. They were arguing. I could hear them yelling at each other."

"What were they arguing about?"

"I think it had to do with what the artist was getting paid."

"Do you have a name for this artist?"

Gomez referenced a visitor's log. "Romero. Jason Romero."

There was only 35 miles between the Pueblos of San Juan and Taos. But the winter storm that started the night before was only getting worse. Aquino didn't want to risk getting stuck on the roads.

"Do you have a phone number for Mr. Romero?"

"I'll check the directory. I'm sure I have his name." She pulled a thin phone book from a desk drawer and started thumbing through the pages. When she found Romero's information, she wrote his name, address and phone number on a piece of paper and handed it to the officer.

"Thank you." Aquino thought for a moment. "Did you keep track of Diego's phone calls?"

"I only wrote down incoming calls. I couldn't tell you who he called."

"Can I see your log?"

The secretary readily handed him her notebook. For the entire week leading up to New Year's, the only name that stood out was Alan Goldman, Adams Gallery, Boston. Thursday, 9:00 am.

"What can you tell me about this call from Boston?"

"Not much. But they did talk for a long time. Thirty minutes."

"How could you tell? Diego was in his office, wasn't he?"

"Yes, but when he is using his phone, this light is on." She pointed at the phone on her desk.

"When we talked Monday, you said your office only dealt with one gallery . . . some place in Santa Fe."

"Yes, *Galeria de Magdalena.*"

"Why would a Boston gallery be calling?"

Gomez shrugged. "Maybe they heard about our artists."

"Do you have a number for this Santa Fe gallery?"

"I do, but Mr. Bryce, the owner of the gallery called this morning. He said he was on his way up here. Since Diego Salazar had died, he needed to talk to someone in charge."

"Why does he need to talk to someone in charge?"

"I don't know." Connie shrugged again. "He said it was important for our artists."

"Who was he going to talk to?"

"I was going to send him to Isaac Yope's office. He's the council's director."

Aquino considered the situation. He had nothing on his plate. Maybe he should be the one to talk to this gallery owner. "When was Mr. Bryce going to be here?"

"Soon. He said he wanted to visit before the storm got worse."

"Is the door to Diego's office unlocked?"

"Yes."

"I'm going in there and closing the door. When Bryce gets here, tell him there's a MR. Aquino waiting for him. He doesn't need to know it's the police."

Before he closed the office door, "Can I call Jason Romero from in here?"

"You should be able to."

"Okay. Thanks."

Chapter Thirty-Five

"Hello?" the man's voice asked.

"Is this Jason Romero?"

"Yeah, who is this?"

"I'm Police Chief Joseph Aquino, San Juan Pueblo."

"What do you want?" Romero didn't come across surly, just cautious.

"You came to visit Diego Salazar at the Northern Pueblo Indian Council last week."

"Yeah. So?"

"Salazar's secretary said you two argued. Can you tell me what that was about?"

"I came to see him because I found out he was cheating me . . . and not just me . . . probably every Pueblo artist he deals with."

"So, you were arguing about money?"

"Yes."

"If he was cheating you, how did you find out?"

"Taos Pueblo has a small gallery where the artists display their work. I show my paintings there. But Santa Fe gets a lot more traffic. The Northern Pueblo Indian Art Council negotiates fees and makes sure our works are shown.

"A couple walked into the gallery early last week. They came for the skiing, but also wanted to do some shopping.

"They saw one of my paintings. It was priced at two hundred and fifty bucks. The *Galeria de Magdalena* would have only paid me two hundred. The galleries always take their cut.

"Anyway, this couple told the Taos salesperson they had seen a painting of mine hanging in a Boston gallery. They were asking a thousand dollars there."

"Do you know which gallery?"

"No, and I didn't get to talk to this couple, either. I heard the story second hand from the Taos clerk."

"So, you think Diego Salazar was cheating you?"

"If he isn't cheating us, he probably knows who is. I'm getting as many of the artisans together as I can. We're going to come to the council and have a little meeting about this."

"You know, Diego Salazar is dead." The silence from the other end of the line told Aquino this was news to the painter.

"What? When did this happen?"

"We found his body Monday morning. He drowned in the Rio Grande."

"Is that why you're calling me? Do you think I had something to do with it?"

"Not at the moment, Jason. I'm just getting a feel for who Diego talked to last week. Someone picked him up on Sunday afternoon. His body was found the next morning.

"You weren't here at San Juan Sunday, were you?"

"No. I was working in my studio."

"Can people vouch for that?"

"I-I'm sure somebody saw me there."

"If I needed to talk to you again, could you come to my office?"

"Not in this blizzard!"

"Maybe after the storm, but this is only if we need to talk again."

"Yeah, sure. I guess."

"Fine. Goodbye, Jason."

As soon as he hung up the phone, it rang.

"There is a Mr. Bryce to see you," Connie said.

"Send him in."

William Bryce entered the office. In his late fifties, he had a mani-
cured look about him. Despite having come in from a snowstorm, he
looked fresh, his suit pressed and expensive. He carried a hat with an
overcoat over one arm. His plastic smile melted at the sight of the Police
Chief's uniform.

"Mr. Bryce, please, sit down." Aquino indicated a chair in front of
the Art Director's desk.

"Thank you." The gallery owner recovered his smile and took a seat.

"I'm Police Chief Joseph Aquino."

"William Bryce, *Galeria de Magdalena*, Santa Fe." Bryce nodded,
but didn't extend his hand.

"What brings you up here in this weather?"

"I found out Tuesday about Diego Salazar's unfortunate death. First,
I wanted to extend my condolences. Second, I wanted to assure the
council there would be no changes with our arrangements. My gallery
will continue to represent Pueblo interests in the same manner as we have
in the past . . . I was hoping I could talk to someone with a little authority."

"Oh, I have lots of authority, Mr. Bryce."

"I meant someone who could talk on behalf of the artists."

"I think I have a handle on what their interests are. What would you
like to discuss?"

"Nothing in particular, really. We have contracts in place that Mr.
Salazar signed. I just wanted you people to know there would be no need
to renegotiate anything."

"You could have called."

"I believe the personal touch is important. Face-to-face. Besides, it's
not that far a drive."

"How did you hear about Diego Salazar's death?"

"I called here to talk to him. Tuesday. His secretary said he was found in the river."

"When was the last time you saw Salazar?"

"Around Thanksgiving, I suppose."

"You didn't pick him up Sunday?"

"N-no. Of course not. I was nowhere near here." He looked out the window behind Aquino. "It looks like it's coming down pretty hard out there. Perhaps I need to get back to Santa Fe." He stood.

"When was the last time you talked to him?"

"It's been a couple of weeks."

"He didn't call you New Year's Eve?"

"Why would he?"

"Just curious . . . Have you ever heard of the Adams Gallery in Boston?"

"I'm sure I have."

"An Alan Goldman called Salazar from there. Do you have any idea what that was about?"

"I'm sorry. I don't have a clue, Mr. . . . ."

"That's Chief," Aquino corrected.

"Chief," Bryce said hurriedly, "I should get going before the roads close. If you need to talk to me again, I'm sure the secretary has my number."

He was out the door and gone.

Bryce denied Salazar called him. That would be easy enough to check. The phone company kept records.

Aquino had only stopped by to ask a couple of questions. Things were a lot more complicated than he expected. Diego Salazar drowned in the river. It didn't look like much of an accident anymore.

Chapter Thirty-Six

Early afternoon brought more snow and more frustration for Lansing. Despite his better judgement, deputies had to be dispatched to accidents. Jack Rivera coordinated with road crews, State Police and towing services. A five-car pileup near the Quincy Game Ranch blocked traffic on Highway 64. Snowplows were having to operate as far south as Segovia.

His lunch with Tina was hurried. Before he left the diner, he had them prepare a dozen sandwiches for the office staff. Morales drove him the one block to his office. The winds had died down, but they still had a bite.

Now that she had a warm meal in her, the teacher was going to risk hitting the IGA for groceries. She promised Lansing she would let him know that she got home safely.

The issue of the John Doe at the funeral home was becoming more complicated. They contacted the Oklahoma DMV. The owner of the license plate was Charles Williams of Oklahoma City. The problem was, the plate had been issued for a Dodge Caravan. The SUV at the lodge was a GMC Yukon. The plate was stolen.

After the storm, someone needed to go back to the lodge and pull the VIN from the car. They would track down the owner's name that way.

The FBI had announced the creation of the Integrated Automatic Fingerprint Identification System. But it wouldn't be available until July. They were still compiling prints from around the country to build the database. For John Doe to be ID'ed, his prints would have to be in the system already. That was a problem if he had never been fingerprinted before.

Then there was the money. It was mostly smaller denominations, 10s and 20s. Was it John Doe's money, or was it stolen?

Lansing was betting he would get his best identification results through the ATF. But answers wouldn't come quickly. He had contacted the ATF Tracing Center in Martinsburg, West Virginia. He provided them with the manufacturer, Smith and Wesson, along with the model, caliber and serial number.

The AFT would contact Smith and Wesson with the serial number to see how that gun entered the distribution chain. ATF then would contact the wholesaler to track down the specific gun dealer. Finally, each dealer was required to maintain a Form 4473, that had the buyer's name and address. When the Tracing Center had that information, they would get back to the sheriff. The entire process could take as much as 24 hours.

Of course, this process only worked if the original gun buyer still owned the gun. If it was sold, traded, pawned or stolen, the chain of custody would be broken. Then all bets were off.

With Rivera and Lopez benched for the moment, it eventually became Lansing's turn to get on the road. John Gutierrez called from the Western Auto. After lunch, his wife, Jessica, was bringing their youngest son to the clinic. She never made it there and she wasn't at home. John couldn't look for her. He took car number two to work, and it barely ran. He was afraid he might break down.

The Gutierrez family lived on a small acreage northwest of Las Palmas on Aspen Road. It was a large family—seven living sons, ages 10 to 20. The eldest, Charlie, had been killed by a classmate six years earlier. The result was both parents were overprotective, especially for their youngest, Stanley.

John's job at the Western Auto barely paid the bills. Their two-acre garden produced enough surplus that they could sell produce at the farmer's market on weekends. But finances kept the family from owning a cell phone.

There had been no accident reports along Highway 15 between Las Palmas and Aspen Road. Lansing would search along the five-mile stretch from the main highway to the Gutierrez place.

Most of Aspen Road ran parallel with Rio Cohino and the tiny farms along its banks were fertile. The acreage was a mile north of the bridge on the river. Since the beginning of the blizzard, the road had been plowed once. But it had continued to snow, and another four inches had accumulated.

The sheriff could tell few vehicles had ventured out that day. He hoped that would make finding Jessica's car easier. Gutierrez told him to look for an older, red Chevy Caprice station wagon.

Lansing wanted to be meticulous in his search, but he couldn't go too slowly. He needed momentum to push through the snow. The further he went down the road, the more disconcerted he became. There was no sign of the station wagon.

It wasn't until he crossed the bridge that he saw the tracks. Jessica had lost control and veered off the road and down the bank of the river. Lansing slammed on his brakes and jumped out of his Jeep.

He ran to where the tracks left the road. The Chevy had skidded down the bank and slipped into the river. This time of year, the Rio Cohino was barely 3-feet deep. But that still put the water within 4 inches from the top of the doors.

Lansing didn't think twice. He removed his coat and gun belt, then bound down the riverbank and waded into the frigid water. He went to the passenger side first, grabbed the handle and pulled the door open. Stanley could barely look at him. He shivered so violently his teeth chattered.

The boy was nearly unconscious. Lansing reached into the water and unbuckled the child. Scooping him up in his arms, Lansing carried him to the bank. He stopped just for a moment and looked back at the station wagon. He decided he needed to put the boy in his patrol car first. The child needed warmth.

The road sat eight feet above the river. Fortunately, the slope was gradual. That didn't keep him from slipping a half-dozen times as he scrambled toward his car.

He pulled the rider's side door open and set the boy inside. The rush of warm air invigorated him. A moment later he was down the bank and into the river again.

The mother had hit her head on the steering wheel. Between the knock on the head and the freezing water, Jessica was incoherent. Again, Lansing reached into the icy water, unbuckling the driver. She couldn't walk. Her legs were numb from the cold.

The sheriff picked her up with both arms. Nearly to the bank, he slipped on the rocky riverbed, plunging them both into the water. He quickly recovered and a moment later they were on the bank.

Leaning her against the side of his vehicle, he opened a rear door and helped her in.

With both safely inside the warm Jeep, the sheriff looked for anything to wrap them in. He knew they would be better off not wearing wet clothes, but he didn't have the time to disrobe them. He needed to get them to the clinic as quickly as possible.

Lansing retrieved his coat and slipped it on. He grabbed his gun belt, then climbed into the driver's seat. "Dispatch, Patrol One. I've just recovered a woman and her son from the Cohino. They're soaked. Tell the clinic we're on our way. ETA, fifteen minutes."

"Dispatch copies."

"Also, call John Gutierrez at the Western Auto. Tell him to meet us there."

"Copy."

It was still snowing. Aspen road had nearly six inches of snow now. Turning around was a challenge. Heading back to Highway 15, the sheriff followed the track he had made through the snow earlier.

The adrenaline surge that served him so well during the rescue began to ebb. He realized he was freezing, even in the heated Jeep. The shivering kicked in so badly he could barely hold onto the steering wheel. He couldn't quit. His two passengers were going to die if he didn't get them to safety.

As soon as he hit the main highway, he turned on his siren and emergency lights. Help was just minutes away.

Chapter Thirty-Seven

Lansing knew the doctor was right. He needed to be treated for hypothermia. But his passengers needed help more desperately than he did.

John Gutierrez was waiting for them at the clinic. He carried his wife into the building. Lansing, with the help of a nurse, followed with Stanley. Rooms had been set aside for all three.

First order was for each of them to strip. Jessica and Stanley each had two handlers. They were nearly comatose. Their clothes were cut away. Both had quit shivering, which meant their bodies were shutting down. Their core temperatures were below 85°. Hypothermia protocols were implemented. They both had to be closely monitored for high blood pressure and cardiac arrest. Ideally, they would have been airlifted to one of the Santa Fe hospitals, but nothing was flying in this weather.

The sheriff was in much better shape. Once his clothes were off, he wrapped in an emergency thermal blanket. A nurse brought him apple juice that had been warmed in a microwave. In addition to the blanket, they were warming him from the inside out. As far as rivers went, he could care less if he ever saw one again, let alone put a foot in one.

For the moment, warmed juice couldn't be used on the other two patients. They might choke trying to swallow anything.

Within an hour, Lansing was ready to leave. He needed a change of clothes and, after the dip in the river, a new phone. Jack Rivera dispatched Jerry Lopez to the Lansing ranch to retrieve a dry uniform. Oscar Vega was there, so getting in wasn't a problem.

It was 5:00 by the time the sheriff headed out the door.

Jessica and Stanley were improving but both were still in the danger zone. The husband and father drifted between the two rooms, trying to hold back tears, trying to be strong. He had six other sons at home to worry about. He couldn't understand what caused the accident. His wife had driven that road thousands of times in all sorts of weather. It made no sense.

Lansing's other major concern at the clinic was Maria Alba. She was lying in bed, eyes open, oblivious to anything around her. Klara Alba just shook her head when he looked in on her daughter.

Back at his offices, Chief Deputy Rivera gave Lansing a quick summary of the accidents from the day. Besides the five-car pileup on Highway 64 and the sheriff's own rescue, a total of 10 additional wrecks had been reported, and that didn't include any handled by the State Police.

The blizzard had abated only slightly since it began 24 hours earlier. They still had another 24 to go. Today was Thursday. Lansing didn't think Friday would fare any better.

The road crews were struggling to keep the highways clear. The sheriff wasn't sure he should try to make it down to his ranch.

"Oscar, this is Sheriff Lansing," he said into his office phone. "I just wanted to check up on things."

"They're doing okay."

"I know you have plenty of food there."

"Oh, yes, sir."

"The horses doing all right?"

"Yeah, I let them out of the stalls, so I could clean them. They walked around in the barn for a while, but they didn't act like they wanted to go outside."

"That's just called 'horse sense,' Oscar. Listen, I may not make it down there tonight. That's not going to be a problem, is it?"

"Oh, no, Sheriff. I'll be all right."

"Good. By the way, don't try to reach me on my cell phone. It's not working. Just call my office if you need to contact me."

"Yes, sir."

Lansing's next call was to Tina Morales.

"Did you know your cell phone keeps going to voice mail?"

"Yeah, my phone got soaked this afternoon."

"What happened?"

He described the river rescue from earlier.

"My God, Cliff. Are you all right?"

"Yes, yes. Doc Picado released me. Said I was fine. By the way, did you make it to the store?"

"Yes, I did. I'm all stocked up, now."

"I don't suppose I could wrangle a couple of meals off you, could I?"

"I don't know. Which meals are you talking about?"

"Dinner tonight. Breakfast in the morning."

The other end of the line was quiet for a moment. "And just what are you planning to do between these two meals?"

"The doctor said I needed fluids and rest. And to keep warm."

"I see." She paused. "I've heard body warmth is a good way to recover from hypothermia."

"I think they mentioned that at the clinic."

"How does this sound? A hot meal tonight, a hot meal in the morning, and lots of hypothermia therapy in between."

"Expect me around seven."

As Lansing hung up, Deputy Lopez knocked on the door frame.

"What's up Jerry?"

"We got a call from the ATF earlier. They have a name and address for the owner of that gun." He held up a sheet of paper.

"Let me see."

Lopez handed him the paper. He stood by, just in case the sheriff couldn't read his writing:

Seller—Brothers' Sporting Goods Outlet, Terre Haute, IN

Purchaser—Walter Deming, 119 S.14th Street, Terre Haute, IN 5/21/91

"What happens now?" Lopez asked

"I'll call the Terre Haute PD. Ask them to see if Mr. Deming is around. If they can't find him, maybe they can find a picture to send us."

"One step at a time, huh?"

"That's all we can do."

Chapter Thirty-Eight

"It's about time you answered your phone," Bryce groused. "Where the hell have you been?"

"I've been busy," Murdock snapped. "You're not my only client, Mr. Bryce."

"I got questioned today by the police."

"What police?"

"The ones at San Juan Pueblo, when I went there this morning."

"Why did you go there?"

"That's where I do business. The Northern Pueblo Indians Council. I needed to make sure everything stayed the same after Diego Salazar died."

"Salazar's dead? When did that happen?"

"Sunday night." Bryce paused. "You mean you didn't know?"

"Why would I know about that?"

"I thought it was you . . . I thought you got carried away . . ."

"All I did was talk to the guy like you said. I explained to him he had contracts, obligations."

"You didn't threaten him?"

"I might have hinted he didn't want me coming back. But I didn't get physical with him. I sure as hell didn't kill him. Why? What did the police say?"

"They said someone picked Salazar up at his house Sunday. The next morning, they found him in the river. Dead. They're trying to tie the two things together."

"Yeah, I picked him up. We drove around. We talked. That's it."

"So, you dropped him off at his place?" Bryce was not sure about the level of honesty he could expect from his henchman.

"Naw. I dropped him off at some old, rundown adobe buildings be-hind the Pueblo offices. He said he needed to meet someone. He was going to call his wife to pick him up."

"Did anyone see your car?"

"I'm sure they did. So, what?"

"Just asking." He hoped someone had seen Murdock. The man's black Lincoln looked nothing like Bryce's light blue Mercedes. No one could link the gallery owner to Salazar's Sunday visitor.

"What did you say to the police?"

"They asked if I was at the Pueblo Sunday. I told them 'no.'"

"You didn't mention me, did you?"

"No. Why would I?"

"You called me up to see if I killed the guy, didn't you?"

"You do have a reputation."

"You know, Bryce, I think it's time to terminate our association. I don't need to work for anyone so willing to throw me under the bus."

"I didn't do that."

"Maybe not, but you would if you had to. I don't trust you."

"The feeling's mutual. Consider our business dealings over."

"And if the cops ask, Bryce, I'm telling them YOU sent me."

The click at the other end told the gallery owner the conversation was over.

Chapter Thirty-Nine

"Cliff!" Tina Morales whispered.

"Hm-m." Her partner was still 90% asleep.

"Cliff, there's someone in here!"

"What?" Lansing said, groggily. "In where?"

"In the room . . . I can sense them."

"Well, turn on your light."

The teacher did as she was instructed. The small table lamp lit only a small patch near the bed. The rest of the room was darkness and shadows.

Lansing sat up. He rubbed his eyes, then tried to focus on his surroundings. Movement would have caught his eye, but nothing moved. He couldn't hear anything, either.

"Why do you think someone is in here?"

"It's a feeling I got. It woke me up. You know how you feel when someone's staring at you? It was like that."

"Stay here." Lansing swung his feet to the floor. He wore a T-shirt, boxers and socks. His holster hung from a chair within arm's length. He grabbed the pistol and went to the bedroom door. Reaching around the frame, he flipped on the living room, overhead light.

Tina Morales rented a small, one-bedroom house six blocks from the courthouse. Besides the bedroom with bath, the frame structure had a living room and a kitchen. She had been told she was getting 800 square feet living space, but she had her doubts.

The two sixty-watt bulbs lit the whole room. The sheriff could see nothing unusual. He checked the front door. It was locked. He went to the back of the house and checked the kitchen door. It was locked as well.

"I don't know what to tell you," he said. "Everything's secure."

He returned his pistol to the holster, then got back into bed. Pulling the covers over him, Lansing leaned toward Tina and gave her a quick kiss on the lips. "Satisfied?"

"I suppose." She turned off the light and laid back down.

Everything was quiet for five minutes, then: "What the hell, Cliff!" Morales yelled, sitting up in bed and turning on the light again.

"What? What's wrong?" He sat up as well.

"Your toenails! You just scratched me!"

"How? I'm wearing socks!"

Tina was wearing a flannel nightgown. She threw the covers back and pulled up her gown to reveal her legs. The left leg, the one closest to her partner, had four long scratches below her knee. One was deep enough to draw blood.

"Holy Crap!" Lansing swore. He looked around the room. From the corner of his eye he saw movement. He turned his head. In the darkened corner, a shadow seemed to dissolve into the wall. He rubbed his eyes for better focus. When he looked again, there was nothing in the room except the two of them.

"What happened?"

"I don't know," Tina whimpered.

"I'll get a washcloth." Lansing went to the bathroom and turned on a faucet. A few moments later he returned with a dampened cloth.

The warm rag felt good against Morales' scratches.

Both were thinking the same thing. The marks on Tina resembled the description of the scratches on Maria Alba. To Lansing, they looked like the scratches on Joey Lopez.

"Are you going to be all right?" he asked, sitting on the edge of the bed.

"I think so."

"Has this happened before?"

The teacher shook her head.

"I'll be right back." Lansing grabbed his gun and searched the tiny house again, and again, with no results. When he returned, he asked, "Are you going to try and get some rest?"

"Rest, yes. Sleep, no . . . but I don't have school tomorrow." Her alarm clock read 3:15. "I know you need rest. Will it bother you if I leave the lamp on?"

"No, since I don't think I'll sleep, either."

Daylight was a few hours away. It couldn't come soon enough.

Chapter Forty

The San Juan Bautista Church at the Pueblo was full for the funeral Mass.

Police Chief Joseph Aquino stood in the back, allowing the many attendees to have seats. He was curious how many real mourners there were, and how many were there out of curiosity.

Before the Mass started, a group of men and women huddled outside the church in the snow in a heated discussion. He only recognized two in the group of over a dozen. They were San Juan Pueblo artists. His guess was the strangers were artists from other Pueblos.

One man vented the most . . . probably Jason Romero, from Taos Pueblo.

If these artists had truly been cheated out of their share of profits, Aquino wasn't sure who they could file a complaint with. They could demand to look at Salazar's books. The Eight Northern Pueblo Indians Council shouldn't have a problem with that.

What if Diego Salazar's books were clean? Whoever was looking into the matter would have to move further up the food chain. That would be William Bryce at the *Galeria de Magdalena*. Aquino wasn't sure he had the right, let alone the obligation, to look into any fraud.

Aquino knew he had no real jurisdiction beyond the reservation boundary. He certainly didn't have the authority to travel the 40 miles to Santa Fe to conduct interviews. What bothered the officer was Salazar's death. He was found two miles from his home. He wasn't drunk, drugged or assaulted. Why was he running around without his winter coat? Why did the man walk into the freezing waters of the Rio Grande?

It couldn't have been a coincidence that he died as soon as this cheating controversy erupted. He had talked to Jason Romero and found out the man was getting short changed on his sales. He had talked to William Bryce who said he wanted to keep the relationship between his gallery and the artists of the northern Pueblos the same. That would make sense if he was cheating his suppliers.

There was one more person he could talk to—Alan Goldman at the Adams Gallery in Boston. Aquino needed to find out what the conversation was between the gallery and Salazar.

The brunt of the January blizzard had stayed to the north, but the Pueblo and Segovia still got their fair share. It was supposed to quit snowing by the evening. The San Juan Cemetery was only a thousand feet away, on the northeast side of the Pueblo. One of Aquino's officers would escort the funeral procession from the church to the graveside. Because of the weather, the gathering would be small—Father Iglesias, the pall bearers and the immediate family.

Aquino stood outside as the church attendees departed. When Constance Gomez emerged, he signaled to her to come over.

"Are you going back to your office?" the officer asked.

"I was going to go to lunch first."

"What time will you be there?"

"It's a little after twelve. I'll be back by one-fifteen."

"Okay. I'll call you then. I need to get that number for the Boston Gallery."

"Sure. Not a problem."

Aquino remained at his post. There was one more person he wanted to talk to. When the man emerged, the officer intercepted him. "Are you Jason Romero?"

"Yes." Romero was a man in his late twenties, a little heavy set with an intense look. He wore a short woolen coat, no hat. His hands were shoved deep into his pockets.

"I'm Police Chief Aquino. We talked yesterday."

"Okay." Romero didn't come across as the trusting type.

"I'd like to ask you a few more questions."

"It's too cold to stand around talking."

"My office is across the parking lot. We can talk there. There's probably some coffee."

"I've heard bad stories about police coffee."

"I can promise you, they're all true. You can try a cup and judge for yourself."

Romero turned to a young woman standing a few feet away and tossed her a set of keys. "Luna, why don't you start the truck, get it warmed up. I'm going with this officer for a few minutes."

"Are you in trouble again?"

"Not this time. We're just going to talk."

Aquino couldn't help but wonder what problems Romero had with the police in the past. It wasn't the current issue, so he pushed it out of his mind.

"So, what did you want to ask?" Romero didn't pose his question until they were in the warmth of the police station.

"Coffee?"

"No." The artist thought about the abruptness of his answer. "No, thanks."

Aquino indicated a chair in front of his desk. Romero sat.

"You said you weren't going out in this blizzard."

"I said 'for a police interview.' A funeral is another thing, all together."

"Fair enough. Have you ever heard of the Adams Gallery? It's in Boston."

"No. Is that the one who had my painting?"

"I'm going to ask them that later . . . when I get their number." He thought for a second before continuing. "That meeting you were having outside the church this morning . . . What was that all about?"

"I was telling them about my painting in Boston and what they wanted to charge."

"What did they say?"

"No one was surprised. The White Man screwing over the Indians again."

"Were they angry?"

"That's really a stupid question, isn't it?"

"Yeah, guess it is. I'm going to approach the Pueblo Council's director, Isaac Yope. I'm going to ask them to open an official investigation about the art sales. They have a lot more clout than a lowly reservation police officer."

Romero nodded. "That's a good thing."

"I thought so, too . . . Do you know William Bryce from the *Galeria de Magdalena*?"

"Yeah, I do."

"What do you think of him?"

"Not much. I liked him at first, then I realized how condescending he was. You get tired of being treated like you're stupid."

It was Aquino's turn to nod, but he kept his opinions to himself. "I appreciate you stopping by."

Chapter Forty-One

When Lansing walked into his office at 7:30 a.m., it had been snowing for 38 hours straight. It was supposed to continue for another ten. Friday morning picked up where Thursday night left off—more snow, more calls, more accidents. Overnight in Las Palmas, two roofs collapsed leaving two families homeless. Fortunately, no one was killed.

To the sheriff, unresolved issues were piling up. Maria Alba was attacked Monday night and went missing for almost 24 hours. She was not talking as of Thursday afternoon. Wednesday night they encounter the unknown shooter at Lookout Lodge. They still didn't know who he was. Thursday afternoon, he rescued Jessica and Stanley Gutierrez from the Rio Cohino. They were recovering at the clinic.

Then last night, Tina Morales was attacked in her own bed. That was the most disconcerting. He was there. He couldn't explain how it happened. He didn't know how he could have prevented it. Until he had answers, at his insistence, she was staying with him at the ranch . . . if she could get down there. Highway 15 would be clear. But the half-mile-stretch of ranch road leading to his house would have over a foot of snow on it.

He'd drive down and check it first before he gave her the all clear to go.

Jack Rivera reached the office a few minutes after eight. Before he began checking road conditions, Lansing had him call the Terre Haute, Indiana, Police Department. They needed to find out everything they could about Walter Deming on South 14th Street.

Lansing himself called the clinic to check on the Gutierrez family. He talked to the nurse in charge. Both mother and son were recovering nicely. Their body temperatures were now normal, and they were responsive. Jessica kept asking who rescued them. She couldn't remember a thing. As far as the accident went, all she could tell her husband was she swerved to miss an old lady standing in the road.

The nurse also said the doctor was busy with patients all morning, but could he call the sheriff later? He felt they needed to talk.

***

"Yeah, Sheriff, your deputy explained a gun originally purchased by Walter Deming was used in a shootout," the police sergeant said.

"That's right." It was only 9:30 when the Terre Haute PD returned the call.

"We talked to his wife first. He bought the gun about eight years ago. She gave him so much grief about having a gun in the house, he pawned it."

"So, that's it? We can't track it anymore?"

"Not true. We called him at work and he gave us the name of the pawn shop. If pawn shops are licensed to sell guns, they have to go by the same rules as anyone else. We talked to Ready Pawn and they had the Form forty-four seventy-three.

"They sold it in ninety-three to a James Forrest. He had an Indianapolis address."

"Indianapolis isn't close, is it?"

"It's about an hour away."

"That's a long drive to look for a gun."

"The Form said they guy was twenty-two. My guess, he went to the university here. Mr. Forrest obviously passed a background check, so the sale was on the up-and-up."

Lansing got the phone number James Forrest provided as well as the address, then thanked the sergeant for his department's diligence. The sheriff's next step was to call Forrest's number. He was rewarded with, "The number you are calling has been disconnected or is no longer in service."

After that he called directory assistance and asked for a listing for James Forrest. He wasn't surprised they had no such name in their system.

The one thing Lansing was sure of was the man in cold storage could not be James Forrest. Forrest would now be about 29. John Doe was at least 10 years older . . . maybe more.

There was one more avenue he could try going down. He could ask the Indianapolis PD if they'd had any crimes where a 40-caliber handgun was used. The briefcase with $10,000 might be from an armed robbery. After being transferred 3 times, he finally reached the violent crimes division. He was glad he could give the sergeant at the other end such a good laugh.

"Sheriff, we have over six million people in our metropolitan area. We had over four hundred and fifty murders last year and twenty-five thousand violent crimes. I don't think we even know the caliber of all the weapons used."

"Well, here's my name and number, just in case something comes up."

Lansing refused to be embarrassed over the call. The police sergeant probably thought he was a rube. He could care less. He was doing his job. All that the conversation did was reinforce the wisdom of his decision to leave the Albuquerque Police Department. Who needed all those big city problems? San Phillipe County kept him busy enough, as it was.

Chapter Forty-Two

After Lansing left for work, Tina tried to keep busy. She had cooked and cleaned in her nightgown and robe. The kitchen was spotless, the dishes put up and the bed was made by 8:30. It took her a long time to get dressed. After her shower, she stared at the scratches on her leg for thirty minutes, trying to make sense of them.

She had been attacked by some "thing"—not some "one." There was no one in the room besides herself and the sheriff. He had gotten up and checked the rest of the house, what little there was of it. There was no one there, either.

At school Monday, she thought she had seen a figure outside her classroom. When she investigated and found nothing, she had dismissed the matter as just her imagination. Maybe she had been too hasty with that conclusion.

When she finished dressing, she stepped outside to look at the snow accumulation. She needed to see if her Chevy Cavalier could make it through the streets. The teacher wasn't worried about reaching the Lansing Ranch. She only wanted to go as far as the clinic. She needed Dr. Picado or Jan Silver, the nurse practitioner, to look at her leg.

Morales knew she only had scratches. She only hoped they could explain how she got them. She checked. The clinic took walk-ins. With the blizzard, they were seeing fewer patients than usual.

Her street had been plowed once since the start of the storm. What might have been 18 inches of snow for her to fight was now only nine. Lansing's Jeep had plowed furrows down her driveway. She managed to use those grooves to maneuver onto the street. Even then, it took her 15 minutes to travel the 2 miles to the clinic.

Tina arrived at the clinic at 10:00. There were only two patients in the waiting room. The four exam rooms were occupied.

"While I'm waiting, I'm going to check on Maria Alba," she told the receptionist. "I won't be long."

Klara Alba sat with her daughter. Her husband was busy plowing roads. He couldn't afford not to be out making some much needed money.

"How is she doing?" Tina whispered.

"We've gotten her to eat a little. Because of the storm, the insurance company has cut us some slack. She can stay here till Tuesday."

"That's great!" She paused. "The scratches she got . . . Are they healing?"

"Yes, for the most part. Why?"

Morales was curious if her scratches looked anything like Maria's. She realized how crazy a thought that was. "No reason. Just hoping she was getting better. I guess I need to get back to the waiting room."

"You're here to see the doctor?"

"Just feeling a little peaked. The weather, I guess."

Alba nodded. "Take care."

"Yeah. You, too."

It was 10:30 before Ms. Silver could see her.

"What brings you in today, Miss Morales?"

"Something scratched my leg last night."

"Can you show me?"

"I'll have to take my jeans off."

"Would you like a gown? It might be a good idea if Dr. Picado has to see you."

"Okay."

The nurse practitioner located an examination gown in a cabinet and left the room. Morales disrobed and covered up. A few minutes later, Silver returned.

"When did this happen?" she asked after studying the marks.

"Around three this morning."

"Were you alone?"

"No, I was with . . ." She struggled to find the right word. "I had a visitor."

"I take it, they didn't do this?"

"Absolutely, not."

Silver's eyebrows knitted in concern. "And there was no one else in your room?"

"There was no one else in my entire house."

"These weren't self-inflicted?"

"No, they were not!" Morales said, indignantly.

The NP sighed. "Dr. Picado needs to look at your leg."

Chapter Forty-Three

Tina sat in Dr. Picado's office, looking at the Polaroid photos he had handed her.

"The first three are of Maria Alba. We found scratches on her legs, arms, and her torso, front and back. The last photo we took this morning. A ten-year-old boy came in yesterday with his mother. They had an accident and ended up in a river."

"Yes, I heard about that."

"When he first came in, his legs were so discolored from the cold we didn't notice the marks."

The teacher looked closely at the picture. The scratches resembled hers, only there were more of them.

"Mrs. Gutierrez, the mom, was bringing him into the clinic. He told her something scratched him in his sleep the night before. He was complaining about the pain. When she saw his legs, she knew something had to be done.

"I notified the sheriff this morning that we needed to talk. I wanted him to know how similar the marks were on the two children. Now, you come in. If you don't mind, I should tell him about you, as well."

She cleared her throat. "He knows about mine."

The doctor raised an eyebrow.

"We spent the night together. He was there when I was attacked."

"You're saying you were attacked?"

"I don't know what else to call it, Doctor. Assault causing bodily injury . . . that sounds like an attack to me. Isn't that what happened to those children?"

"Yes, it is. That's why I wanted to talk to the sheriff."

He pondered the situation for a moment. "I'm from big cities. I haven't spent much time in rural communities. I've only been here in Las Palmas for three months. Do things like this happen . . . often?"

"Beats me, Doctor. I'm from the big city, too. I've been in Las Palmas barely a year longer than you."

"Something physically happened to the three of you. Whatever this is, I guess we should be thankful no one else has been harmed."

"That may not be true, either, Dr. Picado."

Tina recounted the story Lansing told her Monday evening. The sheriff had gone to a home. The parents said their son had been attacked in his sleep the night before. According to the boy, he was hurt by a ghost. He had been scratched on his legs, as well.

"I thought he had been abused by his parents," the teacher admitted. "That's what I told Lansing. The boy made up the ghost story to protect his real tormentor."

Picado shook his head. "I'm at a loss. The Gutierrez boy doesn't know what happened. You don't! We have another kid saying he was hurt by a ghost. And the Alba girl? We don't have a clue."

"Maybe I can talk to her," Morales offered.

"We've all tried talking to her. How could you make a difference?"

"When you went to medical school, was there much discussion about alternative medicines?"

"Yes. We were told to avoid them."

"For a hundred years, western medicine didn't think there was anything to acupuncture. Now it's used all the time."

"It has it's applications."

"They've also discovered some folk remedies really work."

"Some. What's your point?"

"I'm a science teacher. Specifically, chemistry. But my interest in those things sprang from how I was raised."

"How were you raised?"

"My mother and grandmother were both *curanderas*."

"Herbalists?"

"That was a lot of my education. But there was a spiritual aspect to our practices."

"So, you think you're a witch?"

Morales realized they were getting ready to bump heads. "Maybe . . . in the broadest sense of the term."

"In that case, I really don't think you should be talking to that young lady."

"Why, because you've done such a good job, so far?" Tina regretted the question as soon as she said it. "A minute ago, you asked if things like this happen much in small towns like Las Palmas," she said, apologetically. "Maybe they do."

"It makes sense. They're full of superstitious people."

"Some people. Others are just more willing to have open minds about . . . how things work."

"Let me guess. Make up stuff to explain what we don't understand?"

"Science does . . . all the time."

"How?"

"There's a new trend in Cosmology. It's called Dark Matter. These brainy astronomers say the universe is expanding because of unseen gravitational forces. They also say they can only account for about five percent of the matter in the universe.

"To explain both things, they invented Dark Matter. Can't see it. Can't feel it. Don't know where it came from. But it's there . . . How much more 'made up' can you get?"

"We're talking about medical science at the moment?"

"How much does a soul weigh?"

"What?"

"How much does a human being's soul weigh?"

"I don't know what the hell you're talking about?"

"Is a soul a metaphysical concept or can it be quantified? A hundred years ago, an American doctor named MacDougal measured the weight of patients just before and after they died. There was a difference in their weight of twenty-one grams, consistently. He attributed that to the departure of the soul at death."

"I don't know what this has to do with Maria Alba."

"'There are more things in heaven and earth, Doctor, than are dreamt of in your philosophy.'"

"So, you're quoting Shakespeare now."

"Let me talk to her." Tina was pleading.

"Why?"

"I don't know what attacked me. Maybe she doesn't, either . . . but it's also possible we experienced the same thing. Mine just to a lesser degree."

Picado shook his head. "It's not for me to say. You'll have ask her mother."

Chapter Forty-Four

Tina sat in a chair next to the bed. Jan Silver closed the blinds. As she left the room, she turned off the lights. As soon as she did, Maria began to whimper.

It wasn't that Klara Alba didn't want the chemistry teacher to speak to her daughter. She didn't see the logic of Morales talking with her in a darkened room. And she certainly didn't want to leave her daughter alone with this stranger.

"She's trying not to remember what happened to her," Tina argued. "That's why she's avoiding the darkness. You've sat with her for over three days. You're her cocoon, her protection. I want her to know she's strong enough to face what happened to her."

"I don't know," Alba said.

"You and the doctor will be in the hall, next to the door. You can listen to everything going on."

"I'd like to talk to the doctor about this. Alone."

Morales waited outside the closed door. Klara Alba and Dr. Picado talked and argued for five minutes. The teacher wondered if Picado was pleading her case.

Finally, the door opened.

"Before you get started, I'm going to give her a mild sedative," Picado explained. "It will keep her calm, but it won't knock her out."

Morales took the girl's hand. "It's all right, Maria. Nothing can harm you here."

Maria turned her head and gave the teacher a confused look. "Who . . .?"

"It's me. Miss Morales. From school. Do you remember me?"

The girl stared blankly.

"The night you were... taken... You waited on me and Sheriff Lansing at the restaurant. Do you remember?"

Maria closed her eyes. Her brows knitted in concentration. "The restaurant?" she whispered, opening her eyes.

"Yes, Maria. The restaurant." Morales spoke to her quietly. "Do you remember what happened after you left?"

The teenager began to shiver and shake her head. No . . . No."

"*Meja*, I know you don't want to. But we need your help." She paused, then squeezed the girl's hand. "I need your help."

Maria looked at her. "Wh—why?"

"Someone . . . some 'thing' hurt you. Whatever is out there is doing this to other people. The past few days, two little boys were attacked . . . in their beds. Last night, it attacked me. No one suffered as much as you. But we need you to remember something . . . anything at all."

"I can't . . ."

"Maria, please. I know you're strong. I know you can do this."

She closed her eyes, trying to remember. "I didn't see anything. It was like I fell asleep." Tears welled in her eyes. A single drop ran down her cheek. "I could see my house. I was running. I was almost there. Then the shadow wrapped around me."

"What shadow?"

"The one chasing me. I couldn't get away." There was more sadness than fear in her voice. Hopelessness. "I woke up in a room. I was cold. I felt like I had been cut all over."

"Were you dressed?"

The girl nodded. She spoke slowly and deliberately. Words came out as she remembered. "It was completely dark. I felt around. I found a door. The knob . . . it was unlocked. But the door was stuck." She curled her fingers into claws. "I had to dig. I had to pry it with my fingertips. I don't know how long it took . . . but I finally got it open."

"Where were you? Can you remember?"

"It was a tiny, little house. I was in a kind of living room. The window . . . I could see the stars. I opened the outside door and I started running, and I kept running, and running." Her voice drifted off. "Then I wasn't running . . . and then I was here . . . in this room . . . my mother . . . she was with me." Her last words were a whisper.

"Your shoes . . . They found you with no shoes."

Maria shook her head. "They came off, I guess . . . in the snow . . . when I was running."

"You never saw who did this to you?"

"No," she whimpered. The fear was creeping back into her voice. "What did you see when it attacked you?"

"I'm sorry, Maria," Morales said, sadly. "I didn't see anything, either."

Chapter Forty-Five

"Mr. Goldman, my name is Joseph Aquino," the officer said into his phone. "I'm Chief of Police at San Juan Pueblo in New Mexico."

"Yes, Chief, how can I help you?"

"I'm looking into a suspicious death on my reservation. Diego Salazar."

"Diego Salazar? He's with the Eight Northern Pueblo Indians Council."

"That's right. The Council offices are on my reservation."

"I can't believe he's dead. I just talked to him last week. New Year's Eve, I believe."

"I know. That's why I was calling you. Can you tell me what you two talked about?"

"He's director for the Arts Council."

"He was. That's correct."

"My gallery has carried numerous pieces of Native American artwork over the years. Our 'go-between' for New Mexico has been William Bryce out of Santa Fe."

"I've met Mr. Bryce."

"Adams Gallery has been very successful with handling those paintings. But we weren't convinced we were getting a particularly good deal. I sent a buyer to *Galeria de Magdalena*. Of course, this was unbeknownst to Bryce. In his Gallery, he was asking half of what he's been charging us."

"Somehow, that doesn't surprise me."

"We decided here at Adams that we should eliminate the middleman. I had to make a few calls, but I finally found out about Mr. Salazar and the Northern Pueblo Indians Council. When we talked, I told him that we wanted to deal directly with the artists through him. I guaranteed him we could offer a much better package than he was getting.

"I was curious what happened. He told me he would call back after the first. I've been expecting to hear from him all week."

"You didn't mention any of this to Bryce, did you?"

"Of course not. To be honest, I don't plan on ever dealing with that man again."

"Before we hang up, does the name Jason Romero sound familiar?"

"Oh, yes. In fact, we have one of his pieces on display right now."

"Is that the one you're asking a thousand dollars for?"

"I believe it is. How did you know?"

"We heard a rumor."

"Do you know who's replacing Mr. Salazar?"

"No. Not yet. But I'm sure they'll be calling you."

Chapter Forty-Six

It was midafternoon. The snow was finally letting up. The plows had kept the main highways clear. After a late lunch, Lansing and Morales were taking a run down to the ranch. She followed the sheriff's patrol Jeep. They needed to see if her little Cavalier could negotiate the half-mile from Highway 15 to the ranch house.

The topic at lunch had been Tina's visit with Maria. The teacher had hoped for solid answers. It was wonderful that the girl was talking. But she didn't think they were any closer to finding out what was going on.

Despite the question over what tormented San Phillipe, Lansing was interested in where the Alba girl had escaped from. Just as important, how did she get there.

Tina talked in terms of shadows and shadow beings, whatever the hell those were. She claimed she had seen one at school on Monday . . . the same day Maria was abducted. Lansing refused to admit to himself he might have seen something similar the night before.

Morales also mentioned demons and phantoms.

That was all well and good. But a shadow wasn't going to pick up a girl and carry her twenty miles from her home. It was going to need a little help from something a bit more temporal.

Lansing slowed as he approached the turnoff to his ranch. Instead of having to guess where the ranch road was, he was greeted with a freshly plowed access. There was no more than an inch accumulation.

He headed for the ranch house. Morales followed.

"Who plowed the road out there?" Lansing asked, once he was inside the house.

"Oh, hi, Miss Morales." Oscar gave a short wave. "My dad came down with the tractor this morning," he explained. "I meant to call you. I got busy with the horses."

"Why'd he do that?"

"I told him you stayed in town last night because of the storm. He figured you couldn't get down the drive. He did a couple of other places, too."

"I'll need to pay him back, somehow."

"He said, don't worry about it." He thought for a moment. "Are you all right from falling in the river?"

"Yeah. Lost my phone, but I'll be okay."

Oscar looked at his former teacher. "Why are you here?"

"I'm going to stay for a day or so. I followed the sheriff here to make sure my car could make it down the drive. I guess we didn't have anything to worry about."

"Are you going to cook?"

"Yeah, I had planned to."

"Good," the boy said, smiling. "I don't think the sheriff knows how to shop for food. No offense sheriff."

"None taken . . . The horses doing okay?"

"Yes. You want to come out and see?"

"Later. We need to get back to town."

"I need to pick up a few things at my house," Tina elaborated. "Sounds like I need to visit the grocery store, as well. Any requests?"

"I like your spaghetti," the Vega boy suggested.

"Me, too," Lansing agreed.

"Spaghetti it is."

Chapter Forty-Seven

By 5:30 the snow had stopped completely. Lansing couldn't believe there had been half as many accidents on Friday than the day before. Maybe the word got out that driving in a blizzard was unwise. He knew dozens of mishaps would go unreported. That didn't bother him as long as no one was seriously injured.

He didn't imagine the weekend would be any less busy. With the storm over, people would want to be out and about. The opportunity for more accidents was less than a day away. He could hardly wait.

Besides the day-to-day operations, there were other issues he needed to resolve. He caught Rivera before the deputy headed home.

"Jack, do you know any Auxiliary Office that might own a snowmobile?"

"I can check around. Why?"

"It may be weeks before the road to Lookout Lodge is clear. I need someone to take a run up there. I want them to get the VIN off that Yukon. We need to find out who the owner is. If we're lucky, it'll be the guy at the funeral home."

"How soon do you need it?"

"I'd like it tomorrow. Whoever you get will have to pick up the keys. They'll be at the front desk."

"Can't he get the number off the dashboard, through the windshield?"

"Just in case he can't, have him get the keys."

"Will do."

"By the way, we haven't heard anything more about that Ralph Miera character, have we?"

"I haven't. But we have been a little busy around here."

"Can't argue with that. I'll ask Clem if he's seen anything come over the wire . . . Is Jerry back from his errands?"

"Check the day room."

The sheriff found the deputy cleaning up around the coffee pot. "You haven't talked to Jonah about your nephew, have you?"

Lopez looked up with a blank look, then a quick realization he had forgotten something. "I'm sorry, Sheriff. I meant to talk to him last night. It completely slipped my mind."

"Things have been hectic," he agreed. "Listen, some other things have been happening around town. I don't think what happened had anything to do with your brother or you sister-in-law."

"What do you mean?"

Lansing listed the other three cases - Maria Alba, Stanley Gutierrez, and, now, Tina Morales.

"You were in the room when Tina was attacked?" Lopez was shocked. "And you didn't see anything?"

Lansing shook his head. "How old is your nephew?"

"Nine."

"Right now, his explanation that a ghost is responsible makes as much sense as anything. My problem is I don't believe in ghosts."

"Maybe it's time you started believing," the deputy suggested.

Chapter Forty-Eight

Even though the snow had stopped, there were few cars out, even on Highway 74. Police Chief Aquino stopped his car on the shoulder of the road. He was heading west and was at the edge of the Pueblo. He slipped on a reflective vest, grabbed a flashlight, then began walking.

After dinner, the tribal officer couldn't relax. The events of the past week kept playing through his head. It was after 10:00 when he finally put on his coat and headed for the door. When his wife asked where he was off to, all he could say was, "Out."

The blanket of snow muffled every sound. The low clouds gave the impression he was not outdoors. It felt like he was in a giant cavern with darkness on all sides. The reservation plows had kept the roads open. The bridge was clear from the concrete barriers on one side to the barriers on the other.

It was a hundred yards from where Aquino parked to the center of the bridge. As he grew closer, he could hear the quiet babbling of the Rio Grande.

If someone stopped and asked why he was there, he would have struggled to come up with a rational reason. In his own mind, he kept wondering why Diego Salazar had stumbled into the river five nights earlier. Maybe that was why he was there. Looking for an answer.

He was half-way across. He stopped and faced the river as it flowed from the north. He turned off his flashlight and stared into the inky darkness.

There were no cars. There were no lights. Just Aquino and the murmuring river below . . . and then came the sound of a woman's voice. She was singing. Somewhere behind him.

The officer turned and faced the opposite side of the bridge. He hurried across, then stopped and listened.

He could hear the voice more clearly now. It was coming from the river below him. It was a sad, beautiful lullaby. The woman was singing in Spanish. He thought he recognized the melody. It seemed fresh, a tune he had heard as a child. It also sounded ancient, a canticle from a forgotten time.

He resisted turning on his flashlight. He didn't want to break the spell.

Instead, he peered into the darkness, looking for anything.

Then he saw her. A faint wisp, hovering over the icy waters, lit from within. A vision dressed in white buckskin, her arms outstretched, a mother about to embrace her children. She was as beautiful as the song she sang. He could feel her yearning, her sense of loss. Her melancholy music squeezed his heart and tears stung his eyes. He wanted . . . he wanted to be with her . . . to hold her . . . to ease her pain. Deep inside, he wanted the beautiful sorrow to never stop.

It was the splashing, coughing and gurgling coming from the river that woke him from his trance. He turned on his flashlight. The singing stopped. The vision disappeared.

Aquino pointed his beam into the black water. A man was struggling against the current. His head popped above the water. Unseen hands dragged him back under before he could catch a breath. He couldn't even yell for help.

"Hold on!" The officer yelled.

He ran the 300 feet to the end of the bridge, climbed down and raced to the river's edge.

He ran south along the riverbank, yelling, "Hey, can you hear me? Are you all right?"

He swept his flashlight up and down the rippling waters, looking for the drowning man. His efforts were greeted by the quiet splashes of water against the bank.

He chased the river, struggling through the branches of trees, shrubs, and undergrowth, until he reached the Yunge Owingeh Bridge, 200 yards south of Highway 74. At that point he stopped. Nearly out of breath, he realized his efforts were useless. This could no longer be a rescue.

In the daylight, it would be a recovery.

Chapter Forty-Nine

Aquino and Juan El Tano searched the east side of the Rio Grande, starting at the Yunge Owingeh Bridge. Daniel Martinez and Tribal Police Officer Henry Calvert were on the west side. In the mostly flat valley of the San Juan Reservation, the river cut rivulets and channels to either side of the main course. The searchers sometimes had to backtrack to cover all the places a body could hide.

***

The conversation Aquino had with his wife when he got home kept playing in his mind. Sharon was still beautiful after nearly twenty years of marriage. She was also his best friend and confidant.

"I saw her, Sharon."

"Who, Joe?"

"*La Llorona*. Tonight, I saw her. I heard her singing."

"What are you talking about?"

"She's real . . . *La Llorona* . . . The Weeping Woman . . ."

"The Weeping Woman—that's a story grandmothers tell little kids to scare them."

"I always thought that, too. But the stories . . . they have to be true."

"Where were you?"

"On the bridge . . . the Highway seventy-four bridge . . ."

"What were you doing there?"

Aquino shook his head. "I was looking for . . . something . . . anything to explain how Diego Salazar ended up in the river."

"Is that why you went out?"

"Yes."

"And you found the Weeping Woman?"

"I didn't find her. I mean, I wasn't looking for her. I was just there when she appeared."

"What did she look like? What was she doing?"

"She was . . . a spirit . . . floating over the water. And she was singing the most haunting lullaby I've ever heard. I got choked up . . . It was . . . so . . . sad."

"What happened?"

"Someone fell in the river."

"What? Who?"

"I don't know . . . I was listening to the song, then suddenly I heard splashing. Somebody was drowning . . . right next to the bridge. I flashed my light on the river. I saw him go under.

"I ran from the bridge, down to the bank. I looked all over. I followed the river down to the Yunge Bridge, but I couldn't see anyone."

"What happened to the Woman?"

"I don't know. I didn't notice. I was concentrating on the guy in the water." He shrugged. "She disappeared."

"What about the man in the river?"

"I'm afraid he drowned. I'll have to look for him in the morning."

The conversation didn't end until the early hours. Every time Aquino answered a question about the Weeping Woman, his wife came up with another: What was she wearing? What did the song sound like? What were the words? Where did she come from? Where did she go? What did she want?

***

"Look!" Henry Calvert shouted from the opposite bank. "I see something! On the island."

149

Around a bend, a thousand feet south of the Yunge Owingeh Bridge, the river was divided by a small island. On its bank, nestled under one of the scrub trees sprouting from the snowy bar, was the body of a man.

All four men converged, getting as close as they dared without getting wet.

"I think the water is about four feet deep on my side," Aquino guessed.

"It's only a couple of feet on our side," Calvert said. "But I'm not getting in that water without waders."

It took most of an hour to retrieve two sets of fishing waders. Aquino and El Tano joined the other two on the west side of the river. In short order, Aquino and Calvert, the two officers, had waded to the tiny island and dragged the body back to shore.

"Who is it?" Daniel Martinez asked

"Carlos," Aquino said grimly. "Carlos Dominguez."

Chapter Fifty

The Twenty-First Century was less than twelve months away. Cliff Lansing wanted his offices to be a part of it, but the county commissioners fought him all the way. When he first ran for Sheriff in '92, one of his campaign promises was to modernize the Department. He was naïve to believe he would get cooperation from the commissioners. It was always about money.

The Sheriff's Department got its first computer in '93, but it was mostly used as a word processor. Three years later, they had three computers in the office and were finally hooked up to the Internet. Lansing was amazed at what information was available at his fingertips. One day, he was told, computers would be available in patrol cars. He wasn't going to hold his breath as far as San Phillipe County went. He felt like he was lucky to even have patrol units.

Even though it was Saturday, for the sheriff it was just another workday. He hadn't taken time off since before the New Year's. With Tina Morales back in Las Palmas, he looked forward to some down time.

He had the 17-digit Vehicle Identification Number from the Yukon by 9:45. He sat down at one of the terminals in the front office and logged on. (One day he would have a computer in his private office. Again, he wasn't holding his breath.)

DMV.org gave him the name and address of the owner: Samuel Livingston of Chesterfield, Missouri. Had he found the identity of John Doe at the funeral home? On a hunch, he went to the National Insurance Crime Bureau and did another check. The NICB kept a nationwide list of all stolen vehicles that hadn't been recovered. Samuel Livingston's Yukon had been stolen two weeks earlier.

Information provided Livingston's home phone number. The man was home when Lansing called.

"Mr. Livingston. My name is Cliff Lansing. I'm sheriff in San Phillipe County, New Mexico. I'm calling about your stolen Yukon."

"New Mexico? You found my car?"

"Yes."

"Was it in a wreck?"

"Not as far as I know." The sheriff explained where it was, how they stumbled upon it, and why it may be a week or two before it can be recovered. "I was curious. How was it stolen with the keys?"

"It was in valet parking at Lambert International Airport here in St. Louis. I was on a business trip and flew home on Christmas Eve. That's when I found out it was gone. Let me tell you, I was not a happy camper. Secure parking my butt!"

"Yeah. Well, sorry about that. When we get it back here in town, we'll let you know. You can figure out how to get it home after that."

"I do appreciate the call. Thank you."

After hanging up, Lansing leaned back in the chair he was using. Whoever John Doe was, the sheriff could track the man's journey. He called up a road map of the United States.

John Doe started in Indiana, probably around Indianapolis, and took I-70 west, across Illinois to St. Louis. Ditched his car there and got on I-44. It was a straight shot to Oklahoma City. That's where he stole the license plate. I-40 took him into New Mexico. U.S. Highway 285 brought him north to Santa Fe. Highway 15 got him to San Phillipe and Lookout Lodge.

From appearances, it looked like the man intended to hide out for a while. Why was he there? What was he running from? Where was he going to go after his food ran out?

He wished John Doe was his only problem. Something had attacked Tina while he was in bed with her. She seemed to be safe at the ranch, for the moment. But at least three other people had been assaulted as well. The worst part was they were only kids.

Maria Alba was finally talking. She didn't know who kidnapped her. She had no idea where she was taken. Lansing had a guess. He needed to go back to Route 182. He also wanted to talk to the rancher, David Robles, again.

On the weekends, Deputy Sid Barns pulled double duty as dispatcher and desk sergeant. He was across the room from Lansing. He held up his phone. "Sheriff, I think they want to talk to you."

"Who is it?" Lansing asked, reaching for the phone.

"It's the San Juan Reservation . . . The police."

"This is Lansing."

"Good morning, Sheriff. Joe Aquino. I need to ask another favor."

Chapter Fifty-One

"Hi, Pauline," Aquino said, stepping inside the house. For the recovery that morning, he chose not to wear his uniform. "I'm sorry to bother you, but I need to talk to you about Carlos."

"Carlos isn't here," the school nurse said. She stood in the small living room, her two children huddled around her.

"I know . . . Do you think we can talk alone? Maybe put the kids in their room."

Pauline ushered her children to a back room and pulled the door shut, then returned.

"I hate to tell you this, but we found Carlos' body in the river this morning. It appears he drowned last night."

She nodded, expressionless. "So, he's . . . gone."

"Yes." The officer had seen a wide range of emotions from people first confronted with a tragedy. He could tell when a loved one steeled themselves, wanting to save their emotions for a more private moment. He didn't get that impression from Pauline. She seemed almost unaffected by the news. "Can you tell me what he did yesterday?"

"He started the new job at the construction site. Came home. Had dinner. Then went out again."

"Do you know where he went?"

"No. Probably out drinking."

"The judge said if he started drinking, he'd end up back in jail."

The mother shrugged. "I heard he wasn't supposed to beat on his family anymore. That didn't stop him from knocking the kids around last night and slapping me when I stopped him."

"Why was he hitting the kids?"

"He said they were making too much noise."

"What time did he leave?"

"I wasn't watching the clock."

"And you don't know where he went?"

"No."

"So, you don't know why he went to the river?"

The school nurse just shook her head. She turned her attention to her four-year-old daughter. The child ran into the room, wrapped her arms around her mother's legs and said something. "Yes, we'll go to grandmother's later." She stroked the child's head.

"I'm sending Carlos' body to Albuquerque. They'll do an autopsy. It sounds like he might have gotten drunk and fell in."

"I guess I'll talk to Father Iglesias," Pauline said. She seemed resigned to the situation. "I suppose we'll bury him next week."

Aquino suddenly felt awkward. "Is there anything I can do? Would you like me to get your neighbor?"

"We'll be all right. Thank you for stopping by, Chief."

Aquino had driven his personal truck to retrieve the body. He was still driving it when he went to the Dominguez home to deliver the news. He started the engine but remained parked. Pauline worked. Carlos worked . . . most of the time. They each had their own car. Both cars were still parked on the side of the house. Tire tracks in the snow showed both cars had been driven after the snow stopped, about 5:00 the night before.

Carlos probably got home from work after 5:00. That explained his tracks. Did Pauline go somewhere last night?

It was a mile from the Dominguez house on Sage Lane to the river. Dominguez obviously didn't drive himself there. The storm had stopped. He could have easily walked to the river. Then again, his wife could have driven him.

The clouds from the storm had moved on. The blue of the New Mexico sky was a welcomed site.

The officer's visit to the bridge the night before seemed more like a dream now. He had asked Sharon to keep his ghostly encounter a secret. In the sobering sunlight, he was beginning to wonder if it really happened.

But it must have. How else would he have known Carlos drowned?

He put his truck in gear and headed to his office. The EMS would be there soon to recover the body.

Chapter Fifty-Two

San Phillipe County was clawing itself back to normal after the winter storm. The road crews had worked round the clock to keep highways clear. They were now working their way through the streets and back roads. The sunny skies helped lift spirits.

Lansing was back in his office after a quick visit to the cellular store, his new phone in hand. He called Morales to let her know he was online again. Tina had just finished taking Oscar back to his family's ranch and was on her way into town. The two were making lunch plans when Deputy Danny Cortez, dressed in civilian clothes, knocked on the doorframe.

The sheriff waved for the deputy to come in. "I need to get off, Tina. Just come to the office. We'll figure it out from here." He closed the flip phone. "What's up, Danny?"

Cortez stood in front of the desk. "Sheriff, I can't go on patrol tonight."

"Why? What's wrong?"

"Something happened. I can't leave my family alone again tonight."

"What do you mean? What happened?"

"Last night while I was on patrol . . . Ebbie said it must have been around midnight . . . she heard James screaming. She ran to the room. When she opened the door, there was someone standing over his bed."

"Who?"

"She couldn't tell. She said it was all black. The only light was from the hall. But when she opened the door, it turned and looked at her . . . then disappeared out the window."

"The window was open?"

"No. That's just it. It was closed. Ebbie said it was like a shadow . . . or smoke. It just dissolved."

"Did it have a face?"

"She didn't see one. Like I said, it was dark."

"This thing . . . did it hurt your son."

"No, thank God. I think Ebbie got there just in time."

"What did James see?"

"He said he thought he was dreaming. He opened his eyes and saw this shadow standing over him. The eyes were glowing red. He tried to move, but he said he couldn't. It sounded to me like he was paralyzed. Somehow, he was able to scream."

"I don't know what's going on, but whatever it is, I don't think you'll keep it from happening."

"What do you mean?"

Lansing told him about his experience with Tina two nights earlier.

"What did you see?"

"I thought I saw a shadow, in a corner. It looked to me like it . . . dissolved, too."

"What the hell is going on?"

"I'm going to find out. I promise you." Lansing shook his head. "In the meantime, I'm going to need you on patrol, Danny."

Chapter Fifty-Three

Saturday and Sunday were Deputy Jack Rivera's scheduled days off. Lansing hoped the County Prosecutor could review the Lookout Lodge shooting by noon Monday. He was sure both River and Lopez would be cleared of any wrongdoing. At the moment the Chief Deputy had information Lansing wanted.

"Jack," Lansing said into his office phone. "This is Cliff. Sorry to bother you at home."

"No problem. What's up?"

"I need to get the name and phone number of the couple who plowed into the snow drift New Year's Day."

"Let me check my notes." Rivera was off the phone for a long minute. "It was Mr. and Mrs. Robert Paul."

Lansing wrote down the name and phone number. "Do you remember exactly where you found their car?"

"Yeah, it was four miles west of where County Road five-thirty-five 'Tees' into Route one-eighty-two. Remember that old barn that burned down last Summer? About two miles past there."

Lansing remembered the barn very well. It was where Tina Morales' ex-boyfriend died. "Thanks for the info. See you Monday"

The sheriff was getting ready to call Robert Paul when Tina Morales gave a short rap on his door frame. "Are you ready to discuss lunch?"

Lansing nodded toward a chair, indicating she should sit. "I need to make a quick call."

The number he called rang six times before the answering machine kicked in. Lansing explained who he was and, despite his better judgement, gave out his cell number. He needed to ask about their wreck on New Year's Day.

"What was that all about?" the teacher asked when he hung up.

"How hungry are you?"

"I'm not starving, yet. Give me time."

"Let's take a ride in my Jeep. I'll explain on the way to the clinic."

"The clinic?"

"Like I said, 'I'll explain.'"

***

Now that she was awake and talking, Maria Alba had been released from the long-term-care wing of the clinic. Jessica and Stanley Gutierrez were still recovering, though Dr. Picado was confident they could go home on Monday.

He found the woman in her son's room, sitting next to the bed. When she saw the Sheriff enter the room, she jumped up and gave him a hug.

"I can't thank you enough for saving me and my son, Sheriff," Jessica said. This was the first time she had seen her rescuer since the accident.

"I'm just glad I got there in time," Lansing said, a little embarrassed by the mother's attention. He turned and gestured toward his companion. "This is Tina Morales, one of the teachers at the high school."

"Pleased to meet you," Mrs. Gutierrez said.

Tina nodded. "Same here."

"Please, sit back down."

Jessica returned to her seat. The boy smiled and gave the sheriff a small wave.

"How are you and Stanley doing?"

"We're getting better every day."

"If you don't mind, ma'am, I'd like to ask you about your accident?"

"Sure."

"I heard that you told your husband, you swerved off the road to avoid hitting an old woman."

"That's what I remember. I don't think John believes me. He kept asking, why would an old woman be out in a blizzard like that?"

"Do you remember what she looked like?"

"Not really. I didn't see her face. Her back was to me. It looked like she was wrapped in an Indian blanket. It was pulled over her head."

"How do you know it was a woman?"

"She was wearing a dress. It hung down to the ground."

"You didn't hit her, did you?"

"No. No, I'm sure I didn't hit her!" Jessica said anxiously. "Did you find something?"

"No, and I'm sure we won't. A tow truck is fishing your station wagon out today. One of my deputies will be there to assess the accident."

"Do you believe me? That I saw a woman in the road?"

"I'm looking at all angles. Why do you think it was an 'old' woman?"

"I know her back was to me, but it looked like she had a dowager's hump."

Tina interrupted. "They said you were coming to the clinic because something scratched your son. On his legs. Could I see them?"

Lansing understood her concerns and said nothing.

Jessica turned to her son. "Honey, do you mind?"

Stanley shook his head, then pulled back the covers. Of all the scratches Morales had seen, the Gutierrez's boys were the worst. They were deep, more like gouges. They had bled a lot. They probably hurt, as well.

Both the sheriff and the teacher now understood Jessica's urgency to get him to the clinic despite the storm.

"Stanley, do you remember what did this to you?" Tina asked.

The boy's face clouded into a painful pout. "No." The response was a whisper. If he did remember what happened, he was too scared to say anything.

Chapter Fifty-Four

Despite the sunny day, it was still cold outside. For lunch at *Paco's Cantina*, Lansing opted for a bowl of chile. Morales was satisfied with a cup of the same.

"So, you're coming around to my way of thinking?" Tina asked.

"I'm not sure what I think," the sheriff admitted. He took a spoonful of chile and savored the flavor.

"You're not sure Mrs. Gutierrez saw a real woman standing in the road, but she did see something."

"I wish Robert Paul would call back. I want to hear about what he saw."

"Do you think he saw the same thing?"

"Maybe." He thought for a moment, not sure he wanted to pursue the topic. Then he told his partner about Deputy Cortez's visit that morning.

"We ARE dealing with 'shadow people,'" Tina said, definitively. "That's what his wife saw. A shadow, bending over her son's bed." She poked at her cup of food. "The little boy you told me about Monday . . . he said he was attacked by a ghost. Maybe that was a shadow person, too."

Lansing was sorry he brought up the subject. "I hate to tell you this, but I don't believe in ghosts."

"I didn't say it was a ghost. That's what the boy thought he saw."

"So, you're not saying shadow people are ghosts?"

"No."

"Okay. What are they?"

The chemistry teacher thought for a moment, trying to come up with the right term. "They're demons . . . At least, they're a type of demon."

"And they look like shadows?"

"Yes, except they're not flat like a regular shadow. They have depth. They're more three dimensional. And some have glowing red eyes."

"Have you ever seen one?"

"Years ago, when I was a little girl."

"Where was this?"

"In Nogales. I was visiting my grandparents in Mexico. It scared the bejesus out of me."

"What happened?"

"It just showed up in my bedroom one night. I told my *abuela* about it the next morning. She told me not to worry. She would take care of it, and she did. That was the first time I heard about demons and *brujas* and other kinds of witches. That's when I found out my grandmother was a *curandera.*"

"I'm not saying we are dealing with shadow people here. But if we are, do you know how to handle them?"

"No," Morales admitted. "But my *abuela* does."

Lansing's cell phone began to ring. "Excuse me." He retrieved his phone from his pocket. "Lansing."

He listened for a moment, then said, "Yes, thank you for calling back, Mr. Paul. I wanted to ask you about your accident on New Year's Day."

Tina listened to Lansing's end of the conversation. Everything Robert Paul said, the sheriff repeated aloud so the teacher could hear. The sheriff again thanked the man, then hung up.

"It sounded like Mr. Paul saw the same thing Mrs. Gutierrez saw."

"It does," Lansing agreed. "An old woman standing in the road with her back to him, wrapped in a blanket. So, what do these old women have to do with your shadow people?"

Tina shook her head. "I don't know."

Lansing took another bite of soup. He was almost finished. "Do you have any plans for this afternoon?"

"Other than hanging out with you, no."

"I thought we'd take a drive out to the country."

"Where are we going?"

"I want to see where Mr. and Mrs. Paul had their accident."

"Think we might see an old woman?"

"Who knows? We might."

Chapter Fifty-Five

"It's Raymond Mesa," Sharon Aquino said, handing the phone to her husband.

"What in God's name does that man want?" the officer swore under his breath. He took the phone. "This is Aquino."

"Yes, Chief. Sheriff Mesa here."

It grated on the Police Chief every time he heard Mesa use his new title. "Yes, Sheriff, can I help you?"

"I had a talk with Henry Calvert after lunch today. He told me you, he and a couple of other men recovered Carlos Dominguez's body from the Rio Grande this morning."

"Yes, we did."

"He said it was around the bend in the river, something like three hundred yards south of the Yunge Owingeh Bridge."

"Yeah."

"How did you know he drowned? You couldn't possibly see his body from the bridge."

"I heard him. The night before. I was on the highway bridge. He was splashing in the water, trying to swim. I turned on my flashlight and saw him go under."

"Did you try to help him?"

"Of course, I did. I came down from the bridge and ran to the river. I looked for him everywhere. I went all the way down to the Yunge Bridge. I couldn't find him anywhere."

"What time was this?"

"I'm not sure. Ten-thirty, eleven o'clock. It was almost midnight by the time I got home."

"What were you doing on the bridge, Officer Aquino?"

The Police Chief didn't like the direction of the discussion. "What are you hinting at, Ray?"

"I prefer to be addressed as Sheriff Mesa. I'm making an official inquiry."

"Well, Sheriff, I prefer to be addressed as Police Chief Aquino. And exactly what are you officially inquiring about?"

"Yeah, you are Chief of Police, for now. I'm trying to find out how Carlos Dominguez ended up in the Rio Grande around 'ten-thirty, eleven o'clock' last night."

"You and I are asking the same questions, then."

"Police Chief Aquino," Mesa tried to sound as condescending as possible, "it's no secret you didn't like Carlos."

"I barely knew the man. I'll agree, though, I didn't care much for how he treated his family."

"You didn't answer my question. What were you doing on the bridge in the middle of the night?"

"I was doing my job."

"I see." Mesa was quiet on the other end. Then, "I think it would be better if we conducted this interview in person."

"If that's what you want. I'll be in my office Monday morning. We can talk all you want there."

"No, I was thinking a more neutral location. Say, President Kata's office."

"Give me a time. I'll be there." The chief hung up the phone before Mesa could respond.

Sharon Aquino saw the grim look on her husband's face. "What's wrong, Joe?"

"That worthless Raymond Mesa." He thought old rivalries were dead and buried. They weren't. It took that brief conversation for Aquino to realize how much Mesa despised him. That was a problem because the lawyer/sheriff was in a position to get the Police Chief fired.

"What did he do?"

"It's what he's trying to do." He saw the questioning look on Sharon's face. "He's going to say it was my fault Carlos Dominguez drowned."

"Why? Because you couldn't save him?"

"No. He's going to say I murdered him."

Chapter Fifty-Six

On their drive to the countryside, Lansing mentioned his conversation with Police Chief Aquino. "Do you remember earlier this week, when I drove down to San Juan Pueblo?"

"Yes. It had to do with arranging an autopsy for a man who drowned."

"I got a call this morning. They had another drowning and need another autopsy."

"What's going on down there?"

"I wish I knew. Police Chief Aquino and I talked for half an hour. He thinks something strange is going on. He just can't put his finger on it yet."

Lansing followed Rivera's directions. He took County Road 535 to Route 182, then hung a left. The county got a Winter's worth of snow in the blizzard. The southern part got six inches. Las Palmas got nearly two feet. The mountains got three. The snowplows had been busy. The back roads were clear.

The sheriff watched the odometer. Two miles from the "Tee," he slowed and pointed out a clump of charred trees to their right.

"That's where the barn was. That's where we found Poncho's body."

Tina nodded, but said nothing.

Poncho Chamorro, her controlling and abusive ex-boyfriend, had stalked her from Albuquerque to Las Palmas. In fact, she ended up in San Phillipe County trying to escape the man. When he did show up, she nearly took his head off with a shotgun blast. He somehow escaped from police custody and ended up dying in a barn fire. She doubted anyone missed him.

Two miles past the charred trees, Lansing pulled to the side of the road and stopped.

"According to Jack, this is where the Pauls' got stuck in a snow drift."

They got out of the Jeep and looked around. It was midafternoon. Despite the cloudless skies, it hadn't warmed above freezing.

The plows had piled the snow three-and-a-half feet high on either side of the road. The shoulder was only two feet wide. Lansing could see how easily a person could get stuck if they swerved very far off the road.

"Exactly, why are we out here?" Morales asked.

Lansing didn't respond. Instead, he started walking further down the road. In this section, Route 182 ran east to west. Fifty feet from his Jeep he turned and faced north.

Tina came up to him. "What are you looking at?"

He pointed to the west. "David Robles picked up Maria about three miles from here." He nodded toward a small shack next to a line of trees a quarter of a mile away. "That cabin is the only building around for miles."

The teacher looked down the road, then back to the run-down structure. "Do you think that's where she was taken?"

"It has to be, unless Robles lied and found her somewhere else."

"Why would he do that?"

Lansing shook his head. "Let's assume he's telling the truth." He looked at Tina. "Do you recognize that place?"

She looked around. With the blanket of snow, everything had a sameness, with no distinguishing features. "No. Should I?"

"You were here once, last Summer. When we buried Berta Chavez."

The memory of the events from last year came flooding in. From Chamorro kicking in her front door to Chavez plunging into the Rio

Cohino, the only good thing that happened to her was she met Sheriff Cliff Lansing.

Berta Chavez had been a *bruja*, a witch. After wreaking havoc across San Phillipe County, she drowned in the Rio Cohino near *St. Anthony's Monastery in the Canyon.* When her body was recovered, Lansing arranged for Chavez to be buried on her own property, paying all expenses out of his own pocket.

"You don't think the old woman in the road was Berta, do you?" Tina sounded concerned.

"I told you, I don't believe in ghosts."

"Hrmpf." Morales sounded exasperated at the man's stubbornness. "Are we going to check that cabin?"

"I am. Tomorrow. When I'm dressed for trudging through two-foot deep snow."

"I'm coming with you."

Lansing knew better than to argue with her. "Then we'd better swing by your house and get you warmer clothes."

Chapter Fifty-Seven

"*Mi borregita* [my little lamb]," Tina's grandmother exclaimed, "it is so good to hear from you! Did you make it back to New Mexico all right?"

"Yes, I did, Grandma. And you wouldn't believe all the snow we got."

"Snow? I don't like snow."

Abuela Sanchez was eighty. Her husband was almost ninety. Both were still active and very sharp, mentally. Even at thirty, Tina Morales wasn't above asking her elder's advice . . . especially when it came to *burjas, demonios,* and *figura oscuridad.*

"Grandma, I called because I need your help."

She described the sudden appearance of *figura oscuridad*, shadow people. In fact, she explained, she herself had been attacked. As far as she knew, though, she was the only adult that had been hurt. The rest were children.

"How do you know it was shadow people? Did you see them?"

Morales gave the description Ebbie Cortez provided. She mentioned the glowing red eyes that James, her son, had seen. Also, his sleep paralysis.

Another child thought he was attacked by a ghost.

Almost all the assaults were the same—scratches on the legs. The exception was a sixteen-year-old girl whose whole body was clawed.

"I would suspect," Sanchez said, thoughtfully, "if all the attacks were the same, that you are dealing with one entity, not several."

"I thought a shadow person attached themselves to a single person . . ."

"Or to a single location," the grandmother said, completing the thought. "I have known that to be true. You are dealing with something different."

"There's something else," Tina added. She described the old woman on the road in two different locations. Is it the same woman? Different women? Is it a ghost? Are they in some way related to the shadow people?

"No one saw a face?"

"No, *Abuela*, they did not."

"The two people who saw the woman in the road . . . what do they have in common?"

"I don't know. They live miles apart. Plus, one couple saw the woman at night. The other lady saw the old woman during the day, in a snowstorm."

"From your description, I would say, yes. This is the same woman. Is it a ghost? Maybe. Does it have anything to do with the shadow person? I don't know. I would have to know more.

"I believe your shadow person IS a demon. A ghost can't inflict the harm to people you describe. But for it to migrate from one location to another, it must be anchored to a nest."

"A nest?"

Grandma Sanchez struggled to find the right word. "Yes, a nest . . . a home . . . a sanctuary."

"If it's a demon, how do I stop it?"

"Purifying fire. If you destroy its sanctuary you may be able to destroy it. But you can stop it from attacking."

"How, Grandma?"

"To protect a child, or even yourself, at night, pour salt on the floor all around the bed. And not just a little. It must be a visible, unbroken line. The demon cannot cross the salt."

"What about the ghost, if that's what it is?"

"Has it caused harm?"

"Two car accidents. A mother and her son ended up in a river. They nearly froze to death."

"*Meja*, I don't know what to tell you. Maybe we should pray on the matter."

"I will, Grandma. I will."

Chapter Fifty-Eight

"Good morning, Sharon," Lucia said, sweetly.

Sharon Aquino almost regretted answering the phone. Lucia Ortega was the reservation's biggest gossip. You never knew where a conversation with her would go. It could be a malicious rumor about a friend or a sneaky bit of news about someone you didn't like.

Aquino had to admit Ortega always seemed to know what was going on.

"Hi, Lucia. It's early for a call."

"I went to seven-thirty Mass."

It wasn't a brag. It was simply a statement of fact. Nearly the entire reservation was Catholic. The 7:30, 9:30, and 11:30 Masses were always well attended. The Aquino's usually attended the late Mass.

"So, what happened at the Mass?"

"This isn't about the Mass. It's what I heard being discussed when church was out."

"All right. What did you hear?"

"I need to ask you something, first."

"What?"

"Is Joseph in trouble with the Tribal Council?"

"No. Not that I know of. What did you hear?"

"Raymond Mesa is the new Tribal Sheriff."

"Everyone knows that." Sharon snapped.

She knew Raymond Mesa, maybe better than most. They dated one summer when he was home from college. She was still in high school. He made plans for the two of them after his graduation. Fortunately, she found out early on that he couldn't be trusted. She thanked God every day for Joseph Aquino.

"In the parking lot, after church, he was talking to Berto Cruz."

Roberto "Berto" Cruz was one of Aquino's police officers. Of the three, he was the most senior.

"Exactly what were they talking about?"

"Raymond wanted to know if Berto was interested in becoming Chief of Police."

"What?" Sharon was shocked.

"I'm just telling you what I heard."

"Who have you told this to, Lucia?"

"You're the first person I called. I just wanted to find out what was going on."

"Nothing is going on . . . And you better keep your big mouth shut. As far as I know, Joe, the new sheriff and President Kata are having a meeting tomorrow morning. That's the only thing that's happening."

"Now I was told this whole thing was about Carlos Dominguez."

"Who told you that?"

"I can't remember. It's just something I heard."

"I'm nipping this in the bud, Lucia Ortega. There is nothing going on, and if there was, it's none of your business. If you're going to spread stories, tell everyone that Joseph tried to save Carlos. Do you understand?"

"Yes."

Sharon Aquino slammed the phone down before Ortega could mount a defense. At that same moment, her husband entered the kitchen.

"What was that all about?"

"The Pueblo Gossip was handing out her most current bag of crap."

"Who's Lucia going after this time?"

"Remember yesterday when you were talking about Ray Mesa? You thought he was after you. I said you were blowing things out of proportion."

"Yeah."

"I was wrong."

Chapter Fifty-Nine

Most people didn't understand how labor intensive owning and caring for your own horses could be. Lansing had been out to the barn before 7:00 to feed the animals. After his own breakfast with Tina, he was out to the barn again to clean the stalls. It was a daily chore he happily left for Oscar Vega. But Oscar was home for the weekend.

Wood shavings in the three stalls had to be shoveled out and hauled to the compost pile behind the barn. In the Spring, the manure would be distributed across the ranch as fertilizer. Once the concrete was hosed off, new shavings were spread in the stalls.

The stalls needed extra attention in the winter. The horses spent more time inside and left more to clean up. Growing up, Lansing resented the day-to-day ranch chores. As the proprietor now, he understood and accepted the responsibility of ownership. His horses, especially Cement Head, were not pets. They were tools of his trade. At one point or another, all three had been used in policing San Phillipe County. It was important for the sheriff to keep his charges healthy and comfortable.

Lansing didn't use the word often, but he "loved" his horses. He was giving Little Orphan Annie a good brush down when Tina entered the barn.

"Still playing with the animals, I see." She walked up and stroked the horse's neck. Annie was her favorite.

"I'm almost done here. How was Mass?"

"It was good. You should have come."

"I know, but I needed to get this work done before we make our run out to that cabin."

"I need to change my clothes, first. Should I make a pot of coffee? We can take some in a thermos."

"That's a good idea."

For Lansing, taking care of his horses was therapeutic. In the three hours he spent cleaning the stalls and grooming the animals, he didn't think once about his sheriff duties. It wasn't until after he closed the barn door that he allowed his law enforcement responsibilities to occupy his thoughts.

John Doe's body had been retrieved and was at the MI's office in Albuquerque. That was fine. The autopsy would be out of the way, but it didn't bring him any closer to identifying the man. Maybe a thorough search of the Yukon would yield a name.

Lansing would be the first to admit he had seen things in his life he couldn't rationally explain away. However, he wasn't ready to accept the existence of ghosts . . . and demons ran a close second.

Shadow people? He found those a possibility. Ebbie Cortez saw one. Her son saw it. He might have even seen one in Tina's bedroom.

The teacher had a long conversation with her *curandera* grandmother. The old lady concluded that the "shadow person" Las Palmas was experiencing was something else. A single demon was responsible for inflicting all the pain and suffering across the county.

The sheriff wanted more tangible evidence. That was the purpose of the trip back to Route 182 and a visit to the lone cabin. If that indeed was where Maria Alba had been kept, it was possible he could discover who was really involved. He didn't mind Morales' company. Two sets of eyes were always better than one.

***

It was warmer than the day before, but barely. Lansing parked close to the same spot on Route 182. The two investigators got out of the Jeep and studied the quarter-mile track to the cabin. They were ready to tackle the snow this time. They both wore hiking boots, heavy coats and fur-lined gloves. The sheriff wore his ever-present Stetson. Tina had donned a stocking cap.

The blinding sunlight bouncing off pristine snow forced them to wear sunglasses.

Lansing climbed to the top of the snowplow drift, then helped Tina up.

"Let me go first," he suggested. "You can step in my tracks."

"All right, but don't take big steps."

"I won't."

It was more of a struggle to get through the deep snow than the sheriff would have suspected. With each step the snow was above his knee. He wished he had brought a walking stick for balance. When they reached the cabin, they were both grateful they only had to travel a quarter of a mile.

Two snow covered steps led up to the cabin door. The door was un-locked. Lansing pushed it open and the two stepped inside.

The shack was small, with three rooms—a kitchen in back, a bed-room to the side. They stood in the living area. Lansing had been inside once before, months earlier. What little furniture had been there was gone now. The place was dreary and barren.

"Maria said she had to pry a door open." Tina stepped to the bed-room and examined the edge of the door. "Cliff, look at this."

Lansing came closer. He could see the tiny scrape marks where someone tried to dig into the wood with their fingernails. Splinters had broken off. Miniscule, dark stains were inside the scratches. He guessed that it was Maria's blood.

"This has to be where Maria escaped," Morales concluded. "She said she ended up in a kind of living room. She could see the stars through the window."

"Not that window." He pointed at the dingy panes of glass. "She probably imagined she saw the stars. Or she misremembered. She couldn't have seen the stars till she got outside."

"You agree with me, though. This must be where she was taken."

"Looks like it. If she lost her shoes running to the road, they probably won't turn up till the Spring thaw."

Tina thought long and hard about something, then asked, "Do you think Berta Chavez had anything to do with this?"

The sheriff shot his partner a doubtful look.

"Cliff, think about it. The old woman in the road? That might have been her."

"Berta Chavez is dead," he said with finality. "We buried her next to her *horno* out back there."

"Do you remember exactly where?"

"No. Even if I did, we won't find it with all that snow."

"I'm going to look." Tina headed out the back door. If she wanted to fight with the snow, that was all right with him. He had no desire to trudge in more snow than he had to.

"Cliff!" she yelled. "Come here!"

Chapter Sixty

Tina stood twenty feet from the back of the cabin, near the *horno*, the domed, dried-mud oven so popular in the Southwest. As he approached, he could see a patch of bare ground close to her. About three feet wide and seven feet in length, it looked like a grave plot.

There was no snow on it.

It had not been shoveled clean. It looked like the snow never settled on it. The snow on the sides and either end was steep. The earth was dry.

The ground had been disturbed, as if something had been digging in it. But the grave looked intact.

"I found it!" Tina said, announcing the obvious.

"What on God's green earth is going on here?"

"I don't know." The teacher stepped closer, her bravery bolstered by the sheriff's presence. To touch the dry soil, she had to kneel in the deep snow and removed a glove. She looked back at Lansing. "It feels warm."

"The sun's been out all morning," he pointed out.

Morales struggled to stand. Lansing helped her up.

"Cliff, there's something going on. Have you ever seen anything like this before?"

He tried to avoid the question. "Well, we don't normally get that much snow around here."

"So, snow doesn't fall on graveyards in New Mexico?"

"I don't know. I don't hang out in cemeteries."

Morales ignored his efforts at denial. "I need to talk to my grandmother again."

"Why?"

"She said the demon had a nest somewhere. If all this was because of Berta, I was thinking she was using the cabin as her sanctuary."

"Why are you zeroing in on Berta Chavez?"

"The old woman on the road. Maria Alba kept in Berta's cabin. No snow on the old witch's grave. It has to be her!" Morales was emphatic.

"She's a ghost standing in the middle of the road? She's a demon attacking kids? What?"

"That's why I need to talk to my grandmother again."

"Okay. For the sake of argument, let's say it's Berta. How do we stop her?"

"At first, I thought we could burn her cabin down."

"We can't go around burning up other people's property."

"Who own's this place?"

"Berta's relatives, I guess."

"Who are they?"

"I don't know."

"It doesn't matter. I don't think that's her sanctuary."

"Then what is?"

"That's what I need to talk to my *abuela* about."

"Are we ready to get out of here?"

"Yeah, I suppose."

Lansing turned and headed back to the cabin. "I'm going to send Willie Estrada out here. She's my forensics expert. I want her to dust for fingerprints. Maybe she can pull a blood sample off the door. I want to make sure this is where Maria really ended up."

"You're not convinced Berta Chavez is involved?"

"I'm sorry. I'm a cop. I need something a bit more solid to go by."

"What if we could find something that links all the victims to the old *bruja*?"

They were both inside the cabin again. The sheriff closed the back door, then they headed out the front.

"That might be a start," he agreed, though, deep inside, he thought she would find nothing.

"We could stop by your office and start making a list."

Trudging through the snow, back to the Jeep, they used their original tracks.

"First, I'm going to warm up with some of that coffee we brought. Then we're going to the diner. I'm starving."

"Okay, but after that, we make a list."

Chapter Sixty-One

Carla Naranjo handed her mentor a cup of hot tea. "Are you sure that's all you want, Mama Agustina?"

"I'm sure." The old woman took a sip, jerking slightly from the scalding liquid.

"Is it too hot?"

"It's fine."

"Father Iglesias' Mass was good this morning. You would have enjoyed it."

"What did he talk about?"

"Fellowship, brotherly love, and New Year's resolutions. Mostly New Year's resolutions. He said we always make great plans, but never follow through.

"He also said we should all pray for the soul of Carlos Dominguez. He was found in the river yesterday."

"Ah, Carlos. Did you see Pauline at the church?"

"She wasn't at the Mass I attended."

"Maybe tomorrow we can visit her. Offer our condolences."

"You know that she works. At the elementary school."

"Surely, they will give her time off. My goodness, she just lost her husband."

"I didn't think of that. Of course, she'll be home." She thought for a moment, as if remembering something. "People were talking about Carlos after Mass."

"What were they saying?"

"That maybe it wasn't an accident."

"What?" the old woman asked, warily. "What do they think happened?"

"That someone killed him on purpose. They were saying it was too much of a coincidence that two men drowned in a week."

"Who do they think would do such a thing?"

"Someone said Joseph Aquino, the Police Chief."

"Who started such a rumor?"

"I don't know who started it. Like I said, people were talking after church. Then I heard it again from Lucia Ortega."

Jacona allowed herself a grim little smile. "If you heard it from Lucia, it must be true."

Chapter Sixty-Two

Lansing and Morales decided to skip the visit to his offices. Instead, after lunch at the diner, they went back to the ranch. They now sat at the dining room table compiling a list of people who had encountered either the "shadow person" or the old woman in the road.

It was Tina's goal to link every contact with Berta Chavez.

The first reported assault was Joey Lopez. They couldn't think of a time his parents, Elena and Jonah, might have interacted with the old witch. They decided to come back to Joey's name later.

The next victim was Maria Alba. Again, there was no obvious reason for the assault.

"What about the Gutierrezes?" Tina asked. "Is there a connection there?"

"There definitely is."

Lansing recounted the story of Berta's son, Bernardino. Six years earlier, the Chavez boy was eighteen. He and Charlie, the oldest of the Gutierrez kids, were rivals for the same girl. Bernardino decided to eliminate the competition by beating him to death with a bat. Bernardino crossed paths with the wrong person in prison and was killed.

Morales knew the rest. Berta Chavez went on a rampage, cursing and killing anyone she remotely blamed for her son's death. That meant Lansing and anyone else in San Phillipe law enforcement, including their families.

"So, do you think Berta's after the entire Gutierrez family?"

"Yes . . . If it's her. And for me, right now, that's a big 'if.'"

"It's obvious she's coming after me," Tina argued. "She isn't done with what she started in Rio Cohino Canyon last summer." She pondered the other possibilities. "James Cortez. He almost drowned Memorial Day weekend. She was coming back to finish the job."

"You're saying she picked up where she left off last year?"

"Yes."

"I'm sorry, Tina. That's a stretch."

"The old woman in the road. She caused the Gutierrez car to go in the river. That had to be Berta."

"Then why did she run Robert Paul off the road?"

"I don't know. Maybe she was lost, trying to get her bearings. He was at the wrong place at the wrong time."

They had beaten their heads on the table for over an hour. Lansing stood.

"Where are you going?"

"I'm going to check on the horses."

"You're not taking me seriously."

"I am. I just have to make the connections in my own mind for any of this to make sense." He put on his hat and coat and went out the door.

Tina leaned back in her chair, disappointed and angry that the sheriff didn't believe her.

Lansing suddenly opened the door and came back in. "Jonah Lopez works for the county road department. You met him last summer. He's the one that operated the backhoe to dig Berta's grave. That's their connection."

Chapter Sixty-Three

During Summer vacation, Tina Morales had visited her grandparents in Nogales, Mexico. While she was in Nogales, she gave her grandmother a complete account of her interaction with Berta Chavez. Naomi Sanchez now listened intently while her granddaughter described her visit to the old *bruja's* cabin and gravesite.

"Chavez has become a *lechuza*," Sanchez said. "She is a demon, in league with Satan. She can still take the form of an owl. That allows her to travel from one place to another.

"But she can no longer physically become human. She is a phantom."

"The old woman in the road?"

"No more than an apparition."

"When she appears as a shadow person?"

"Just an entity in the shape of a human."

"Why couldn't the people see her face?"

"There is no face to gaze upon. Just those burning red eyes."

"If she's just an apparition, how can she inflict pain? How can she scratch and claw?"

"*Bioquinesis*. She has no physical hands or nails. She uses her mind to cause harm."

"When we first went to the witch's cabin, I thought that was her lair. That's where that student of mine was taken. Am I wrong?"

"Tell me about the grave, again."

Tina described the grave site once more. The barren ground. The absence of snow. The warm earth.

"Just as a yucca plant repels water, the *lechuza's* burial pit rejects life giving moisture. This Berta Chavez may be dead . . . but she is still very active."

"Should I burn down her cabin?"

"That is not where she is operating from."

"Her grave?"

"Yes. You said the soil was disturbed. That is from her demonic force coming to and from."

"How do I stop her?"

"As a minimum, you must burn her heart until there is nothing left."

"You mean, we have to dig her up?"

"If you want to be rid of her, yes."

"I'm not sure how much Cliff will like that idea."

"I can't help what your sheriff likes. I am just telling you what must be done."

Morales was quiet, thinking over the situation. "*Abuela*, this biokinesis? Could Chavez use that to transport Maria Alba twenty miles from her home to the cabin?"

"No, my child. She is not that powerful. She enlisted help . . . from someone living."

Chapter Sixty-Four

"How are you feeling, honey?" Klara Alba asked.

"I'm okay." Maria Alba sat in a chair, alone in her bedroom. She had been home for 48 hours. In that time, she had taken three showers. It was as if she was covered with a stain she could never remove. She needed clean pajamas each time she showered.

Her interactions with her parents and her two younger sisters were brief and infrequent, which was tough to do in their small house.

"Have you thought about going to school in the morning?"

The girl nodded. "I guess I'll go." Her answer dripped with reluctance.

"At least you only missed two days last week. Everything was closed Thursday and Friday because of the storm."

Afraid of her mother's reaction, Maria said her next words cautiously. "Mom, I don't want to work after school."

"I don't think it will hurt you to miss a few more days."

"You don't understand. I don't want to go back to the restaurant. I can't walk in the dark anymore."

Klara thought about what her daughter said. She was not going to force her oldest to do anything she couldn't handle—not school, not work, not even eating meals at the kitchen table with the family. "You don't have a thing to worry about, my baby. I don't want you walking those streets at night, either."

Now Maria was sorry she even brought it up. "What about the money? I know we need the money"

"We'll work out something. When you're ready, if you want to go back to work, you can. But your father and I are not going to make you go back to the restaurant if you don't want to."

Maria was overcome with relief. That had been her big worry, ever since coming home. She didn't want to disappoint her parents. But she also knew she couldn't walk home after work. Not yet. Maybe, not ever again. She started crying.

Klara stepped closer and hugged her. "Maria, my baby, we're just glad that you're home. That's the most important thing: That you're home and safe with us again.

"God brought you back. He'll see us through anything else."

Chapter Sixty-Five

It was Monday morning. The forecast was for sunny skies and warmer temperatures the entire week, provided the Jet Stream stayed to the north. Some of the snow might even melt.

Lansing was filling his coffee mug when Jack Rivera walked into the day room.

"You look like something the dog dragged home," the sheriff observed.

"Thanks," the Chief Deputy said. "I love you, too." He found his own mug and held it out for Lansing to fill. "I'll be fine. I just need some coffee."

"It looks like you haven't slept in days."

"I haven't."

"What's wrong?"

"Deedee," Rivera said, referring to his now five-year-old daughter. "The last two nights she's been waking up screaming. Something about a monster in her room.

"We finally put her in bed with us. She started crying every time we turned off the lights. I can't sleep with the lights on. If I left the room to get some sleep on the sofa, she started the waterworks all over again."

Lansing let out a long breath. He suspected he knew what Deedee's monster was. But that meant he had to completely buy into Tina Morales' and her grandmother's theories. He wasn't ready to run around declaring a demon was on the loose. However, telling Rivera to protect his daughter with a barrier of salt would require him to do just that.

"Did she say what the monster looked like?"

"All she talked about was the red eyes that glowed in the dark."

"That's really weird," Lansing said, trying to sound nonchalant. "Danny Cortez's son said he saw something like that Friday night."

"What in blue monkey butts are you talking about?"

Lansing recounted his conversation with Deputy Cortez on Saturday morning. He described the shadowy form Ebbie saw bending over the bed and the red eyes James had seen. He wanted to make sure Jack heard it from him first.

"What the hell is going on, Cliff?"

"I'm not really sure," the sheriff said. He knew the statement was a half-truth. But he wanted to contain the situation, if he could. "Let's hope they're just nightmares. They'll probably go away."

He steered the conversation in a different direction. "The county prosecutor should finish his review of the shooting this morning. Are you ready to get back on patrol?"

"I will be, after a gallon of coffee . . . By the way, did you get that VIN like you wanted?"

"I did. Turns out that GMC Yukon was stolen from a St. Louis airport parking lot."

"So, we still don't know who that shooter is."

"Nope. We should get John Doe back from the MI tomorrow. I'll check and see how long we need to hold onto a cadaver. No one's going to claim it, I'm sure.

"I also need to look into the Maria Alba case."

"How's she doing?"

"Better. She's home. I'd like to interview her, see if she remembers anything. I'm also going to drive out to David Robles' place. He and I need to talk."

"What about?"

"I want him to go over exactly how he found her on the road. It was a miracle she was rescued. The thing is, miracles are hard to come by."

"You doubt his story?"

"He's the only connection we have to the girl's abduction." He was also thinking about what Naomi Sanchez told Tina. If Berta Chavez was in the middle of all the chaos, she had help from someone living.

"Tina and I went out to an old cabin yesterday. It's down the road from where Robles picked her up. In fact, it wasn't far from where the Pauls' got stuck.

"The point is, that cabin looks like the spot Maria was taken. I'm sending Willie out to pull prints. I'm also going to ask David Robles to come in, so we can get a set of his for comparison."

"Do you think he'll cooperate?"

"It will be mighty suspicious if he doesn't"

Chapter Sixty-Six

Joseph Aquino stepped out of his office, into the bright sunlight. Across Po'Pay Avenue was the *Ohkay Owingeh* Tribal Office building. A block to the north was St. Chapelle Chapel. Behind the chapel was *Owe'neh Bupingeh*, the oldest part of the Pueblo structures. They were originally built around 1300, already 300 years old when the Spanish took over the Pueblo.

The *Ohkay Owingeh* people were entering the 21st Century with a renewed interest in their tribal heritage. Only 300 residents still could speak the original Tewa language. Classes were being taught to keep their ancient tongue alive.

There was a desire to rebuild the old Pueblo structures, not with modern-day materials, but with plain old adobe. They would include electricity, modern plumbing and heating, but the exterior walls would be the ancient, mud-dried adobe bricks.

Aquino knew two things stood in the tribe's way—money and the knowledge of how to actually make adobe bricks. It had been over forty years since the last craftsman needed to make new bricks. A new generation had to learn the old art.

The Police Chief knew it would be years before something would actually happen. The Federal Government could cut loose funds for the Bureau of Indian Affairs to build new, wood-frame houses for the tribal members. But adobe was not an approved building material. The tribe would have to come up with their own dollars.

As much as Aquino loved his Pueblo and its residents, he had more pressing concerns. He wasn't sure he still had a job. Saturday, Sheriff Raymond Mesa was very clear—he was Chief of Police, for now. Sunday, the Pueblo gossip machine was in overdrive, speculating on his future unemployment. Today, Rebecca Luna, the office reception-ist/secretary, Henry Calvert and Berto Cruz all looked at him like he was a dead man walking. Their greetings were cool and distant.

The worst part of his treatment was the speculation that he might have killed Carlos Dominguez.

He knew he hadn't.

Aquino's own theory was that Dominguez was so enchanted by the Weeping Woman, he tried to approach her. When he did, he got caught in the river's current and drowned.

Why the man wasn't shocked back to reality as soon as he stepped into the cold water, the officer couldn't explain. Maybe he was drunk.

The similarity between Salazar's and Dominguez's deaths couldn't be a coincidence. But when they conducted the autopsy, the coroner found no alcohol or drugs in Salazar's system. What if the autopsy on Dominguez produced the same results?

Was the Weeping Woman responsible for both deaths?

Would anyone believe him when he claimed he had seen her?

He waited for a car to pass, then crossed the boulevard. It was time for him to meet with Tribal President Manuel Kata and Sheriff Raymond Mesa.

***

Manuel Kata had been appointed as permanent President of the Tribal Council two years earlier. Prior to that he had served as Governor four years in a row, appointed alternately by the Summer and Winter chiefs. He had been a member of the National Congress of American Indians. A retired Electromechanical Systems Engineer, he had worked at both Los Alamos and Sandia Labs, as well as taught at the University of New Mexico.

Kata was highly respected, both on and off the reservation.

When Aquino arrived at the President's office, the secretary instructed him to go in, Kata and Mesa were waiting for him.

"Joseph, please sit down." Kata indicated a chair in front of his desk.

Mesa was already seated. The sheriff looked at Aquino, barely acknowledging him.

"Do you know why we're having this meeting?" Kata began.

Aquino knew the accusations being leveled against him. At least, he had heard the rumors. He wanted a clear explanation. "No, President Kata, I really don't."

"Sheriff Mesa says he has issues with the death of Carlos Dominguez."

"Just what are those issues?" Aquino directed his question at Mesa.

"How did you know Carlos drowned and how did you know where to find him?"

Aquino turned to Kata. "I told Mesa Saturday, I was on the Highway seventy-four bridge Friday night. I heard splashing in the water. I turned on my flashlight and pointed it at the sound. I saw a man drowning.

"I ran from the bridge down to the bank. I followed the river all the way down to the Yunge Owingeh Bridge looking for the guy. My only conclusion was the man drowned and was swept further down the river.

"I didn't know it was Carlos Dominguez until we found the body the next morning."

The lawyer started his cross examination. "Exactly, why were you on the bridge?"

"I was trying to find out how Diego Salazar ended up in the river."

"At night?"

"During the daytime, I couldn't find a reason for Salazar to be at the Rio Grande. I thought a clue might turn up at night."

"And you just happened to be there when Carlos died?"

"Yes."

"You said you heard splashing in the water, 'then' you turned on your flashlight. There aren't any lights on the bridge. Weren't you afraid of getting hit by a passing car?"

"I was wearing a reflective vest. When I first walked out there, my flashlight was on. I turned it off when I got to the middle of the bridge. I was looking for any lights or sounds that might have drawn Diego to the river."

"And that's when you heard Carlos in the river?"

Aquino hesitated. "No." He considered the wisdom of explaining what he thought he saw, then pressed on.

"I was on the north side of the bridge. Somewhere behind me I heard singing. I ran to the other side and looked down. That's when I saw her. She was singing the most beautiful song I had ever heard."

"Saw who?" Kata asked.

"*La Llorona*," Aquino said softly. "The Weeping Woman."

Chapter Sixty-Seven

The school bell rang, announcing the end of second period. The students in Morales' room stood, grabbed their books, and hurried to their next class. All except Maria Alba. She remained seated while the others filed out.

The teacher approached. "Maria, I'm so happy to see you in school today. How are you feeling?"

"I'm better than I was. I wanted to thank you for coming to see me on Friday. I think I'd still be in the hospital if it weren't for you."

"I'm glad I could help."

Students for the next class were filling seats.

"I think you need to go to your next class," Tina suggested.

Maria stood reluctantly and picked up her books.

"What's wrong?"

The girl cringed. "Everyone keeps looking at me like I'm a freak."

"I'm sure they don't mean to. If anything, they're just curious about what happened."

Maria wore jeans and a long-sleeved sweater. She wanted to ensure none of the scratches showed. "My friends keep asking me what happened. I don't know what to tell them. I don't even know what happened." She was on the verge of tears.

Tina wanted to hug the poor girl. She knew such a gesture in front of a class full of 8th graders would cause problems for both of them. Instead, she placed her hand on Maria's shoulder and walked her to the door.

"Everything's going to be fine, Maria. Are you going to work today?"

"No." She didn't feel like elaborating.

THE WEEPING WOMAN

"Do you want to talk after school?"

Maria nodded. "I'd like that."

Chapter Sixty-Eight

Tomasita Salazar claimed she never saw the car that picked up her husband the Sunday before yesterday. Two of her neighbors on Kennedy Loop were sure they had seen a black Lincoln Continental and saw Diego get in. No one could remember seeing either the car or the Art Director return.

Aquino finally had a lead. There were no Lincolns on the reservation. He was beginning to think an outsider caused Salazar's death. He was sure William Bryce was involved. But then how did the Weeping Woman fit in?

He canvased the neighbors around the Dominguez house. No one had seen Carlos leave. They couldn't remember Pauline driving anywhere once she was home from school.

As a follow-up question in both neighborhoods, he asked if there had been any unusual activities at either house. No one remembered any out of the ordinary events, but the people who talked saw the same two visitors, just before or after the drownings—Agustina Jacona and Carla Naranjo.

Jacona's visits were striking because she never left her apartments. She was the cacique of the Women's Society. People came to her.

Other than drowning in the river, this was the first link Aquino found between the two deaths. It was tenuous, at best. It might not lead anywhere. But he had to ask about the visits.

Carla Naranjo lived on Yucca Street, just a couple of blocks from the Dominguez house. She was surprised at Aquino's visit. At first, she was pleasant, asking about Sharon and their son. When he broached the subject of her visits to Pauline and Tomasita, her attitude changed. Initially, she feigned ignorance. She couldn't remember any visits.

When he mentioned neighbors had seen both her and Jacona at the two houses, her memory improved. The visit to the Salazar home was the day of the Buffalo Dance. But they had visited several places that day, that was why it didn't stand out.

What did they talk about?

Well, of course, Diego's untimely death and how sorry they were at hearing about it.

The visit to Pauline Dominguez was the day after Carlos had been arrested. They only stopped by to give the poor woman moral support. That was at the end of a long day for Carla. She had been so busy she barely remembered going there.

Aquino thanked her for her time. When he left, he was confident Agustina Jacona would be alerted that he was coming. That was all right with him. All he wanted to do was see if both women agreed on why they made their visits.

"Please, sit, Joseph," Jacona indicated a wooden love seat with two cushions. She turned off the radio she had been listening to and returned to her own wooden chair.

The old woman's two-room apartment was still warm from the morning sun. This was Aquino's first visit to Jacona's home. He could sum up its appearance in two words – organized clutter. The living area had shelf after shelf of earthen pots and small glass vials. Dried flowers and thin branches from an assortment of plants protruded from taller vases on the floor.

Jacona noticed the officer's glances around the room. "I am an apothecary of sorts, Joseph. The Bear Chief of the Medicine Society is not the only one who needs to concoct remedies, from time to time."

Aquino nodded, but said nothing.

"I understand you asked Carla why we made visits this past week."

"I did," the officer affirmed. He wasn't surprised that she knew he had just talked to Naranjo. He was surprised at the old woman's directness.

"Long before the PeaceKeepers came along, The Women's Society was the only place abused wives could turn to for support," Jacona explained. "Just because the tribal government offers programs now to protect families does not negate my society's role. We still play an important part.

"Tomasita had just lost her husband. I stopped by to offer my condolences and support. You had just arrested Carlos Dominguez for hitting Pauline. Again, I was there offering support."

"Did you know Tomasita was being abused, as well?"

"How would you know that?"

"I saw the bruises on her arms. She tried to hide the marks with long sleeves, but I saw them. She never filed a complaint with my office, though. She never said anything to the PeaceKeepers, either. I checked.

"Did she ever say anything to you?"

The old woman shook her head slowly. "No, I don't believe she did."

"You sure about that?"

"I still have a sound mind, Joseph," she snapped. "I would have remembered."

"When I arrested Carlos, Pauline said that wasn't the first time he had hit her. Did you know anything about that?"

"This is the first I've heard . . . Let me ask you a question, Joseph. Why all of this interest in my visits?"

"I'm trying to find out why two men drowned in the river within a week of each other."

"Are you sure you're not trying to point fingers away from yourself?"

"What do you mean?"

"It's common knowledge now throughout the Pueblo. You didn't like Carlos Dominguez. Everyone's saying how cruel you were to him in court. Then the day after you release him from jail, he ends up dead."

"I had nothing to do with that." He tried not to sound defensive.

"But I heard you were near the river when he drowned."

It didn't matter if President Kata believed him or not. Kata had been explicit at the end of the meeting with him and Mesa. No one outside of his office was to hear talk about the Weeping Woman. He didn't want people crowding the Rio Grande at night, getting hurt or drowning because they wanted to get a glimpse of a ghost. Aquino knew it was a risk, but he decided to bring Jacona into his confidence.

"I was on the bridge. I heard singing coming from the river?"

"Singing?"

"I looked down. I saw *La Llorona*. She was floating above the water and singing."

Jacona was visibly shaken by the news. "You saw her?"

"I think that's what attracted Carlos into the water. It could be why Diego drowned as well."

"Do you have any proof?"

"No, of course not."

The cacique began rocking slightly forward and backward in her seat. She was silent for a long time, engrossed in her thoughts, her eyes fixed on nothing specific.

"Are you all right?" Aquino finally asked.

Jacona suddenly looked up. "I have nothing more to say to you," she hissed. "Leave my home!"

Shocked at how nasty the old woman had suddenly become, the officer retreated without saying a word.

He was barely a dozen steps outside Agustina's home when he was confronted.

"What the hell do you think you're doing?"

Chapter Sixty-Nine

It was before 10:00 a.m. when Joseph Aquino returned home from his meeting with Kata.

"What happened?" Sharon asked, following her husband into the bedroom.

He didn't look at her as he removed his uniform. "I've been suspended?"

"What does that mean?"

"That means I'm no longer Chief of Police, pending an investigation." He looked at his wife. "Don't worry. I'm suspended with pay."

She sat on the bed. "At least, they didn't fire you."

"Not yet." He hung his uniform in the closet, then slipped on jeans and a flannel shirt. "Ray Mesa was in with President Kata for an hour before I even showed up. I'd bet a barrel of blue corn he tried to do just that. Get me fired." He tucked the shirt into his pants.

"What happens now?"

"Kata's going to put together an independent committee of former governors and sheriffs to look into Mesa's accusations."

"So, Raymond Mesa won't investigate?"

"No, thank God. Sounds like he plans to be the prosecutor. After the meeting, he informed me he was going to look for his own evidence against me."

"There is no evidence!" Sharon complained.

"We know that." He slipped on his boots. "You haven't told anyone about the Weeping Woman, have you?"

"Of course not. You said keep it between us. Why?"

"I told Kata and Mesa what I saw. Mesa just laughed at me. The president took my claim more seriously, but I think he has his doubts. He told me and Mesa to keep my story about *La Llorona* to ourselves. It's a safety issue. He doesn't want people storming the river looking for her."

"That was smart."

Aquino headed to the front of their house. Sharon followed.

"Where are you going?"

"I have to prove that I didn't kill Carlos Dominguez. That won't happen if I sit around the house and do nothing.

"I need to talk to neighbors. Find out what they saw."

"Can you do that? I mean, while you're suspended."

"How does Lucia Ortega get her information?"

"She pokes her big nose in places it doesn't belong."

"Yup, and she does it all without a police badge. Why would I need one?"

***

Aquino had visited six houses on Kennedy Loop and four on Sage drive before he ever talked to Carla Naranjo. It wasn't until after his stop at Agustina Jacona's house that he met any resistance. Berto Cruz, the "acting" Police Chief was waiting for him when he came out.

"I asked you, Joe. What the hell do you think you're doing?"

"I'm just gathering facts, Berto. Raymond Mesa wants to charge me with a crime. I have every right to defend myself."

"I'm getting complaints."

"People are complaining that I'm asking questions?"

"At least one person says you were harassing them."

"I'm not in a position to harass anyone. I have no authority."

"Did you make it clear that you were no longer Police Chief?"

"Why would that make a difference? Exactly what did Carla Naranjo tell you?"

"I didn't say it was her."

Aquino pushed past Cruz, heading for his truck. As far as the suspended officer was concerned, the conversation was over.

"Don't make me lock you up, Joe."

Aquino considered flipping him the bird. Ignoring Berto would be even more insulting.

"You could be charged as a public nuisance!" Cruz yelled at his suspended boss. "Getting fired won't be the worst thing that happens to you."

Aquino stopped, his back to Cruz. He had just been threatened and that made him angry. He was angry at being suspended. He was angry that Berto Cruz shouted out his situation to the entire Pueblo. But he wasn't going to stand in the plaza and get in a yelling match. Instead, he continued walking, got in his truck and drove off.

Chapter Seventy

David Robles was a sheep rancher. From all appearances he had been quite successful. At least, to Lansing, he had. Besides the ranch house, there was a barn, two sheep sheds, large enough to house a thousand animals, and two large trailers for his permanent workers.

The sheriff showed up unannounced. He knocked on the ranch house door. It took a minute, but it was finally answered by Robles' wife, Anna. She was a small woman and frail. This was the first time they had met. On Lansing's previous visit he was told she was in bed, not feeling well.

"Can I help you?" There was a deep sadness about the woman.

"Yes, Mrs. Robles. I'm Sheriff Cliff Lansing. I was wondering if your husband was available. I needed to talk to him."

"David's not in the house," she said, absently. "He's probably feeding the animals. You might check the pens."

"Thanks."

Lansing stepped down from the porch. It was sunny and cold.

A lot of the recent snow had been removed from the barnyard and piled near the animal pens. Three hundred head of sheep bleated in three separate enclosures. One pen was set aside exclusively for pregnant ewes. Two of Robles' workers were filling feeding troughs with a barley and oats mixture.

The sheriff called to the workers, "Robles?"

One of the men pointed toward the barn.

Three dogs ran past Lansing as he crossed the open area, beating him to the barn. The double-wide doors were open, letting in as much light as possible. Robles was crawling out from beneath a tractor when he entered.

"Hi, Mr. Robles. I was wondering if you had time for a few questions?"

"I'm a little busy, right now."

"It won't take long."

"What do you want from me, Lansing?" The question was abrupt and harsh. "I told you everything I know. I even showed you where I found the girl."

In Lansing's previous two encounters with the rancher, Robles had been pleasant and cooperative. He didn't expect this response.

"This isn't about when you picked her up," he said sternly. If the rancher wanted to play tough guy, so could he. "What were you doing Monday night?"

"Monday night?"

"The night the girl went missing."

"I was home. Where else would I be?"

Lansing studied the man's face. There were bags under Robles' eyes. He looked tired. His response was nervous, anxious.

"You didn't take a drive to Cohino?"

"Why would I?"

"You may not know this, Robles, but Maria Alba was not the only child attacked in the last week. One boy and his mother were almost killed. Something's happening around here. I'm going to find out what it is.

"Maria Alba ended up in a shack seven miles from your ranch. She didn't walk there. She didn't fly there—someone drove her. Someone who knew about that place."

"I'm sure lots of people knew about that cabin." He was shaken now.

"Why would anyone know about that cabin?"

"Because that's where . . ." Robles struggled to finish the sentence. "Because that's where the old hag lived!"

"Berta Chavez?"

"Yeah. Chavez."

"Lots of people knew about her?"

"Come on, Sheriff. You're not stupid. Don't treat me like I am. People knew about her a long time before her kid went to prison. She was a friggin' witch. She made her living selling potions and casting spells."

"You don't believe in those fairy tales, do you?"

Robles shot him a withering look. "I wish they were fairy tales."

Lansing considered the response. "We need to talk, David," he said calmly. "You have to tell me everything you know."

Robles stood, wiping his hands with a rag, thinking. Finally, resigned, he gestured to a side room near the front of the barn. "We can use my office. Its heated."

Chapter Seventy-One

"The old hag moved in twenty-one years ago. From what I heard, the Apaches ran her off the reservation because she killed her husband. Poisoned him or something."

Robles produced a bottle of tequila from a file cabinet. He gestured toward a cup. Lansing sat in a chair next to a cluttered desk. He shook his head. It was still morning. Too early for a drink.

Robles sat at his desk and poured a shot. After he downed it, he continued. "The rumor going around was she was a *bruja*. Everyone was afraid of her, even the Apaches.

"One of my shepherds had a crush on a gal over in Estrella. He went to the old hag for a love spell. Before you knew it, the two were engaged, got married and ended up moving to Albuquerque."

"Sounds like a happy ending."

"It wasn't. Potions and spells can go stale. Their love affair sure did. I heard he caught her in bed with some other guy. Shot both of them before he killed himself."

Robles cleared his throat. He was starting to relax. Lansing thought it could be the tequila. Or, it might be the rancher was clearing his conscience. Possibly both.

"I had a small operation back then. I wanted to expand. Money was tight. Adjacent land wasn't available. I saw what the hag did for my shepherd. I thought maybe she could help me.

"You couldn't go to the hag and just say, 'Make me rich!' She insisted that you be very specific. Her spells needed a target. Someplace to direct the energy.

"I told her I wanted to own a five-hundred-acre ranch adjacent to my property. It would put me next to the Estrella Ditch and access to more

water. The old man who owned the property wouldn't sell. He said he was keeping it for his kids.

"We agreed on her fee. I figured the hag would cast a spell and suddenly the old guy would want to sell me his property. Something stupid like that."

"What did happen?"

"He kept about a dozen hogs. As best anyone can tell, he fell in their pen and they ate him."

"They ate him alive?"

Robles shrugged. "Who knows."

This was the first time Lansing had heard the story. He was on the Albuquerque Police Force at that time. "So, you got the property?"

"Yup. His kids didn't want to have anything to do with the place after that." Robles downed another shot.

"The hag showed up here, demanding payment. I told her I didn't think she did anything. The old man had an accident. I certainly wasn't going to pay her property note for six months. That had been her fee.

"She agreed. Accidents do happen. I got up the next morning and found ten of my sheep dead. Doc Bertrand couldn't find a reason. They just keeled over.

"I went back to the hag. She didn't admit to anything. All she said was, 'Yeah, accidents do happen.'"

"She got her fee."

"So, it cost you the price of her property note?"

Robles nodded. "Yes, for six months . . . that and a piece of my soul."

He poured another shot, but just stared at the glass. "I couldn't leave well enough alone. I got greedy. Every time I thought I wanted something, I went back to the hag. The trouble was, I wasn't dealing with an old woman. I was dealing with Satan, himself.

214

"Oh, yeah. I got rich. I also ended up paying off the hag's property note.

"About five, six years ago I decided I had everything I wanted. I wasn't going to deal with her any longer. That was about the time her kid went to prison.

"She showed up on my porch. Had a list of demands. She needed money for food. She needed her roof repaired. She needed a new *horno*. She wanted her garden tilled, plus seeds for planting.

"I told her to get lost. We were no longer partners. No more business between the two of us." He stopped and downed the shot. "That's when my daughter got sick. She was eleven.

"We took Jeanie to specialists in Santa Fe and Albuquerque. They couldn't find what was wrong. She was just wasting away.

"I was so damned stupid. I didn't put two-and-two together. The old hag put a curse on her. By the time I went to the witch, it was too late."

"Chavez cursed your daughter for a few shingles?" Lansing said in disgust. For years he had wondered how the old witch supported herself. Now, he almost regretted knowing.

"I threatened to kill her. The old hag said I couldn't. She owned my soul. She told me to go home and take care of my wife. Anna was going to get sick and would stay that way for a long time—as long as the hag lived, so did my wife.

"When I heard the witch died, I was afraid something would happen. When Anna didn't die, I thought I was free and clear of her. But Anna's still sick . . . and the hag came back."

"When?"

"New Year's Day . . . at night."

Chapter Seventy-Two

The evening of New Year's Day was when Robert Paul and his wife swerved off the road to avoid an old woman. The pieces to a big puzzle were starting to fit together for Lansing. "What happened that night?"

"It was around ten. We were getting ready for bed. Anna said she heard something on the porch. She swore it was a baby crying. When she opened the door, there was nothing there.

"It happened two more times. She kept running to the door, looking for an abandoned child. I never heard a thing. But the fourth time she wanted to go, I went, instead.

"I turned on the light and went out. That's when I heard the hag."

"Did you see her?"

"No. Not really. Just beyond the porchlight, I saw a dark shadow. And I saw her eyes . . . red, glowing eyes. That's when she told me she was back. She said I was going to help her. If I didn't, Anna would die."

"She wanted help that night?"

"No." He shook his head. "I asked her what she wanted me to do. She didn't say anything. She just disappeared.

"I went back inside. I didn't get much sleep. When I woke up Saturday morning, I thought I'd dreamed the whole thing. It was Monday night when she showed up again."

Robles explained how he was told to drive to Cohino. On one of the back streets was an old shed. That's where he found Maria, unconscious. The hag directed him to bring her to the old cabin.

Robles put her in the back room and left.

"I couldn't sleep that night. I couldn't eat the next day. Anna asked me what was wrong. I told her everything," he said, sadly, "just like I'm telling you now.

"She never knew about the old hag. Now, Anna's angry with me . . . No. More than angry. She's disgusted with me. She knows now, it was my fault Jeanie died. She said she didn't care if she lived anymore. She also told me I couldn't leave that poor girl in the hag's hands.

"That's when I drove back to the cabin and found her walking down the road."

The two men sat in silence.

"Are you going to arrest me?" Robles finally asked. "For kidnapping."

Lansing was angry at the man for what had happened to Maria Alba. He tried to find a spark of sympathy for Robles. After all, he did lose his daughter. His wife was ill and had been threatened. But the rancher made a pact with the Devil. He had brought it on himself.

"Why did Chavez come back?"

"I don't know. She died seven months ago. I was sure she was burning in Hell. Maybe she was too evil, even for Satan. He couldn't stand to have her around. That's why she's here. He wanted to get rid of her."

The sheriff guessed it had more to do with the new year, but he kept his speculations to himself. It didn't matter.

"Why Maria?"

"I have no idea."

Lansing had no more questions. He wanted to know how Maria Alba ended up in the old cabin. Now he knew. Just as important, he found validation for Tina Morales' claims. Berta Chavez was back and responsible for all wickedness taking place. He stood.

"What now?" Robles asked.

"You might want to get your affairs in order," the sheriff said. "I will come back for you. For the time being, take care of your wife".

Chapter Seventy-Three

Unsure what his next step should be, Aquino realized he was hungry. It was midafternoon and he hadn't eaten lunch yet. He lived near the end of Jackrabbit Trail, a mile and a half south of his office and the Pueblo adobe buildings.

"Sharon, I'm home," he announced, slipping off his coat.

His wife came out of the kitchen, her apron dusted with flour. "What have you been up to?"

"I've been making house calls. Trying to find out if anyone saw something."

"Any luck?"

"Agustina Jacona's name kept popping up. She and her assistant made trips to see Tomasita Salazar and Pauline Dominguez. Carla Naranjo claimed she couldn't remember making any visits. The old woman didn't deny them, but had her reasons for going. I really upset her when I mentioned the Weeping Woman."

"What was she upset about?"

Aquino shrugged. "Beats me."

"I thought that was a big secret?"

"It slipped out," the suspended officer said innocently.

"By the way, someone called for you."

"Who?"

"She said her name was Connie Gomez."

Aquino nodded. "She's the secretary at the Art Council. Used to work for Diego Salazar."

"She sound's young. Should I worry?"

"No, you shouldn't . . . What did she want?"

"I'm not sure. She got a call from someone in Santa Fe. She called your office, but they said you didn't work there anymore. She would only talk to you, so they gave her our number. Then she called here."

"When was this?"

"An hour ago."

Aquino started putting his coat back on.

"You haven't had lunch yet, have you?"

"Hopefully, I won't be gone long."

"Can't you just call her?"

"I could. Berto Cruz followed me when I left Agustina's place. He's keeping track of me for some reason. I'm going to drive over to the Northern Pueblos' offices. Let him follow me over there. It'll drive him nuts trying to figure out what's going on."

***

By taking a 200-foot long gravel cut-through from Jackrabbit Trail to Highway 68, the offices for the Eight Northern Pueblo Indians Council were closer than the police station. It took Aquino less than five minutes to get from his house to the council parking lot.

Connie Gomez looked up when he entered her office. "Chief Aquino!" she exclaimed, surprised at his arrival.

"It's just 'Joe' these days, Connie."

"I called your office. They said you don't work there anymore. You're not Chief of Police?"

"Temporarily." He noticed the questioning look on the secretary's face. "It's complicated. You called about a phone conversation you had?"

Gomez handed him a note from a sticky pad on her desk. "He said his name is Edmund Murdock. He wants to talk about Diego Salazar."

Aquino took the note. "Can I use the other office again?"

Connie nodded.

Aquino took a seat at Salazar's former desk, then dialed the number on the note. The call was answered after two rings.

"Murdock," the man at the other end said.

"Yes, Mr. Murdock. My name's Joseph Aquino. I'm up at San Juan Pueblo. I understand you called about Diego Salazar."

"Are you the police?"

"Does it matter?"

"It does to me. I found out Thursday that Salazar died last week. I need the police to know I had nothing to do with it."

"You can tell me anything you want. I'll make sure the right people hear about it."

It was silent at the other end of the line for a long moment. Finally, Murdock continued, "All right. I found out from William Bryce that Salazar was dead. Do you know Bryce?"

"We've met."

"If you've met, then you know what a little weasel he is. I thought about this over the weekend. He essentially accused me of killing Salazar. I want to set the record straight. I only met with the man. I want the police to know that. We met. We talked. When I left, he was very alive."

"Why were you meeting him?"

"Bryce had contracts with the Pueblo Indians that Salazar had signed. He wanted Salazar to know breaking those contracts would carry some heavy penalties."

"You work for Bryce?"

"WORKED for Bryce. We parted ways Thursday."

"Do you drive a black Lincoln Continental?"

"Yeah, I do."

"So, you're the one who picked Diego up at his place." It was a statement, not a question.

"Yes, that was me."

"What happened?"

"Salazar called up Bryce that weekend, complaining about what the gallery was paying for Indian artwork. The Pueblos were going to take their business someplace else. Bryce sent me to San Juan to convince Salazar otherwise."

"You threatened him?"

"I hinted to Salazar that it might be unhealthy for him to change the status quo. But I didn't get physical with him."

"You didn't take him back to his house, though."

"He had me drop him off at an old adobe building behind a chapel, next to the Pueblo offices."

"Why?"

"He didn't say."

"Did he mention who he was visiting?"

"No."

"What time did you drop him off?"

"It was five o'clock. It was getting dark."

Aquino thanked Murdock, reassuring him the proper authorities would get the information. Once the conversation ended, the officer just stared at the phone, thinking. Salazar didn't go from his house to the river. He went from his house to the old Pueblo. He ended up in the river after that.

Agustina Jacona lived in the old Pueblo.

There was a connection. Aquino was sure of it.

Chapter Seventy-Four

Lansing was still angry about Robles and his abduction of Maria Alba when he got back to his office. He could have arrested the man on the spot. Maybe he should have. But the lawman was confident the rancher wasn't going anywhere.

Clem Montoya intercepted him when he came in. "Sheriff, you got a call from a detective in Indianapolis. He'd like you to call him back."

Lansing took the note with the information and went back to his office.

"Detective Burroughs, this is Sheriff Cliff Lansing in New Mexico. I'm giving you a call back."

"Yeah, Sheriff. Thanks for the call. I found a note on an office electronic bulletin board about a shooter you had last week. You said he was using a Smith and Wesson MP Forty. How did you trace the gun to Indianapolis?"

"The gun was last purchased at a pawn shop in Terre Haute. But the new owner had an Indianapolis address."

"That wasn't your shooter, then?"

"Nope. That guy would still be in his twenties. Our shooter was at least forty."

"I take it he didn't survive?"

"No, he was shot by a couple of my deputies."

"Did you happen to pull prints?"

"Of course."

"How about a photo of the corpse?"

"Yeah. We took one when we brought the body in."

"Can you send us a copy of both electronically?"

"I'll get them scanned at the courthouse next door. Give me your information." After he wrote down what he needed, Lansing asked, "Do you think this guy is tied to a crime of yours?"

"Could be. Did the shooter have a car?"

Lansing gave Burroughs what he knew. The car was stolen from the St. Louis airport. It had license plates taken from a van in Oklahoma City.

"That's good info," the detective said, pausing a moment to write something. "We have a place to look for his car now."

"What's he wanted for?"

"Murder," was all the detective said. "I'll call you back after we check out the prints."

Burroughs hung up before Lansing could get a potential name for his John Doe. He also missed the chance of asking about the $10,000 dollars in the briefcase.

The sheriff scanned the prints and the photo onto a floppy disk at the tax assessor's office, then transmitted the data to Indiana from one of his own computers. He wondered how long before he would hear anything back.

It was 2:00 in the afternoon before Robert Garcia, the county attorney, released his findings on Deputies Rivera and Cortez. The shooting was found justified. No further action was necessary.

That was one less problem Lansing had to deal with. This was the first time either deputy had killed a man. They seemed to be holding up all right, though they could get counseling if they wanted it.

Thinking about Robles and the specter of Berta Chavez crowded out every other thought. He was anxious to talk to Tina Morales about his discoveries that morning.

Her grandmother spelled out what she thought should be done about the witch. Dig up the grave and essentially desecrate the body. Lansing

didn't have a big problem with that now that he was certain Chavez was involved. If cremating the old *bruja's* heart put an end to the chaos, so be it.

He wasn't concerned with the legality of such actions. He was certain a court wouldn't grant an exhumation order, just so he could mutilate a body. In this case, asking for forgiveness took precedence over asking for permission. Besides, who would complain?

It was 4:30 before Morales finally called. "I just drove Maria home," Tina said. "I don't think she had a very good day. I tried to discuss what happened to her. She still doesn't want to talk about it."

"I don't think we need her help anymore," Lansing said. "Meet me at *Paco's* in thirty minutes. We have lots to talk about."

Chapter Seventy-Five

Aquino didn't know who left the note on his windshield at the Northern Pueblo Council offices. He had his suspicions. It made him mad.

STOP POKING YOUR NOSE WHERE IT DOESN'T BELONG. BAD THINGS WILL HAPPEN.

The threat made his resolve only stronger. The conversation with Murdock convinced him Diego Salazar was not killed by someone outside the Pueblo. With the note, he was now positive the Art Director's death was not an accident. Why else was he being told to back off?

It was after 4:00 when he got back home. He was hungry. He was angry. He became even more upset when Sharon greeted him in tears.

"Joe, they took him! They took Jacob!"

"Who did? What are you talking about?"

"The bus didn't drop him off. I called the school. They said he was picked up by the authorities."

"Why? What did he do?"

"They said it was protective custody. "

"Protection from who?"

"You, Joe."

Aquino was ready to explode. "What's the number to the school?"

"Segovia Middle School, this is Myra. Can I help you?"

"This Is Police Chief . . ." Aquino stopped. He wasn't Police Chief any longer. "This is Joseph Aquino. I want to know what happened to my son, Jacob."

"I'd better let you speak to the principal."

"This is Dorothy Valdez," the principal said, when she finally came on. "How can I help you?"

"My name's Joseph Aquino," the father said angrily. "Someone took our son out of school today. What's going on? They didn't have our permission."

"I'm sorry, Mr. Aquino. He was released into protective custody under court order."

"Who's court? Who signed the order?"

"It was the San Juan Tribal Court. Judge Paul Lovato signed the order."

"Where did they take Jacob?" he demanded.

"From what I understand, he's at the Butterfly Healing Center in Taos."

"What the hell? That place is for kids on drugs or in trouble with the law."

"It's also for kids from troubled homes and it sounds to me like that's exactly where he should be."

Aquino slammed the phone into its cradle. It rang as soon as he hung up.

"What?" he asked forcefully.

He listened for a moment then handed it to Sharon. "It's for you."

"This is Sharon." She listened to the woman on the other end. This time it was her turn to explode. "I don't know where you're getting your information, but those are all lies. I don't need your help. Don't ever call here again!"

"Who was that?"

"That was the PeaceKeepers. They got a report that you were out of control. They heard Jacob was taken away. They wanted to know if I needed a safe place to go!"

"Come on, Sharon."

"Where are we going?"

"To the Tribal Court. I want to catch Lovato before he leaves. We're going to find out what's going on!"

***

Aquino stormed past Judge Lovato's secretary, despite her protests. Sharon was close behind him. Lovato looked up when the former police chief threw open the door.

"You can't come barging in like that!" Lovato protested.

"Judge?" His secretary had followed the Aquino's into the office. "Should I call the bailiff?"

"And the police," the judge added.

"Why did you take our son away?" Aquino demanded.

"Because of the way you behaved in President Kata's office this morning."

"What are you talking about?"

"I got a full report from Raymond Mesa. He said you were belligerent toward him during the meeting . . ."

"I was belligerent because he accused me of killing Carlos Dominguez!"

Lovato held up his hand to silence him. "You were belligerent at first. Then when President Kata suspended you, I was told you were out of control."

"That's a lie."

"I called up the President. He affirmed you were upset."

"Of course, I was upset. I was angry at all the unfounded accusations coming from Mesa. I was angry that Kata was taking his word against mine. What does that have to do with taking away our son?"

"That wasn't even a consideration until the complaints against you started coming in."

"What complaints?"

"You've been going around to different households on the reservation making threats."

"Who have I threatened?"

Lovato picked up a sheet of paper on his desk. "Carla Naranjo, Agustina Jacona. Lucia Ortega called in and said she heard you were going door to door in two neighborhoods, trying to stir up trouble."

"Lucia!" Sharon rolled her eyes. "That's always a reliable source."

"What does that have to do with Jacob?"

"When Raymond said you had been abusing your wife, the court was afraid for you family's safety."

"He's never abused me!" Sharon protested.

"I want my son back!" Aquino yelled. "Now!"

Al Feliz, the court bailiff, and Officer Henry Calvert tumbled into the room at the same time. They both grabbed for Aquino. He pulled free.

"Let go of me!"

"You can't have your son back." Lovato raised his voice above the commotion. "Not tonight!"

"Why not?" Sharon asked, upset.

"He's on a seventy-two-hour hold. It's a cooling off period. For him and for you."

"Can we at least see him?" the mother begged.

"Not for three days. He has to be evaluated. You and Joseph need to be interviewed. After that, there will be a hearing to determine whether it's safe for him to go home."

"This is insane!" Aquino said, lunging toward the judge.

The officers each latched onto an arm. The former police chief struggled to pull free.

"You want him locked up, Judge?" Calvert asked.

"Aquino! Joseph! Calm down," Lovato ordered. "Or you're going to jail."

Sharon put her hand on her husband's arm. "Joe, please. Stop. I can't lose you today, too. I need you with me."

Aquino stopped struggling. He couldn't help Jacob, Sharon or himself sitting in a jail cell. He needed time to figure out what was going on.

"All right," he said.

Lovato nodded to the two men holding Aquino. They released the former officer.

"You and your wife need to go home," the judge suggested. "And you, Joseph, need to stay out of trouble."

Aquino scowled at the Tribal Judge. He wrapped his arm around Sharon and led her from the office, without saying another word.

Chapter Seventy-Six

Tina Morales didn't interrupt Lansing once while he described his visit to the Robles ranch. He was surprised. He was sure she would have a dozen questions. Instead, she stared at her cup of coffee, concentrating on his every word.

"When I left," he said in conclusion, "I told him I would be back for him."

"You're going to arrest him for kidnapping?"

Lansing took a sip of his own coffee. "Of course."

"Why didn't you bring him in today?" Morales asked, sounding miffed.

"You would understand if you saw his wife. He's going to end up in prison for a long time. He needs to make sure she's taken care of before he goes away."

She shook her head. "I've been trying to come up with a reason for why Chavez went after Maria. I think it was because of me."

"Why do you say that?"

"I'm the only connection there is between the two. Maria, the Albas, they probably never heard of Chavez before. I think the witch followed us to Cohino. She watched from outside. Hell, she could have been inside the restaurant for all we know. But she saw how friendly Maria and I were. The witch went after Maria to hurt me."

"That could be," Lansing agreed. "Doesn't really matter, anymore. Now, we have to stop her."

"I told you what my *abuela* said we had to do."

"And I'm ready to do it."

"Really?" Morales asked incredulously.

"I haven't thought about anything else since I talked to Robles. I don't have any better solution than what your grandmother suggested."

"When are you going to do it? Tonight?"

"No, not tonight. I'm not going to tangle with that witch in the dark. Besides, I can't dig up that grave by myself."

"Are you getting a backhoe again?"

"I don't think we could get one through the snow."

"Mr. Alba runs a snowplow. He could clear the road back to the cabin," the teacher suggested.

"When we buried Chavez, I paid for county road equipment and personnel to dig the grave. That was a legitimate operation. I was sanctioned by the courts. I'm not going to be able to do that this time. Besides, I want to keep all this business low keyed. The fewer people involved the better."

"Then, how are you going to open the grave?"

"David Robles has men working on his ranch. I'll get them to do it."

"What if he doesn't want to cooperate?"

"He doesn't have a choice."

"They'll want to get paid extra."

"I'm sure they will. That can come out of Robles' pocket." He thought for a moment. "Can you be there?"

"I'd like to . . . I mean, I really think I need to be there. When are you digging up the grave?"

"As early as possible. I'll call up Robles tonight. Tell him what needs to be done."

"It will take them a while to dig up that coffin. I need to teach my morning classes. That will give me time to find a substitute for periods five and six."

Lansing nodded. "Are you hungry?"

"Not really."

"I'm not either, but we need to eat. Are you staying at the ranch?"

"One more night. After tomorrow, it should be safe for me to go home."

Chapter Seventy-Seven

"I don't understand it," Sharon said after hanging up the phone. She was more disheartened than mad. "They were all at our house last Wednesday, after the Buffalo Dance. Everything was fine. Now they sound like you're the Devil and I'm your prisoner."

Sharon had spent an hour on the phone talking to Rebecca Luna, the office secretary, as well as the wives of Roberto Cruz and Henry Calvert. She had hoped she could find out what they knew. The normally talkative group was uncharacteristically mute.

"I know who's behind all this."

"Raymond?"

"Of course."

"Why? Because he and I dated once? That was twenty years ago."

"You're the one who got away. He still blames me for breaking you two up."

"I dumped him a year before we started dating."

"He just got divorced again."

"That's what? Number three?" Sharon asked.

Her husband nodded. "He has to blame someone for his misery. Why not me?"

"So, he's going to ruin you and destroy our entire family?" Sharon was getting angry.

"He's getting plenty of help."

"From who?"

"Berto Cruz. He's the one who turned the office against me. He has to be."

"So, he can be Chief of Police?"

Aquino gave a short nod. "I think there's still one person left on the force I can talk to."

*＊＊

Juan Pico was the youngest officer in the San Juan Pueblo Police Department. He had been there only two years and Chief Aquino was his mentor. Aquino hoped there was still some loyalty there.

Pico shared a trailer with another bachelor on Tortilla Flats Road.

It was after dark when Aquino arrived. When Pico answered the door, he looked up and down the road to see if Aquino had been followed, then ushered him in.

"Pedro, can you take off?" Pico asked. "Chief Aquino and I need to talk."

The trailer mate grabbed his coat. "No problem. I was going to see Pam anyway."

Once they were alone, Pico looked at his former boss. "I know you want to know what's going on. Chief, I don't know."

"Somebody heard Berto was offered my job yesterday. He didn't turn the office against me overnight."

Pico sat on the built-in sofa. "It started last Monday."

"What happened Monday?"

"That was the day you found Diego Salazar."

"What are you talking about? I didn't find him. Pauline Dominguez saw the body from the highway bridge. She's the one who reported it."

"Sheriff Mesa said he was there. That's what he told Berto. You're the one who found the body first and that seemed suspicious to him."

"Did you talk to Henry? He was there with me."

Pico shook his head. "Like I said, Chief, I don't know. I'm just telling you what I heard. Then there was what happened Monday night."

"What happened Monday night?"

"When you beat up Carlos Dominguez . . . after you arrested him."

"What the hell are you talking about? I didn't beat anybody up."

"Berto said he saw him the next morning. He said Carlos was in bad shape."

"He was hung over!" Aquino growled. "Of course, he was in bad shape."

Pico went on to list all of Aquino's alleged offenses, according to Cruz. Aquino mistreated Dominguez during the court proceedings. He knew where to look for the man's body in the river because he killed Dominguez. It was no coincidence that it was Aquino found the body first.

The former police chief felt like blood was getting ready to shoot from his eyes. Each lie was compounded by another one.

"Juan, do you believe any of this crap?"

"Chief, I don't know what to believe. Especially when they said you killed Dominguez because you were having an affair with his wife."

"What?" Aquino exploded.

"I told Berto I didn't think you would do that. But he said that it all made sense now."

On his drive back to his own house, Aquino was beyond angry and frustrated. He knew he couldn't let his rage get the better of him.

He was on his own. No one in his office had his back. He was sure he could clear his name. That is, if they gave him enough time. But what if "they" had other plans.

And who were "they"? Cruz? Mesa? Lovato?

Then there were the two dead bodies found in the Rio Grande.

Something else was at play. He was sure of it.

Chapter Seventy-Eight

Lansing remembered his father talking about getting the first telephone at the ranch. That was in the 1920s. What had seemed like a luxury at the time, soon became a necessity. The ranchers and farmers wondered how they had survived for so long without one.

The sheriff was starting to feel that way about cell phones. He had been without his for only two days. Even though he was constantly next to land lines, he felt a strange disconnect from the rest of the world. The convenience of having your own personal communication device was empowering.

In his patrol unit, he was always in contact with dispatch. Except for a couple of handhelds, his department had yet to invest in individual portable radios. Historically, when he was away from his Jeep, he was incommunicado.

The cell phone changed all that.

Today, while they disinterred the body, he could be a quarter mile from his unit and still be in contact with anyone he needed. That is, if they did disinter anything.

He sat in his Jeep on the highway, next to the track leading to the Chavez cabin. He looked at his watch. It was 8:25. Robles' men were nearly thirty minutes late. Lansing had talked to the rancher around 8:00 the evening before. Supposedly, everything was all set up.

He called the Robles ranch. No one answered the phone. Fortunately, the place was less than ten minutes away.

***

Lansing parked in the same spot he had the morning before. Except for the plaintive bleats of the sheep in the distant sheds, the ranch seemed abandoned. He stepped onto the porch and pounded on the door.

"Robles!" the sheriff shouted. "You in there?"

He waited, then pounded again.

Again, no answer.

He tried the handle. The door was unlocked. He pushed it open.

"Robles?" he called.

The only answer he got was the lonely tick-tick-tick of a wall clock. The sound came from the dining room.

That's where Lansing found David Robles. The body was slumped in a chair next to the table, arms dangling at the sides. On the table was an empty bottle of tequila. On the floor was the 9-millimeter automatic he had used.

Anna Robles was in her bed. Cold to the touch, she had been dead for hours. There was no apparent outward cause of death. Postmortem would eventually show she died of natural causes.

"Dispatch, this is Patrol One," he said into the mic in his Jeep. "I'm at the David Robles ranch on Route one-eighty-two. I have two dead bodies. One is an apparent suicide. I need Deputy Estrada out here with her forensics gear. If other units are available, send them out. I'll also need a couple of ambulances for transport."

Berta Chavez's grave would have to wait.

Lansing's first impression was correct. The ranch had been abandoned. Both trailers were empty. There were no workers in the barn or back in the sheep sheds.

The penned-up animals complained. They hadn't been fed.

Robles had killed himself after the two of them talked the night before. The workers evidently heard the shot, found the bodies, and realized there was no future for them at the ranch. The office in the barn had

been thoroughly ransacked, someone looking for anything valuable. Fear of the dead kept them out of the ranch house.

The sheriff was disgusted. There was obviously no loyalty to their employer. No sense of decency, either. They simply left David and Anna Robles to be found by the first person to come along.

Lansing made another call to dispatch. He needed Jack Rivera. Deputy Rivera coordinated the animal control agencies in the county. Someone needed to take charge of 300 sheep before they starved to death.

It would be a long morning.

Chapter Seventy-Nine

Arthur Orante sat in his living room. On a shelf behind him were the two symbols of his position—the decorated ceramic bowl signifying his status as Made Person and the carved stone mountain lion symbolizing his role as Chief of the Hunt Society.

Joseph Aquino had been pledged to the Hunt Society at birth, as had his father and grandfather. When he was eight, he underwent the Water Pouring Ceremony, initiating him as a Dry Food Person in the Winter Moiety. It was then that he began studies, learning the prayers and rituals of the Hunt Society. He completed his Made Person finishing ceremony when he was twenty-one.

He adhered to the Hunt Society requirements as best he could, but policing duties often took precedence. Orante had no problem pointing that out when the former officer sought his advice.

"I am sorry for my lapses in the past, Arthur. But I have nowhere else to turn." He explained his situation. His biggest concern was getting his son back. Beyond that, he had to fight the loss of his job and the charges Raymond Mesa made against him.

Orante listened thoughtfully. "Outside of the Hunt Society, I have very little influence," the seventy-year-old chief finally admitted. "I can talk to President Kata about your job. I can speak on your behalf before the Tribal Council. If you do come to trial, though, I am only one vote."

Aquino thought for a moment. He wasn't sure Orante could answer his next few questions, but he had to ask. "Agustina Jacona is now the *Apienu* of the Woman's Society. Carla Naranjo is one of her principals. Why would they tell lies against me?"

"What did you do?"

"I just asked questions. I was curious why they visited the homes of men who drowned in the river."

"What did they say?"

"Agustina said it was for moral support."

"What were their words against you?"

"They said I threatened them, that I was out of control. I didn't threaten them. But Agustina was upset about what I saw at the river."

"What did you see?"

Aquino described his encounter with *La Llorona*.

"It has been years since people spoke of the Weeping Woman," Orante admitted. "But she is very real."

Aquino asked what the role of the Woman's Society was now, and why were they against him.

"Because we no longer need to hunt for our food, the Hunt Society has lost much importance. Because we have fought no one in over a hundred years, the Scalp Society is a ghost of what it once was. The Women's Society took care of the scalps taken in war. No war, no scalps.

"Agustina is reinventing the society in her own image."

"Can she do that? Does tradition allow that?"

"One would think not. Each society has its own secrets and rituals. She could well be operating within the scope of her duties. But we don't know her motivations."

"How could we ever know her motivations?"

"You must know her history. Visit *P'oe Tsawa*, the archives at the Community Library.

Talk with Sophia Nuno, the *conservadora*. She would know about Agustina Jacona."

"After that, what should I do?"

"That's up to you, Joseph."

***

Sophia Nuno was a trained Genealogist and Archivist. In her mid-fifties, she had been documenting the history of San Juan Pueblo for thirty years. She knew the family stories. She knew about skeletons hidden away that no one talked about—secrets that were carefully guarded.

It was only after Aquino pleaded his case that Nuno opened up about Agustina's story.

The future head of the Woman's Society was married at age fifteen. She had two sons before the age of twenty. Her husband, Pardo Jacona, was a cruel drunk. He beat her and the boys often. She completed the finishing ceremony for the Women's Society when she was 25 and became a Blue Corn Woman, one of the three women that headed the society, when she was thirty.

It was soon after that when Pardo died. He drowned in the river. Probably, people guessed, because he was drunk.

She was a principal in the society, a Blue Corn Woman, for 35 years. She had only recently become *Apienu*.

The former police officer had to ask—did the Women's Society have a special relationship with *La Llorona*?

No. Not that Nuno knew of.

Aquino felt he had learned all there was to learn. On his way out of the archives, he asked, almost as an afterthought, what was Agustina's maiden name.

It was Cruz.

Chapter Eighty

Deputy Willie Estrada took a dozen photos in the dining room. A single shell casing had ejected onto the table. There was gunpowder stippling around the entry wound at the temple, indicating a gun had been fired at close range. A Gun-Shot-Residue test confirmed Robles had recently fired a gun with his right hand. It was reasonable to conclude the rancher had taken his own life.

Chief Deputy Jack Rivera made a half dozen calls trying to determine what to do with 300 sheep. There appeared to be plenty of feed for the animals. It made sense to leave them on the ranch. David Robles' nearest relative needed to be contacted. They would decide the animals' fates. In the interim, the County Extension Service would look after the flock.

The house and barn office were searched for names and contact numbers. Lansing would like to talk to the most recent employees about what happened. Deputy Lopez was assigned the task of making phone calls.

It was noon before the bodies were removed. The Sheriff's department completed evidence gathering by then. Yellow "Police Line Do Not Cross" tape was stretched across the ranch house door. It would remain there until autopsies were completed.

Lansing got into his Jeep as the other vehicles pulled out. His cell phone rang. "Lansing."

"Hi, Cliff," Tina said. "I have one more class before I can leave. How's the digging going?"

"We haven't started yet."

"What? Why? What's going on?"

"It looks like David Robles killed himself last night. His workers took off."

"My God! What about his wife?"

"She's dead, too. I found her in her bed. I'm praying she passed away in her sleep."

"For her sake, I'm really sorry to hear that. I guess you've been too busy to worry about Chavez."

"True statement. I'm finished at the Robles ranch now. I need to come up with another plan for opening that grave."

"You haven't changed your mind about using a county crew, have you?"

"No. That's still out of the question."

"Cliff, I have to get to class. I have one suggestion. Ron Alba. He might be able to help."

"Thanks. I'll look into that."

Lansing didn't have Alba's number handy. He would have to drive back to the office. Besides, even if Alba could help, it might take hours before he could get to the cabin. The hope of putting an end to Berta Chavez that day was fading.

There was a note for the sheriff when he got back to Las Palmas. Detective Burroughs had called again from Indianapolis. Lansing would return the call once he finished talking to Ron Alba.

"Mr. Alba, Sheriff Lansing."

"Afternoon, Sheriff. What's going on?"

"We found the man who took Maria from Cohino."

"Who was it?" Alba demanded.

"The same man who brought her into the clinic, David Robles."

"That son-of-a-bitch. He's the one who hurt my daughter? I don't suppose you could leave me alone with him for ten minutes?"

"That won't be necessary. Robles is dead." Lansing described his discovery that morning.

"I hope that bastard is burning in Hell now," the angry father growled.

"I'm sure he is," Lansing said. "But you need to know something. He didn't act alone."

If he was going to enlist Alba's assistance, the man needed to know why they were digging up a grave and who was in it. The sheriff was reluctant to talk about witches and Shadow Demons. Rational people didn't believe in such things. But, he thought, when was this ever a rational world.

Alba listened to the story Lansing told, interrupting only occasionally. At the end, he asked, "How many men do I need to round up and when do you want us there?"

***

"I have a name for your shooter," Burroughs said. "Doug Wilson."

"Doug Wilson," Lansing said, jotting the name down. "You said he was wanted for murder. What happened?"

"He killed his entire family. A wife and three kids. Someone found the bodies Christmas Day. They were all laid out together in a row in the basement. He shot them all in the head."

"Damn," the sheriff said.

"They had been dead a few days. He shot them that Monday or Tuesday. The kids were out of school for Christmas break."

"We searched the cabin he was using. There was a briefcase with ten thousand dollars."

"He cleaned out his life savings from the bank before he skipped town. That was on Tuesday. That's why we think the family was dead by then.

"We also managed to track down the family car. You told us where to look. It was at an impound lot in St. Louis. He abandoned it at the airport."

"Do you have any idea why he ended up in New Mexico?"

"We don't have a clue here. Maybe you can dig up something."

"What am I supposed to do with the corpse?"

"We'll make arrangements to have it shipped back to Indiana. Just let us know where to pick him up."

When he was finished talking to Burroughs, Lansing called Sam Keller, the owner of Lookout Lodge.

"Mr. Keller, this is Sheriff Lansing. I have a question for you."

"Shoot."

"Do you keep records of Lodge visitors?"

"Sure do."

"Can you check if a Doug Wilson ever stayed there?"

"Might take me a day or two. All the records are at the Lodge House. That the name of the guy who shot at me?"

"Yes, we believe it is."

"Let you know what I find out."

Tina knocked on the office door frame. Lansing looked up as he finished the conversation.

"You hungry?" he asked after hanging up.

"I could eat. What about the grave?"

"Ron Alba's meeting us there at three. We're going to get this over and done with today."

Chapter Eighty-One

Sharon Aquino rushed to the front door when she heard it open. "Did you talk to Chief Orante?"

"Yes. We had a talk," he said, taking off his coat.

"Is he going to help?"

"He said he would speak to President Kata about my job."

"What about Jacob?"

"He said he didn't have much influence anymore. There was nothing he could do. Did you check and see how Jake's doing today?"

"Yes, but they still said I couldn't talk to him."

The Butterfly Healing Center in Taos was operated by the Eight Northern Pueblo Indians Council. The Center was a live-in facility for Pueblo youths, ages 13 to 18. Its programs were designed to help kids with drug problems, behavioral issues, and from broken homes.

The Aquino's called the night before to make sure their son was indeed there. They would call every day to check on his status. They wanted the Center and the courts to know they were caring parents and that theirs was a safe and loving home.

"Did they say he was all right?"

"All they said was he was 'adjusting,' whatever that means."

"Yeah, I'll bet he is. Just like I'm adjusting to being suspended."

"You were at Chief Orante's for a long time."

"I spent most of my time at *P'oe Tsawa*, at the archives."

"What for?"

Aquino started toward the kitchen. "How about some coffee. I'll tell you all about it."

Her husband recounted Agustina Jacona's history as closely as he could remember it. "So, what does all this mean?" Sharon asked.

"Agustina was an abused woman. She seemed surprised, maybe suspicious, when I told her I thought Tomasita Salazar was abused. And we all know Carlos beat on Pauline. The husbands of all three women drowned in the Rio Grande. That's not a coincidence."

"Do you think Agustina was responsible?"

"I don't know how, but yes. I also think Berto is protecting her."

"Why?"

"Because Agustina is his aunt. I'd bet anything he's the one who left the note on my windshield. He wants me to stay away from her."

"Raymond Mesa's out to destroy us because we're married. Berto is gutting you because he wants your job, plus he's shielding his aunt," Sharon summarized. "What about Judge Lovato? Why is he against us?"

"I hope he's only reacting to the lies he's being fed. The same with President Kata."

"Joe, is there anyone on the reservation we can turn to?"

"I'm not sure anymore."

"Are they going to charge you with the murder of Carlos Dominguez? Do they even know how he really died?"

"The autopsy results will be in today. Just like Diego, it will probably show drowning. But I'm sure now that Carlos was drugged before he got to the river. I'll bet the same thing happened to Diego."

"You said they didn't find any drugs in Diego."

"Maybe they didn't look hard enough or looked for the wrong thing. They said they ran a standard drug panel. Maybe someone used a non-standard drug. Something the coroner doesn't normally look for.

"As for being charged with anything, I'm not sure it will go that far."

"They're not going to blame you?"

"They will. They just don't want a trial. Too many skeletons might come out."

247

"Then what is going to happen, Joe?"

"I hope they'll drop the charges for lack of evidence. But there will be enough suspicion that I won't get my job back. Or . . ." He shrugged, letting the rest of the sentence dangle.

"Or what?"

Aquino dug in his wallet and retrieved a business card. He handed it to his wife. "If something happens, here's who you should call. His cell number is on the back."

Sharon looked at the card. "Are you sure he can help?"

"He's the only one I trust, right now."

Chapter Eighty-Two

It was thirty-six degrees by midafternoon. The roads were sloppy, and everything would refreeze over night when the temperature dropped to seventeen.

Lansing and Tina Morales parked next to the track leading to the Chavez cabin and gravesite. It was 2:45. Ron Alba had assembled four men from the Chisum and Aztec Railroad. They arrived five minutes later.

The five Cohino men climbed out of a F-250 crew cab. They each grabbed a tool from the truck bed. There was a pickaxe and four shovels. Alba had thought ahead. It would be dark a little after five. Their equipment for the dig included two Coleman lanterns.

Introductions were made all around. Eager to get started, Lansing led the work crew toward the grave. The snow didn't seem as deep as it had two days earlier. There had been some warming since the blizzard. The top layer had melted during the days and froze again at night. Their footsteps crunched as they broke through the icy crust.

All seven stopped and stared at the barren ground marking the grave. The railroad crew had not been warned about the eerie absence of snow.

"Well," one man remarked, "we know where to dig."

It was obvious only two men could dig at the same time. That's what Alba expected. Two men would labor for five to ten minutes, then rest while the other two took their turns.

While the excavation progressed, Lansing noticed Alba staring at the run-down shack.

"Is that where they took Maria?" the father asked.

"Yes," the sheriff said. "We're pretty sure it is."

"Can I go inside?"

"I don't know why not. It isn't locked."

Alba headed for the cabin. Lansing and Morales followed.

The inside was just as dark and dingy as it had been on Sunday. Alba surveyed the kitchen and living area, asking no questions, touching nothing. He pushed the bedroom door open. Morales was tempted to point out the scratches and splinters where Maria clawed her way out. She realized that revelation would cause only more anguish.

Alba stood in in the middle of his daughter's former dungeon. It looked like he was trying to imagine what Maria suffered. Again, he said nothing. When he'd had enough, he simply headed for the back of the cabin and the gravesite outside.

Lansing and Morales looked at each other and shrugged. Whatever the train engineer was thinking, he was keeping it to himself.

The hole was four feet deep when the sun dipped behind the Jicarilla Reservation mountains. Dirt shoveled out of the grave was moved further away. When the coffin was finally exhumed, they didn't want to fight a pile of dirt around the opening.

Alba asked what would happen once the casket was unearthed. Tina explained her grandmother's recommendation. Remove the heart and burn it. That would end Berta Chavez's terror forever.

Lansing had agreed to perform the operation once the coffin was open. He had a burn pile at his ranch. The task would be completed there.

Chapter Eighty-Three

Sharon Aquino watched as the Tribal Police car backed out of the parking area in front of their house. Joseph had been waiting to get picked up for thirty minutes. Officer Juan Pico was supposed to be there at 4:00. He didn't arrive till 4:30.

She thought it was suspicious that her husband was being chauffeured to the meeting. St. Chappell Chapel, across the avenue from San Juan Bautista Church, was only a mile and a half from their house. Joseph could have easily driven himself there. For that matter, as late as Pico was, Aquino could have walked to the chapel already.

"Why St. Chappell's?" she had asked just minutes before.

"It's neutral ground, I suppose," Aquino guessed.

"Who are you meeting with?"

"Juan really wasn't clear. Berto set it up. There's supposed to be a discussion about Carlos Salazar."

"I would rather you discuss Jacob or your job."

"I'm sure it will all tie in."

"I don't like it," Sharon said. "Why couldn't you meet at the Tribal Offices or the Court building? Someplace with people hanging around."

"It's the end of the business day. People are going home. I'm sure we can stay in the chapel as long as we want."

"Do you trust Berto, or Mesa, or any of them?"

"Not particularly."

"Then, why are you going?"

"Because nothing's going to get resolved if I just sit here."

"Are you going to bring up Agustina? Tell them what you think she's involved with."

"I think some people already know what she's done. I don't want to advertise the fact that I know it, too. That might be our only ace up the sleeve."

"How long will you be gone?"

"Two hours at the most, I'm sure."

They heard the sound of tires crunching gravel. Aquino looked out the front window. "Juan's here."

"What happens if you don't come home?"

"I gave you a number to call."

"What should I tell him?"

"Tell him about what happened Friday night." With that, Aquino was out the door.

***

The chapel was empty when Aquino arrived.

"Hello?" he called. There was no answer. He checked his watch: 4:40. Sitting in a back pew, he would wait till 5:00. If no one showed up by then, he was gone.

Juan Pico still claimed he didn't know what was going on. Aquino had asked him again during the short ride from his house who would be at the meeting. Pico just shook his head.

"Chief, I really don't know."

Aquino only felt a hollow reassurance that Pico called him "chief." He had been stripped of that title only the morning before. It seemed like a month had passed already.

4:55. He wondered if the chapel had a phone he could use. He would call Sharon to pick him up. Sunset was in 15 minutes. He could walk home, but he was afraid that would offer too convenient a target on the dark road.

The chapel was small. On the outside, it was only thirty feet wide and fifty feet long. The high ceiling kept it from feeling cramped. A sliver of light traced a path across the northern wall of the chapel. The building faced west. The sunlight came through the three decorative windows above the front door. Just inside the entrance, a small chandelier hung from the ceiling. It was the only interior light illuminated.

He heard a door open. The sound came from behind the altar at the front of the room. A figure bathed in shadow emerged.

"Come with me, Joseph," was all that Carla Naranjo said.

Chapter Eighty-Four

Both Lansing and Morales had opted for heavier footwear before heading out to the cabin. He still wore his uniform, though, and she was in the woolen slacks and sweater she had worn to school that morning. When the sun finally sank in the west, they wished they had worn warmer clothing.

It had taken a little over two hours to dig out the first four feet of the grave. It was 6:30 and dark when the first shovel struck the top of the coffin. Enough dirt had to be removed from the ends and sides to allow the workers space to lift the casket out of the hole.

Ron Alba pumped up the pressure in each camping lantern, adjusted the flow valves and lit the mantles before it grew too dark. A lantern was set at either end of the grave to provide as much light as possible.

The coffin was a simple, white pine design, square at both ends. The flat lid wasn't even permanently anchored. Slots in the wood topper fit over notched tabs sticking up from the sides. The lid was then slid beneath the notches holding it in place. The box measured 23"x77"x14". Empty, it only weighed 54 pounds. The body of Berta Chavez barely added another eighty.

Because there were no handles, the casket had to be lifted from underneath. If they had known, they would have made the hole a little longer. As it was, one end had to be tipped up, then the box scooted until that end rested on the lip of the grave. The opposite end was raised, then the entire coffin was removed from the hole.

Berta Chavez's remains had been placed inside a white, linen body bag before the lid had been secured. That's what Lansing expected to see when the lid was removed.

A shovel was used to knock the lid loose. The top slid two inches, then was lifted over the notches. Both lanterns were brought forward so everyone could get a better look.

Lansing got on his knees, jack knife in hand. He punctured a hole in the bag where he guessed the waist would be and cut a slit to above the head. Spreading the cloth aside, everyone could see its contents.

Berta Chavez had been buried for seven months. Lansing had expected some decomposition. In the high desert, he wouldn't have been surprised if it had started mummifying. Instead, the body looked as fresh as the day it was interred. That didn't mean it was in good shape.

The old witch had died from burns on 80% of her body. When she was buried, she wasn't dressed in clothes. A sheet donated by the funeral home was draped over the corpse before it was encased in the body bag. Where the sheet now fell away, the skin was soft and supple, except for where it was burned. The wounds were either black or red, glistening in the lantern light. They looked fresh, painful. The face was a mask of anger and hate, not serene death.

There were audible gasps from the tough railroad workers.

Tina averted her eyes. "Hurry up, Cliff. Let's get this over with."

Reluctantly, Lansing pulled the sheet away to reveal the torso. More gaping lesions were exposed. It was apparent how horrible the old *bruja's* death had been.

He knew he couldn't cut through the breast plate. His plan was to make an incision below the rib cage and remove the heart that way. He had seen plenty autopsies in his career and was sure he could figure out what needed to be done.

As he started his cut, a hand grabbed his wrist, stopping him.

The witch's head turned toward him, and the lids opened revealing milk-white eyes. She began to hiss, warning him away.

"What the hell?" Lansing yelled, struggling to pull free.

The struggle lasted only a moment.

"Watch out!" Ron Alba shouted as he swung the pickaxe.

The tool whooshed past the sheriff's head and buried itself deep into Chavez's chest.

The body jerked and writhed. The hissing became even louder. Lansing was released, as both hands clutched at the metal implement, trying to pull it out.

The tip of the pick had driven through the body and was now embedded in the wood of the coffin.

"Move back!" Alba ordered.

"I have to get the heart," Lansing protested.

"No," the angry father corrected. "You have to burn the heart. Nothing says you can't burn the whole body, as well." He turned to his fellow railroad companions. "Grab the coffin."

"What are you doing?" Lansing asked, scrambling to his feet.

"I decided when I walked through that bitch's dump that I was going to burn it down before I left. She might as well go up with it."

"You can't burn down other people's property just because you want to," the sheriff warned.

"Arrest me! Throw me in jail. I don't give a damn. I'm not leaving here until that shack and that witch are a pile of ashes."

The men who dug the hole were reluctant to touch the casket. Chavez still writhed and hissed, trying to pull free of the pick through her chest.

"I'll drag it in myself if I have to," Alba growled. He took a step toward the box.

One of the other men waved him away. "We've got it, Ron."

The four men lifted the coffin and started toward the cabin. Alba led the way carrying both lanterns.

Tina looked at the sheriff. He didn't seem to have a problem with Alba's plan. They followed the procession into the shack.

Alba motioned to the center of the living room. His assistants gladly freed themselves of their burden. They retreated toward the back door. The engineer set down one lantern, then turned off the fuel flow to the other. Once the mantle extinguished, he opened the fuel cap and dumped the remaining white gas around the coffin.

"Everyone, get out!" he ordered.

Five of the observers quickly exited through the back door. Lansing remained to witness the final end to Berta Chavez.

Alba pulled a wooden match from his pocket. It was the same kind of kitchen match he used to light the lanterns. One swipe against the wooden floor and the matchhead burst into life. He tossed it where he poured the gas. The fumes ignited.

He stood there long enough to ensure the dry wood of the floor and casket was burning. Only then did he and Lansing join the others outside.

Chapter Eighty-Five

It was seven o'clock. Two hours had come and gone. Sharon had yet to hear from her husband. Before she made any phone calls, she would look for Joe herself.

The drive to the Pueblo was quick. She didn't care about proprieties. She parked in the gravel area that separated the chapel from the Business Office building.

The chapel door was not locked. The sanctuary was empty when she stepped inside. The only light came from the lone chandelier over the entrance. She knew it was a waste of time, but she called for her husband anyway. She didn't wait long for an answer.

Back outside, the temperature had dropped below freezing. Her breath hung in the still air. The night was supposed to dip to 20° before morning.

Looking both ways, she ran across Po'Pay Avenue to the Catholic church. Maybe the meeting had moved. The church doors were locked.

She hesitated. Her next stop would be the police station, a long block from the church. She could run there, or she could drive. She decided to take the truck.

The door to the police station was locked as well.

Sharon was becoming frustrated and angry. She jumped back into the truck, turned around and drove into the cluster of old adobe buildings. The truck skidded to a stop in front of Agustina Jacona's home. A moment later, she was pounding on the old woman's door. She banged on the door three separate times, never getting a response.

Five minutes later she was beating on Juan Pico's trailer door. She knew it was futile. The trailer was dark inside and there were no cars present. The bachelors were out for the evening.

Back at her house, Sharon found the business card Aquino had given her. She dialed the cell number on the back. A man answered at the other end.

"My name's Sharon Aquino, Joseph Aquino's wife. Something's happened to my husband. I need your help!"

Chapter Eighty-Six

The four railroad workers grabbed their shovels while Ron Alba carried the two camping lanterns. The group of seven moved from the graveside behind the cabin to the front of the burning structure. They needed to be clear of the building before the flames became too intense.

Ancient resins and oils sputtered and snapped as the old wood heated and burned. Snow on the roof melted, then turned to steam as the fire grew and spread throughout the hovel.

The question in everyone's mind was, "Did the coffin burn?"

The unnerving shrieks of Berta Cortez, or at least the Demon that she had become, filled the night air. The question was answered.

Lansing and Morales held hands. Both remembered the sight and sound of Chavez as a flaming owl, attempting to flee the Sheriff's burning flare the summer before. The beast/witch's tumble from the sky and eventual plunge into the Rio Cohino was still vivid in their minds.

The screams and cries finally faded until the only sound left was the crackle of burning wood. The group stood mesmerized by the dancing flames, each contemplating their own vision of Hell, knowing at this moment it was real.

The sheriff was annoyed when his cell phone rang. He almost didn't answer it. "Lansing."

He listened for a moment. "Mrs. Aquino, I don't know what I can do. The reservation is outside my jurisdiction."

Tina noticed the concern on his face as he listened to the woman's plea.

"It will take me an hour to get down there," he finally said. "Maybe I can get there sooner. I need to get to my Jeep. Let me call you right back. You can fill me in on what's going on."

He hung up.

"What's wrong?" the teacher asked.

"I need to get down to San Juan Pueblo." He addressed Ron Alba. "Can you stay here till the fire's out?"

"Those were my plans," Alba admitted.

Lansing turned back to Morales. "I can drop you off in town."

"Does that lady need help?"

"Yes."

"Why don't I ride along? You might need a woman's touch."

Chapter Eighty-Seven

Lansing sped along the back roads toward Highway 15 as fast as he dared. Icy patches were already forming, and he didn't want to end up in a wreck. When they reached the main road, it was clean and dry. With his blue lights flashing, he started making up for lost time.

He put his phone on "Speaker." Tina held the device while he drove. They both listened to Sharon Aquino describe the situation.

Her husband, Joseph, had been suspended as Police Chief the morning before. He was under suspicion for murder. The man in question had drowned in the Rio Grande three nights earlier.

Lansing remembered the autopsy request, but didn't interrupt her.

After Joe was suspended, he started inquiries around the reservation. There had been two deaths within a week and they were identical. She filled them in on everything: how and why their son was taken; who was accusing her husband and their motivations; and, ultimately, who Joseph suspected in the deaths.

"You said Joe thought they were drugged?" the sheriff asked.

"Yes, but nothing that would show up on a standard drug screening."

"It could be something that dissipates quickly," the chemistry teacher suggested.

"Or something easily detected, but they don't test for," Lansing said.

"Joe said I needed to tell you about last Friday night, when he was at the river.

"He was restless. He went down to the highway bridge, looking for some clue as to why the first man, Diego Salazar, drowned." She was quiet for a moment. "Before he heard Carlos in the water, he saw something else."

"What?"

"He heard her first, then he saw her floating over the water?"

"Who?" Lansing and Morales asked the question simultaneously.

"*La Llorona.* The Weeping Woman."

"What are you talking about?" the sheriff asked.

"I need to tell you a story, first. It's one every *Ohkay Owingeh* child is raised with.

"The Pueblo People drove the Spaniards out of New Mexico in sixteen-eighty. They had made us slaves. Taken away our land and our religion. We wanted to be free, the way we were before they ever came.

"Twelve years later the Spanish returned. Drought and famine had weakened us. We tried to resist, but didn't have the strength.

"Pavi was a young mother here at San Juan. She had two small children who had never known the White Man's cruelty. She dreamed of them growing up free. When her husband died fighting the Spanish, she wanted to flee to the mountains. It was winter. She hid in the brush along the river until night. She needed provisions, so she snuck back into the Pueblo, leaving her babies behind.

"Spanish soldiers were everywhere. Pavi had to evade them and she couldn't get back to the river until morning. But that night a chilling wind blew in from the north. When she finally got back to her children, she found they had frozen to death in the darkness.

"She didn't know what to do. She began singing to her babies. It was a sad lullaby, telling them to sleep the sleep of eternal peace.

"It was the singing that brought the soldiers. They found Pavi kneeling next to her children, rocking back and forth, crying over her loss. When she saw the Spaniards, she grabbed her poor babies and plunged into the river, drowning herself.

"Pavi is still here. Her spirit walks the river, still singing to her children, inviting anyone who hears her to join her in death."

Lansing shook his head. He had heard similar versions of the same story years earlier. Despite what he experienced just an hour earlier, he still had a hard time believing in ghosts. Demons were one thing. Spectral apparitions were something else.

"You're saying he saw a ghost?" Tina asked, obviously caught up in the tale.

"Yes."

"Is he sure he saw this Weeping Woman?" the sheriff asked.

"I've known Joe for over twenty years. He doesn't make stuff up. If he said he saw *La Llorona*, I believe him. It was while he was watching her that he heard Carlos in the river. He's sure Dominguez was drawn by the singing."

"So, are we talking ghosts now and not drugs?"

"Why can't it be both?" Tina asked, sensing her partner's doubt.

"Mrs. Aquino, I'm still not sure what you want me to do when I get to the reservation," Lansing said, ignoring the teacher's quip. "I don't have any authority."

"Please, just call me Sharon. I know this isn't in your jurisdiction. I just want you to help me find my husband."

"How? I wouldn't know where to start."

"I do," Sharon said firmly.

Chapter Eighty-Eight

The first thing Joseph Aquino became aware of was the pain at the base of his skull. His first thought was, "Is this a dream?"

He kept his eyes closed, trying to remember. He had been in the chapel. Yes, Juan Pico dropped him off there. He was supposed to meet someone. He couldn't remember who. Then somebody came in. Who was it that came in? They called his name. He followed them.

That's right, he thought. Carla Naranjo showed up at the front of the chapel. She wanted him to follow her. They went out the side door. He had asked her where they were going.

He couldn't remember what she said. Maybe she didn't say anything.

The sun was setting. Deep shadows engulfed everything. They were heading toward the old adobe structures of *Owe'neh Bupingeh*, the heart of the Pueblo.

He remembered seeing a movement out of the corner of his eye. Then?

He couldn't remember being hit, but the pain told him it happened.

He tried to sit up, only to be greeted with a wave of nausea and dizziness. He laid his head back down.

"Ah, you are alive."

Aquino recognized the voice. It was Agustina Jacona.

He squinted his eyes open. He was in a small, dark room. The only light came from a battery-operated lantern. Except for a table and the chair Jacona used, the room was empty.

He carefully sat up. His only protection from the cold, clay floor was the blanket he had been sleeping on.

Sleeping? That wasn't the right term. He had been knocked unconscious.

"Here. Drink this." The crone handed him a cup of steaming liquid. She had poured it from a thermos.

"What is it?"

"Herbal tea. It will help with the pain."

Aquino hesitated.

"It's not poisoned," she scolded.

He took the ceramic cup. The taste was minty, with a little bitterness.

"Desert lavender gives it the mint flavor," Jacona explained. "The acacia leaves help with the nausea and will calm your nerves. The Brittle Bush numbs you."

Aquino took a sip, then another. His stomach steadied. The pain at the back of his neck lessened. The hint of a headache disappeared.

He looked around. The room was familiar and unfamiliar at the same time. "Where are we?"

"Still at the Pueblo," she reassured him.

"What's going on?" he asked, still unsteady. He didn't think he could stand. Not yet, anyway.

"We are here talking."

"Why?"

"There are things you need to understand, Joseph."

"Like what?"

"You no longer have any influence in the Pueblo. Or on the rest of the reservation for that matter."

"I know that."

"Do you? Is that why you came poking around at Carla's yesterday? Or came to my place?"

"I was trying to find out what's going on."

"Is that why you were at *P'oe Tsawa* this morning? Digging up long buried graves. Resurrecting forgotten memories. How is harming me going to help you?"

"That is not what I was trying to do."

"You are a Made Person, but you have forgotten the teachings. Blue Corn Mother and White Corn Maiden sent us into the world. They were and are the first among our deities. When I assumed the title of *Apienu,* I took on the mantle of White Corn Mother. What I do is always for the good of the Tewa People. What I do cannot be questioned."

Aquino's head began to clear. Beyond the thick adobe wall, he heard the muffled sound of a car on pavement. He was in a house close to Day School Street or Highway 74, near the bridge.

"How is drowning two men good for the people?"

Jacona shook her head. "Men die all the time, Joseph. Sometimes it's for the best."

"So, you admit you were involved?"

"Always with the questions," the old woman asked, admitting to nothing. "Always with the wrong questions."

The former police officer tried to think of a question she might answer. When they talked the day before, she seemed upset over what he saw from the bridge. "Can you tell me about the Weeping Woman?"

"Ah," Agustina said, leaning back in her chair. "You finally asked the right question."

Chapter Eighty-Nine

Agustina refilled Aquino's cup, then sat again.

"When I was four, I was playing next to the river. I was sitting on the bank with the cornhusk dolls I always played with. I was there with my three brothers. We were supposed to go home soon. It was almost time for dinner.

"We all looked up when we heard the singing. My brothers saw her first . . . the Weeping Woman. She frightened them. They were so scared they forgot about me and ran away. I didn't know what to do. But the singing was so beautiful, I didn't want to leave.

"That's when she came to me. Floating over the water. People say ghosts only come out at night. This is not true. They come out as they please.

"She came right up to the riverbank. She stopped singing, looked down at me and smiled. She was the most beautiful woman I had ever seen in my life. Her hair was long and black. She wore white, deerskin clothes. And she was so sad.

"She told me her name was Pavi and that she was lonely.

"I was four. I didn't know I was supposed to be afraid. I asked if she wanted me to come with her. She told me no, I shouldn't. But it was all right if I came to visit her.

"That's when my brothers came running back with my father. She disappeared. She just went away.

"I remember my father being angry and upset. He asked me what I saw. I was afraid to tell him, so, I told him I didn't see anything. He yelled at the river, telling the Weeping Woman to never come back. Then he told me to stay away. Never come close to the water.

"I guess I was not a good daughter," she sighed, "because I didn't listen to my father. I would sneak away and come to the river as often as I could. I had to see Pavi. She was my friend. In fact, she became my best friend. When I visited, she told me her story.

"She had lost her children a long time ago. It broke her heart when they died. She first sang to them, then drowned herself, hoping to join them in death. The people of the Pueblo never found her body. She was never properly buried and so her spirit couldn't return to the *Sipofene*.

"Her spirit still wanders the river, still singing to her children. She invites all who hear her song, if they seek peace, to join her in the waters."

Aquino remembered the singing. He understood the urge to come to the Weeping Woman. "Why didn't you follow her into the river?"

"She didn't want me to. I was destined for more important things. I didn't understand at the time. As I grew older, the visits became fewer and fewer. When I became a wife and a mother, I was young. Then there was no time for such joys as seeing my Pavi.

"It was after I became a Made Person, when I joined the Women's Society, that I saw her again. She had not forgotten me. In fact, she was proud that I too had become a mother.

"I visited the river as often as I could. It was hard to do. My husband had become more and more cruel over the years. I told Pavi. I told my sisters in the Society. The old *Apienu* took pity. Before she passed, she selected me to be the next Blue Corn Woman.

"It was then that I began to learn the secrets our Society kept. I also learned our responsibilities. Protect the women and children of the Pueblo."

"Is that when you killed your husband?" Aquino refused to succumb to her tale of woe.

"No. I didn't kill Pardo. I led him to the river. Pavi sang to him . . . then he was gone."

"Did he go to the river willingly?"

"Very much so. As did Diego. As did Carlos. You see, I fixed them each a tea made of Desert lavender, acacia and Brittle Bush."

"What?" He looked at the now empty cup, then threw it across the room. He stood but needed the wall for support.

"There are other things in the tea. Seeds from Sleepy Grass and Morning Glories. They will take effect soon. When you're ready, we can go."

Aquino shook his head. The world snapped into focus. The clarity he felt when he first drank the tea suddenly intensified. Sounds became sharper, clearer. The lantern on the table blossomed into a bouquet of colors. His eyes dilated, absorbing every sliver of light available. A wave of peace and serenity washed over him.

He felt himself stand straight. He didn't need the wall to lean against.

He could hear the old woman's voice. She said, "Come, Joseph. It's time. Pavi is waiting for you."

Chapter Ninety

Sharon Aquino said there was a reason Joe wanted her to recall the events of Friday night. She guessed that what he saw at the bridge happened twice. Once with Diego Salazar. The second time, the one he witnessed, was with Carlos Dominguez. It was going to happened again. But this time, Joseph Aquino would be the victim. She was sure of it.

She had Lansing and Morales meet her on Highway 74, just east of the bridge. They both parked on the paved shoulder, their vehicles pointed toward the Pueblo.

"We need to be on the bank," Sharon explained. "Joe was on the bridge when he heard Carlos drowning. He couldn't get to the river soon enough."

It was dark. Past 9:30. The sky was moonless. The only light came from the flashlight Sharon held.

Lansing looked toward the river. He could hear the gentle murmur of the water. In the nearly black night, he could see nothing.

"I have two flashlights," he said. He retrieved them from his Jeep, handing one to Tina. Before starting toward the Rio Grande flood plain he asked, "How sure are you that Joe's going to show up?"

"I'm not sure at all. But in the middle of the night, I don't know where else to look."

"What if we're too late?" the teacher asked.

"It was after ten-thirty when Joe saw the ghost. I pray we're here in plenty of time. All I want to do is stop him from drowning."

A well-worn path next to the guardrail and elevated roadway led them to the river's edge. Sharon had no idea where Carlos Dominguez entered the water. They spread themselves along the bank, thirty yards apart. Tina was closest to the bridge. Sharon next. Lansing at the end.

With only six inches of snow during the storm, most of it had melted already. The brush along the bank had lost its leaves. There were any number of open paths that led to the water.

Lansing suggested they stand guard with their flashlights off. If Aquino was being brought to the river, they didn't want to scare anyone off. (He hoped their cars on the road wouldn't give away their presence.)

There was no conversation. All three listened for any sounds other than the babbling river. For a long time, the only interruptions came from the occasional car on the bridge.

The chill was setting in. Standing in one place took its toll. The sheriff stomped his feet to keep warm. He wanted to check his watch for the time but didn't want to betray his position. He had no idea how long they stood in the dark. It could have been fifteen minutes, or thirty. He wasn't sure. He didn't know how much longer they needed to be there, either.

Just when he was ready to say something to Sharon, the singing started.

It was a woman's voice, beautiful, ethereal. The melody came from across the river and grew closer.

The lyrics were in Spanish. An old Spanish. He recognized the words, but they were archaic and seldom used. That didn't detract from the haunting song.

Staring into the blackness, a mist, glowing from within, began to form. It coalesced into the shape of a woman . . . a maiden dressed in white buckskin.

She hovered above the water, drifting closer, singing her lament.

Later, the sheriff would describe the experience as mesmerizing. At the moment, he had no thoughts at all. His heart and mind had been completely captured by the siren's song.

The spell was finally broken when a woman began screaming, "Help! Help! He's drowning!"

Chapter Ninety-One

Sharon had screamed. Her flashlight was now on, the beam trained on a figure floundering in the river.

As he ran toward the frantic wife, Lansing ripped off his coat and dropped his gun belt before wading into the icy current. He had no idea how deep the channel was, but the water was soon chest high. Within seconds he had grabbed the man and helped him stand upright.

It was Joseph Aquino. He was incoherent, unaware of his surroundings. Initially he fought off the sheriff's assistance. He stopped struggling when he realized he was being rescued.

Lansing supported him. With one of Aquino's arms around his neck, they started wading toward the bank.

"Let him go!" a man's voice ordered.

Lansing looked up. Three flashlights were trained on him: Tina's, Sharon's, and now the intruder's.

"I said let him go!" The command came from behind the light in the middle.

"He'll drown!" Lansing protested, stopping.

"That's the idea. Let him go! You're trespassing on reservation land. I've got a gun. I have every right to shoot you."

"I'm the county sheriff!"

"Like I give a damn. Let him go, or you both can die!"

The flash from the barrel and the sound of the blast were simultaneous.

The intruder's flashlight dropped as the man fell to the ground.

"Come on," Sharon shouted, picking up her flashlight. She had let it drop when she grabbed the sheriff's gun from the holster.

Lansing and his burden reached the shallow bank. Tina and Sharon were there to assist.

"No!" Agustina Jacona shrieked, rushing from the darkness. She scratched and clawed at Lansing. Desperate, she tried to grab Aquino and shove him back into the river.

The sheriff fended her off. Tina tried to pull the horrid creature away from the two men.

Sharon Aquino finally had enough. "Oh, no, you don't!"

She grabbed the old woman by the hair, yanked her head back, and violently swung her into the river.

The old hag screamed once. Her last, woeful plea was, "Pavi!"

The icy flow shocked her so severely, she couldn't save herself. She simply disappeared under the inky water.

Lansing started back into the river.

"Let her go!" Sharon begged. "Please, just let her go!"

Chapter Ninety-Two

Tina called 9-1-1 from her cell. An ambulance was dispatched and reached the Highway 74 bridge in 12 minutes. Both Lansing and Aquino were transported to the White Pines Urgent Care Medical facility in Segovia.

Sharon followed in her truck. Tina drove the Patrol Jeep.

Lansing insisted the hospital draw blood from Aquino. The man had been drugged. The authorities needed to know what the substance was. It could have caused two other deaths.

Both men were treated for hypothermia. They recovered quickly and were released the next morning.

An investigation was already in full swing on the reservation. Because there was a shooting and a death, the FBI out of Santa Fe took the lead.

The dead man on the bank of the Rio Grande was acting Police Chief Roberto Cruz. He had been shot once in the head. Next to him investigators found a flashlight and his gun.

A few feet away they recovered Lansing's flashlight, belt and pistol. The pistol had been recently fired.

Interviews had to be conducted. The sheriff was the obvious target for the investigation. His gun was used to kill Cruz. Also, he was completely out of his jurisdiction. He had no reason to be at San Juan.

The FBI took over three rooms in the Tribal office building. One room was set aside for interrogations. Because he was a suspect, Lansing wasn't allowed to go home just yet. During his first interview, he had to wear borrowed clothes.

He explained he was on the San Juan Reservation by request. He was there to help a friend. The visit was not in his official capacity as San Phillipe Sheriff.

No, he did not shoot Cruz. He couldn't have. He was in the water rescuing Aquino.

In a separate interview, Tina Morales backed up everything Lansing said.

Sharon Aquino not only corroborated the sheriff's statements, she confessed to killing Cruz. Her explanation as to why was simple. She was saving her husband's life.

Joseph Aquino was little help in the initial interrogation. His recollection of the night before was hazy at best. He had been knocked unconscious. When he woke, he drank a tea Agustina Jacona gave him. The next thing he remembered, he was in an ambulance.

Later that day, Lansing was released from custody. His firearm was confiscated for the duration of the investigation.

Driving back to Las Palmas, Lansing admitted to Tina, other than the dip in the river, he had one major complaint. He lost another phone when he waded into the Rio Grande.

They drove in silence for a while. Eventually, Tina had to ask. "Did you see her last night?"

"Who?"

"*La Llorona,* the Weeping Woman."

Lansing was quiet for a long time. Finally, he admitted, "Yes. Yes, I did."

Chapter Ninety-Three

The FBI investigation took a week. Besides the four individuals present at Cruz's death, a dozen more reservation members were interviewed. The Bureau wanted a full picture of the events leading up to the shooting.

Agustina Jacona's name kept surfacing. Not only because she drowned that night, but because she seemed to be linked to two other deaths at the Pueblo.

Tomasita Salazar and Pauline Dominguez were brought in for questioning. They seemed grateful for the chance to unload guilty consciences. They had been abused wives and sought Jacona's help. As head of the Women's Society, she advertised her ability to solve domestic problems. They both professed ignorance of the old woman's solutions or how far she would take things. Neither admitted they owed the *Apienu* great favors for her services.

After a day, Joseph Aquino's head cleared. He was able to remember more of what happened that evening. Carla Naranjo had lured him from the chapel. Once outside, he was struck from behind. He woke some hours later in an old adobe hut, close to the bridge he guessed.

Jacona was there when he woke. She had him drink a tea made of Desert lavender, acacia leaves and Brittle Bush. He said she had given the same drink to her husband, Salazar, and Dominguez. When he started feeling strange, she admitted her concoction included Morning Glory seeds and something called Sleepy Grass. After that, everything turned weird, exaggerated. He couldn't come up with the right term. (What he meant was he was hallucinating.) Then he blacked out.

The blood sample the hospital procured explained a lot. It contained the same substance found in the thermos recovered from the old adobe

hut. The active drug was D-lysergic acid amide, a precursor to LSD, something not normally screened for. It was in concentrated amounts and had been derived from the seeds of Morning Glory flowers and Sleepy Grass.

Sleepy Grass was found throughout New Mexico. Ranchers had known for over a hundred years the sedative effect the grass had on livestock. The Pueblo Indians had known about its properties for centuries.

The search at the abandoned hut turned up something else—Diego Salazar's missing winter coat. For Aquino, that confirmed his suspicions that Jacona was responsible for the Art Director's death.

A description of Jacona's activities and statements were reviewed by a Bureau profiler. Her conclusion was the old woman had all the characteristics of a psychopath. She was tied to the death of three men and the attempted murder of Joseph Aquino. Now the sudden death of her predecessor seemed suspicious. No one knew how many more victims she had claimed over the years.

Roberto Cruz's patrol car was found on the Yunge Owingeh Bridge road, 400 feet from where he was shot. It was close to the path Jacona took from the adobe hut to the river. It was unclear if he had helped his aunt or he suspected trouble when he saw Lansing's Jeep parked on the highway. No one would ever know.

Aquino was sure, though, that Berto was the person who knocked him out. Carla Naranjo plead ignorance. With the revelations about her mentor becoming public, she distanced herself as far as she could from the old hag.

The same thing happened with Sheriff Raymond Mesa. He claimed he had no idea any of this was going on. His accusations against Police Chief Aquino were only made with the welfare of the Pueblo as his only

concern. He, too, had been misled by Cruz. He sincerely regretted being taken in by all the lies.

President Kata immediately reinstated Aquino as Police Chief. He accepted under one condition—that he be allowed to replace his two remaining officers. He didn't think he could operate with a staff that refused to back him up.

Kata thought that was harsh. Aquino shrugged off the concerns. If Juan Pico and Henry Calvert still wanted to be a part of law enforcement, they could always get jobs as security guards at the new casino.

Judge Lovato was apologetic about having Jacob Aquino removed from school. He rescinded his orders and the boy was released from the Butterfly Healing Center.

The Tribal Court had no jurisdiction over the killing of Roberto Cruz. That fell under the FBI. However, it was concluded that Sharon Aquino's actions constituted justifiable homicide. No charges were brought.

One of the first things newly reinstated Police Chief Joseph Aquino wanted to investigate was the fraud case against William Bryce. He was sure the gallery owner owed the Pueblo Tribes thousands upon thousands of dollars.

When he asked for help from the Santa Fe Police Department, he was informed he was too late. Bryce was dead. He was found hanging in his gallery two days earlier. Though it appeared to be suicide, the police ruled the death as suspicious. No suicide note was ever discovered, and several paintings seemed to have been removed. What's more, his business ledgers were nowhere to be found.

Aquino had a couple of suspects in mind: a very angry artist from Taos Pueblo and the mysterious Edmund Murdock. He had no proof. Besides, it was Santa Fe's problem, now.

The Weeping Woman was never discussed. Agustina Jacona's relationship with the phantom was a secret Joseph Aquino shared only with his wife.

It was assumed that Jacona or Cruz, maybe both, pushed Aquino into the river. He knew differently. He had walked into the Rio Grande willingly. No one pushed or prodded. In his altered state of consciousness, he was aware of only two things—The Weeping Woman and his desperate need to be with her. It was the lost souls of all the men who went before him that dragged him under the waters. He would have joined them if it had not been for his wife, Sharon, Tina, and Sheriff Cliff Lansing.

Chapter Ninety-Four

Lansing was glad to be back on his own turf. The FBI told him they would be in touch if they had any further questions. They never called.

Thursday morning, Sam Keller contacted him. A Doug Wilson, his wife and three kids had stayed at the Lookout Lodge in June of 1997. In fact, they had been in the same cabin Wilson was hiding in.

Keller said he checked the cabin. He found the remaining cans of food, a suitcase full of clothes, a bible, and a yellow legal pad. Wilson had written in the pad the same line over and over: God, I'm sorry. Please, forgive me. God, I'm sorry. Please, forgive me.

Lansing thanked him for the information. He then called Detective Burroughs in Indianapolis. They compared notes.

Talking with Wilson's neighbors and coworkers, Burroughs discovered the man was very strict in his religious beliefs. He had expressed concern numerous times that he felt his family was drifting away from the church's teachings. The detective suspected Wilson thought by killing his family he was saving their souls.

Lansing offered his perspective. Wilson had done everything possible to escape capture and was doing a good job. He guessed Wilson returned to Lookout Lodge for one reason. The Lodge was the last place the family visited together when they were happy. That's when the guilt took over.

When he burst out the cabin door, gun blazing, he wasn't trying to escape. He was committing suicide by cop. He could kill his own family, but he was too much of a coward to take his own life.

The sheriff would make sure the $10,000 was returned to Indiana to help cover funeral expenses.

***

A warm snap hit the county a week later. Snow melted.

A Ford Explorer carjacked in Santa Fe was found in an arroyo next to Highway 15. It had crashed, probably during the storm. A dead body was found inside. It was Ralph Miera, the escaped prisoner. The manhunt was finally called off.

It was during the warm snap that Lansing and Morales visited the ashes of Berta Chavez's cabin. There was absolutely nothing left. Even the witch's bones had been destroyed. Either they burned, or Ron Alba had beaten the remains to dust. The only thing left was the metal part of the pickaxe used to pin the demon to her coffin.

Anna Robles had a sister in Farmington. She inherited the ranch. The property and livestock were sold to cover taxes and mortgages. What David Robles had sold his soul to build was gone in a few weeks.

There were no more reports of Shadow People. Children were no longer being harmed. They were sleeping in their own beds again, safe and secure.

The scratches on Maria Alba and Stanley Gutierrez soon faded. The memories of what they went through never would . . . not completely.

***

Lansing held the door open as Tina climbed into the Jeep.

"Are you sleeping at your place?" he asked.

"If the invitation's still open, I like staying at the ranch."

Lansing smiled. "I like that, too."

Epilogue

Only four people saw her that night. A few others heard she had appeared.

To those who believe, she is very real.

She still wanders the river, singing to her children . . . inviting all who hear her to join her beneath the waters.

She is *La Llorona*, the Weeping Woman.

Coming 2020!

MOON OF THE BLUE MUSTANG
A Sheriff Lansing Mystery
Book 8
By
Micah S. Hackler

The body-count climbs as Sheriff Cliff Lansing contends with drugs, death, cattle theft and a power struggle with the Forestry Service. The resources of his office are spread thin. Almost too late, he realizes more than one murderer may be involved.

An Apache legend and family secrets weave their way through the action . . . unseen forces play their part . . . providing Lansing with a mystery he may never solve.

For more information
visit: www.SpeakingVolumes.us

Coming 2020!

DEATH AT RAINY MOUNTAIN
A Tay-Bodal Mystery
By
Mardi Oakley Medawar

"Another great storyteller is emerging."—TONY HILLERMAN

As the separate bands of the Kiowa nation gather at Rainy Mountain in 1866, the bands find themselves divided over the choice of a new principal chief, as a cloud of murder hangs over the event.

For more information
visit: www.SpeakingVolumes.us

On Sale Now!

A Sheriff Lansing Mystery
Book 6

On Sale Now!

SHERIFF LANSING MYSTERIES
Books 1 – 5

**For more information
visit:** www.SpeakingVolumes.us

On Sale Now!

HOWARD MOON DEER MYSTERIES
Books 1 - 4

"Terrific…I couldn't put it down."
—Margaret Truman, author of *Murder at the Watergate*

For more information
visit: www.SpeakingVolumes.us

On Sale Now!

THE GLORY DAYS OF BUFFALO EGBERT

"A must read. If you haven't yet read it, get it.
It's a fine reading experience."
—Allan W. Eckert, author of *That Dark and Bloody River*

**For more information
visit:** www.SpeakingVolumes.us

On Sale Now!

STAR SONG *series*
Books 1 – 3

For more information
visit: